The BATTLE *for* ABBESSI

THE BATTLE FOR ABBESSI

Resource Publications
An Imprint of Wipf and Stock Publishers
199 W. 8th Ave., Suite 3
Eugene, OR 97401

www.wipfandstock.com

PAPERBACK ISBN: 978-1-6667-3721-9
HARDCOVER ISBN: 978-1-6667-9643-8
EBOOK ISBN: 978-1-6667-9644-5

FEBRUARY 7, 2022 3:13 PM

The BATTLE *for* ABBESSI

Russell Marrone

RESOURCE *Publications* · Eugene, Oregon

In loving memory of Deborah Mandel

Prologue

It was a cool October evening and the mist from the still warm Clinton River billowed up and rolled through Millar Cemetery. The Millar Cemetery had been on the banks of the murky river for well over a hundred years and the tombstones gave testament to its vintage. Groaning bullfrogs and singing crickets underscored the still blackness of the gentle rolling river. Low-pitched owls cried into the night's darkness. Great oaks planted along the banks overhung the cemetery, maintained the integrity of the shore, and shielded its secrets from the full moon.

The adjacent parking lot, which seemed blasphemous to the sanctity of Millar, serviced a chiropractic office and an insurance company, but at this time of night everything was eerily vacant. Sitting in the lot next to the picket fence that lined the front of Millar Cemetery idled a black limousine.

A dark figure emerged from the cemetery mist and exited through the archway in the picket fence. The clinic security light illuminated the figure, revealing his chiseled jaw, athletic body, and black tuxedo. The limo driver's side door opened and a pale figure dressed in black and sporting a dated taxi driver's hat hurried around the limousine to the rear passenger door. He quickly opened the door for the tuxedoed man. "

So good to see you again, sir," the driver said.

"A pleasure as always, Blisdon," the dark figure replied.

"Where to, sir?" Blisdon queried.

"Take me to West Big Beaver . . . The Capital" the dark figure responded, sliding into the back seat.

"Your wish is my command," Blisdon replied. He hurried around the limousine and jumped into the driver's seat. He pulled out of the driveway and onto Big Beaver. Blisdon knew this would be a long night.

CHAPTER 1

S HE SAT AT A WINDOW overlooking the office building's outdoor patio, watching a homeless man finish his lunch under an awning of walnut trees lining the parking lot. She watched him stand and toss his McDonald's bag onto the patio floor and amble away. Within seconds a dark cloud of cawing birds descended to the ground and a murder of crows began to fight for the leftover fries and hamburger remains. She remembered being told that witnessing six crows congregating was a sign of illness and death.

She shuddered at that thought, and swiveled her chair around to the desk, weary from a day of battles won and battles lost. She won a battle with a title company, but lost to a lender to insure a future closing. She called back all her clients and, after showing three new clients' homes, prepared for tomorrow morning's listing appointment. Only one more late day appointment remained: a five o'clock consultation with Dr. Fineman. She considered cancelling it.

Her typically energetic self had been dragging the last few months. "I'll order a series of tests, Mandy, but my guess is you're overworked. You're pushing yourself." As a former athlete she trained for years. She lived a clean and sober lifestyle, but now approaching forty perhaps Dr. Fineman's premature diagnosis was right. She was feeling the wear and tear of all those years of competition. Simple as that. She reconsidered her appointment with Dr. Fineman to go over her test results.

She glanced at her cell phone and sighed. Mom. She preferred not to answer the call, but she made a promise long ago to her mother that she would always answer "Mom Calls." In return, Mom agreed to only call if it was "really important" and would restrict her social calls to the weekend.

"Hi, Mom," Mandy answered. "What's so important?"

"Well, Amanda, sweetie, I thought I'd remind you of your appointment with Doctor Fineman today. You know you get so busy . . . " Mom said.

"Yes, I remembered my appointment," said Mandy with a hint of sarcasm.

"Well, you know Aunt Virgie just disregarded her health and look what happened to her. You know if she'd been going to the doctor regularly . . . " droned Mom.

"Mom . . . Mom . . . MOM!" she shouted to no avail. Mom was on a roll; she just prattled on.

"Well, when you're finished at the doctor's stop by and I'll make you dinner," said Mom in her annoyingly cheerful voice.

"We'll see, Mom, we'll see," said Mandy, knowing full well the last place she wanted to go after this doctor appointment was her mom's house and face an excruciating cross-examination, regardless of the test results, that would be more tedious than the visit itself. "I'll call you *if* I'm coming."

"OK, but try to call by six so I have time to prepare."

"Mom, if I don't call you by then, I probably won't be coming," Mandy said, pushing to end the conversation.

Mandy contemplated her options. She knew if she ghosted her doctor's appointment, she would never hear the end of it from her mom. On the other hand, going home now, drawing a hot bath, fixing a cocktail, and washing away the stress of the day sounded wonderful. It's the kind of medicine she wanted, but she knew there was only one option. She packed her stuff, and grabbed her coat.

She hurried through the office only to stop at the front desk to inform Sam she'd be leaving for the day. "Sam, please forward all my calls to my cell. I won't be back today," she instructed.

"Anything you say, Boss."

As she turned to leave, a deliveryman entered the glass office doors with an obvious flower delivery.

Bypassing Mandy, he headed straight to the front desk to Sam. "Delivery for Amanda Abbessi."

"Hold on Boss, these are for you."

"Probably from that nice couple from my closing on Monday," Mandy said returning to claim the gift.

She opened the box, stunned to see two dozen red roses. "Seems a bit much from someone I helped find a home." She hastily retrieved the dainty envelope nestled between the stems and perked up slightly after reading the note:

I find myself daydreaming about you all the time. Love, Your Secret Admirer.

"Sam? Do me a favor and put these in water and place them on my desk."

"You got it."

With a new smile, Mandy pushed through the glass doors and headed to the elevators. Preoccupied with her appointment and now having a secret admirer, she literally bumped into her old friend, Brent. "So sorry, excuse me," Mandy apologized, not immediately recognizing him.

"Hey, Mandy, how's it going?" Brent chirped.

"Oh, Brent, sorry, I'm a klutz. It's been a rough day and I have one more appointment before I can crash," Mandy replied. Together they waited for the elevator ding. Brent, an attorney from the third-floor legal firm she had worked with on a few deals over her years in real estate, always made her laugh with his cornball jokes.

"No worry. You do look stressed though," he said.

"Yeah, it's been one of those days," Mandy groaned, ". . . and it's still not over."

"Here you go," Brent said. "What's the difference between a dead squirrel in the middle of the road and a dead attorney in the middle of the road?" He waited for her response. When she didn't react, he finished the joke. "There's skid marks in front of the squirrel," laughed Brent.

"Really?" deadpanned Mandy. "Still the spontaneous jokester, eh? I don't know who needs more therapy. You or me." She had to admit she found him attractive. Well-groomed, early forties, fun. She harbored a small crush for him, but never had time to pursue it.

When the elevator dinged and the doors opened, Mandy slipped in, leaving Brent waiting behind the closing elevator doors. She heard him holler something, but she was so taken in by her own thoughts that his words didn't register.

I feel like shit, she thought. *I've been an athlete all my life . . . I know my body. It's gotta be something serious. Otherwise, why would Fineman call me to his office to discuss my test results? Not tell me over the phone?. . I hope it's something treatable like low hormones.* Mandy tortured herself on the elevator ride down.

A quick peek at her watch told her she was behind schedule, so she picked up pace and jogged toward her car. As she reached the row of her parked car, a blue sedan screeched around the corner, nearly hitting her.

"Slow down, asshole!" she yelled at the reckless driver who flipped her off as he completed his turn.

"Idiot," she mumbled under her breath, her frame of mind moving from self-pity to anger.

Zipping through traffic with the agility of a Formula 1 driver she glanced at her watch again and saw she had less than fifteen minutes to make her appointment. With work traffic getting heavier she bore down and barreled in and out of the traffic flow to exit the freeway. She drove along the service drive until she reached Dequindre Road, then made a quick right and turned into the medical complex across from the hospital and parked. Once again, she looked at her watch, but this time smiled . . . she had five minutes to make it to the office.

Still, she couldn't waste the last remaining minutes. In her haste, she hopped out and heard a crunch under her feet and felt her knee buckle. She didn't need to look down to know the heel of her left stiletto had separated from her left shoe.

"Damn!" she hissed, "Why now?"

Mandy tried matching the wayward heel to the shoe, to no avail. *Now what?* Finally grabbing both shoes and a useless heel she popped open her trunk and threw them in while retrieving the black work boots she wore when showing new construction.

"Well, they ain't pretty, but they'll work," she grumbled while knocking off mud from a construction site.

"Lord, give me strength."

She clomped through the parking lot to the clinic entrance and through the lobby to the bank of elevators. She didn't give a damn if anyone chose to roll their eyes at her foot attire. *Let 'em look.*

CHAPTER 2

S HE ANNOUNCED HERSELF and was told to take a seat. "Anywhere special?" she asked referring to the empty waiting room devoid of patients. *What's that expression? Saving the worst for last?*

She flipped through an odd assortment of magazines, all outdated and well used. She scanned the room for anything to distract her from an increasing sense of dread while waiting to be called. With all his money, the least the good doctor could do would be provide a place of comfort instead of two cocktail tables loaded with dated magazines and a full-length skeleton in the corner of the room. *How bizarre*, she thought. *Speaking of bizarre* . . . she looked down at her black boots.

She diverted her thoughts to imagining the room dressed with watercolor prints of flowers under blue skies. Recessed lighting. A large potted plant or two could certainly liven up the place.

"Amanda Abbessi?"

The sudden announcement of her name startled her from her decorating fantasy. She looked up to see a fresh-faced nurse in the doorway holding a clipboard.

"Yes, that's me."

"The doctor will see you now."

Mandy followed the nurse through the door; by-passing the weight scale she had stepped on years ago and winced, remembering her weight read-out then. After swearing off fast food, her weight eventually came down. Curiously, though, her home scale told her she continued to lose weight even after she went back to her normal diet, which included lots of pasta and bars of chocolate. She wasn't complaining, but it was a bit troubling. She chalked it up to an improved metabolism.

She thought it curious when the nurse walked her by the last examining room and stopped at the oak door at the end of the corridor. She knocked softly, before opening the door to Dr. Fineman's personal office.

"Come in, young lady and have a seat," Dr. Fineman said. With greying temples, he maintained a distinguished air despite his tussled hair, thick black-rimmed bifocals, and bow tie. His worn face showed the decades spent servicing sick patients throughout his years of practice. He reminded Mandy of her late father and that soothed her somewhat.

"Is this a new look you're wearing?" Dr. Fineman asked with a wry smile.

"It's called breaking your heel in the parking lot and having to resort to your new construction boots," she replied sarcastically.

"Please have a seat."

Mandy settled into the office chair across his desk. She checked out the many diplomas behind his desk assuring her she was in good hands. Watching him shuffle through her charts she instantly took note of his frown and solemn demeanor. *This is not going to be good* she thought and braced herself for the worse.

"Miss Abbessi," Dr. Fineman began, coming right to the point, "this has never been an easy thing for me to do, but as your physician I must report the findings of your MRI, CT scan and battery of tests. There is a cancerous mass growing on your ovaries and it has metastasized to your liver and pancreas."

Mandy slumped in the chair after hearing the words pancreas and metastasized in the same sentence. She clutched the arms of the chair to dispel the rising anxiety. Dr. Finemen sat silent while she gathered her composure.

"I know this is a lot to take in, Miss Abbessi . . . take a few deep breaths and we'll continue."

"Are you sure it's me? Do you have the right file?" Mandy asked softly, "There must be some kind of mistake." Her watery eyes pleaded for a reprieve from the devastating diagnosis.

"I'm so sorry, but there is no mistake."

"So," she said with resolve, "what is our plan of attack? How are we going to beat this thing? What's the prognosis, Dr. Fineman?"

Dr. Fineman removed his glasses. Looking directly in her eyes he said, "The best we can do is to start you immediately on intense chemotherapy and try to shrink the epithelial tumors. If we are lucky, we will shrink your tumors and beat it back into remission. But there are no guarantees."

"No guarantees. I understand that, but what are my chances? What are the odds of beating this thing?" Mandy queried.

This was always the most difficult part when delivering bad news to patients. Even though he wanted to sugar coat the diagnosis, his ethics and integrity wouldn't allow him.

"Because it has metastasized, at best, even with immediate and aggressive treatment, your chances of surviving this are not good," Dr. Fineman said stoically.

Shocked into silence, she lowered her head.

"How much time?" she struggled to ask.

She looked up and locked her gaze on Dr. Fineman. His eyes looked sad and tired.

"How much time?" she asked again.

"With the intensive chemo, twelve months."

"And without the chemo?"

"Maybe three months . . . maybe a little more. We could admit you tomorrow and begin treatment. You'll probably be in the hospital three days and then you would switch to outpatient treatment. After that, you'd have your treatments every three weeks."

"I see," choked Mandy. And her words gave way to a low utterance, "I need a little time to think about all this. I'll let you know."

"I don't want to rush you, but the sooner we start the better," Dr. Fineman urged.

"I understand." Mandy thanked the doctor, and slowly removed herself from his office. Her ability to think was trapped in a whirlwind of "what ifs?" She wanted to scramble through all the scenarios that might be in her near future, but she couldn't land on single one. So absorbed, she didn't remember how she got into the elevator or pressed the button that took her to the main floor. Walking through the lobby she fought back tears threatening to swell up. She looked away at staring eyes and hurried her steps to the door. She would beat this just as she had beaten other opponents she encountered throughout her life. She was a champion and champions do not quit.

When she arrived at her car, she fumbled for the keys in her purse, only have them fall to the pavement. Reaching for them, she encountered her construction boots.

"God, what was I thinking?"

She grabbed the keys and, once again, they slipped from her hand.

"Sonofabitch," she yelled and slumped to the hard cement and wept. She sobbed loudly and this time she allowed the tears to flow. She covered her face at the sound of footsteps nearing.

"Honey, are you all right?" a kindly, elderly woman passerby asked. "What can I do to help?"

"Nothing," sobbed Mandy still collapsed to the ground, showing no effort to stand.

"Come now," the old woman consoled as she tried to help Mandy off the concrete. "Take this tissue. Tell me how I can help, dear."

"I'll be fine," Mandy said working to compose herself.

"I will pray for you, my dear. Sometimes it's darkest before the dawn. It will work out for you. God will take care of you," said the old woman, full of empty clichés.

Mandy brushed off her bottom and threw herself into the driver's seat, abruptly slamming the door on the old women without apology. She sat for a second and looked into the visor mirror.

"What a hot mess you are," she mumbled to herself, "I need a drink."

She fired up her automobile, put it in reverse, floored the gas pedal and backed out and then quickly slammed the transmission into drive, peeling out of the parking lot, leaving a trail of vaporized rubber behind her.

The little black Jag blazed in and out of traffic to the front door of her favorite upscale bistro, The Capital, and screeched to a halt. She blasted from the car, tossed her keys to an attendant and marched to the entrance where a stationed doorman, sensing her rush, held open the door. Without a nod or a mumbled thank you she tromped directly into the bistro.

After she passed, the doorman and attendant exchanged smirks. "Don't you just love the new styles," the doorman chuckled, "those boots must be the new business casual."

They both laughed.

CHAPTER 3

ONCE MANDY STEPPED into The Capital she remembered why she instinctively chose this place. She was greeted at the door by soft, smooth jazz orchestrating the dimly lit bistro. Warm cherry wood paneling and a coffered ceiling, both gave an understated elegance to the room. Businesspeople filled the bistro toasting a week well done, and couples celebrated their togetherness. She moved to the bar in keeping to the beat of the music, despite her bad mood and clunky boots dragging her down.

She saddled up on a warm red leather stool and stared across the bar, into the mirror behind the bottle display, hardly recognizing her own frail face.

"Hey, there, what can I get you today? Our martinis are on special and it's happy hour."

Mandy didn't hear the bartender at first, too intrigued by the woman in the mirror.

"Huh?" she asked.

The barkeep gave her a smile and repeated his greeting.

"I'm not sure," she whispered, ". . . a martini."

"What flavor?" the barkeep asked.

"Ah, um, ah," she hemmed and hawed. "You'll need to excuse me, I'm not much of a drinker. I need guidance."

"How about a nice chocolate martini," the barkeep suggested. "It's my specialty. But to be fair, I must tell you martinis are quite strong and . . . "

"Great!" she interrupted. "Chocolate it is. A strong chocolate martini is exactly what I need."

"Coming right up."

9

She returned her gaze to the mirror noting her high cheekbones highlighting her sunken cheeks. *There are models who'd die for a profile like mine.* She swiveled her head to a slight left and caught the reflection of a gentleman in her peripheral vision seated on a stool one down, staring back at her through the mirror. She didn't see him join her at the bar, nor did she sense his presence. He simply appeared. Along with a spark from a fiery red ruby on his index finger. Mandy made a swift turn to find the gentleman now watching the barkeep work on the chocolate martini. His chiseled jaw sported a Van Dyke and a touch of grey highlighting his temples. He looked to be in perfect shape. Mandy's first thought when she looked at him was *What a beautiful man*, her version of a middle-aged Adonis.

Finally, the barkeep delivered the martini and when she reached for her purse she heard: "Her money is no good here. Put that on my tab." It was the tuxedoed man with a smooth English accent ordering to pay her drink.

"No, no, no," Mandy quickly interjected, "I can pay for my own drink."

"Of course you can, but not today." The gentleman raised his glass in toast to her.

The barkeep went back to his chores and Mandy reluctantly accepted the gallant gesture and raised her glass in return. She inhaled the intoxicating aroma of Godiva chocolate before taking her first sip.

"Thank You," she said. "Lord knows I need this."

"Some Lords even encourage it," the tuxedoed man laughed revealing a bright, white smile. He slid his business card down the bar to her.

She looked down and read from the card aloud: "'B. Zagan Bubb, Connecting You to Your Desires'—What the hell come-on is this?" She stared into his eyes for seconds, trying to figure him out before she said, "Well, I desire you take a hike."

"Isn't that a bit harsh? I just bought you a drink and you certainly looked like you needed one," said Zagan.

"Fuck off," Mandy hissed her eyes trained down on her martini.

Her rudeness took him off his game, forcing him to backtrack. "Listen, I don't want anything from you. It's just my deed for today. You looked sad and preoccupied and I thought I'd brighten your mood."

Mandy said nothing.

"I must apologize if you misunderstood me. I'll leave you to your night." He offered a weak smile and stood to leave.

She thought it could be worse. And, *damn, he's so handsome.* She looked back at her chocolate martini. She certainly had no plan to hook up with him, but his company could suppress this growing fear she had of being alone on this particular night.

"Thank you for the drink," Mandy said. "You're perceptive, I had a miserable day. And this drink is perfect."

"Well, I'm happy such a small favor was appreciated," Zagan said.

"Please stay. Actually, I could use the company."

They sat in a quiet hold, each nursing their drink. Mandy began to relax as the martini's magic took hold.

"Where did you get the odd name of Zagan?" Mandy queried without looking up from her glass.

"It's an old family name. An uncle, I believe," he chuckled.

"So, what's the 'B.' for? What's your first name?" Mandy asked.

"It's Bielle. It's French. I was tired of being called "Billy" so I chose to use my middle name instead," Zagan explained.

"Billy Bubb," said Mandy, "that's funny. Bubb, what nationality has a surname Bubb?"

"Bubb is the fine English surname of Henry Bubbe and that dates back to the year 1273 under the reign of King Edward I. It's true origin, though, comes from an even earlier time and the Vikings . . . " Zagan started to explain.

"Well thank you for the history lesson, Zagan," Mandy interrupted.

"Huh, you don't have to take the piss with me," Zagan responded.

"What the hell are you talking about?"

"Oh, I'm sorry. You Yanks aren't familiar with English slang," Zagan explained. "You see, 'take the piss' is English slang for mock or, as you Americans might say, 'poke fun of.'"

"You're right. I'm sorry. Quite honestly this is the best thing that's happened to me today,"

"And how should I address you, young lady?"

"My friends call me Mandy."

"Well, how about we make it even better? Mandy, would you care to join me for supper? My treat."

"I don't know. I mean, I don't know you and I don't want pity, and besides your business card reads slightly shady."

"Pity? Poppycock. You have yet to earn my pity. I'm a businessman and we'll discuss the business of getting to know *me*," Zagan chuckled.

"Barkeep, bring me a Devil's Brew Pale Ale and the lady another martini and we need a table!"

The barkeep bent across the bar and shook his head apologetically. "I believe there are no available tables."

Zagan lunged his face forward, eyes glowing red embers and repeated, "We need a table. I'm sure you can find one."

Momentarily dazed, the barkeep stood at attention and said, "Certainly, sir, I'm on it."

Zagan straightened his bow tie and turned to Mandy with a warm, toothy smile.

"Are you standing up in a wedding?" Mandy asked.

"Are you taking the piss with me again? No, no, no," Zagan chuckled, "I like to look good when I'm out and about."

"Isn't it a bit over the top?"

She surprised even herself with her volley of sarcasm. Perhaps it was her way of proving a point to Zagan that she didn't want anything more from him than his company.

"Well, I'm never underdressed for any event, you see," explained Zagan.

The barkeep brought Zagan the two drinks, and asked, "Will there be anything else, sir? Your table is being prepped and will be ready shortly."

Zagan pulled a crisp one-hundred-dollar bill from his inside pocket and laid it on the bar. "Keep the change."

With that said, Charles, the maître d' and well-known fixture at the bistro, appeared, ready to escort the two and Mandy's martini to their table.

Mandy slid from her stool and accepted the arm of the maître d'. Her clump, clump, clump followed her every step.

Zagan caught view of her foot attire for the first time and set to laughing.

Mandy looked over to him and scowled. "Are you pissin' on me?"

Her question propelled him into deeper laughter. It's obvious the martini was doing what he meant it to do. "Please, please forgive me, Mandy, I'm sorry, but your footwear does not match your persona. Do not be embarrassed. Please let me help you regain your dignity," Zagan said quickly.

Zagan reached into his vest pocket and pulled out his cell phone, hit the speed dial and said, "Blisdon! I need a pair of women's shoes size . . . ?" Zagan trailed off looking to Mandy for help.

"To use a word from your country, I must be blitzed, huh? Or maybe you're a drunken scoundrel. Ya think? You can't have my shoe size, it's too personal." She broke into a giggle and asked the maître d' to explain that to Zagan on her behalf. "To ask a woman for her shoe size after just meeting is deeply . . . utterly preposterous . . . " Changing her mind she spit out "six and a half."

"Six and one half . . . with speed my dear man, with speed," he ordered.

"Who is Blisdon and why is he buying me shoes? Where is the logic in some unknown man buying shoes for me at a classy restaurant? This is nuts."

"Blisdon is my driver and minion," said Zagan. "Don't worry, he does all my shopping."

"Really? You must be joking. I appreciate the thought, but it's unnecessary. I'm the type of woman who's at ease in six-inch heels as well as work boots.

"Have no worries, young lady. It is but a small gesture to make you feel a little more comfortable," Zagan explained. "Now please, let us sit and enjoy the rest of the evening."

"I hope everything is to your liking tonight, Mr. Bubb."

"I'm sure it will be, Charles," Zagan said shaking his hand and slipping a hundred-dollar bill into his palm.

"Your server will be with you shortly."

"Thank you, my good man," Zagan said.

Once seated, the busboy rushed to filled their water glasses and place a breadbasket on the table. Mandy unfolded her linen napkin and placed it in her lap.

"Please excuse me," Mandy said, reaching for a crescent roll, "but this is the first thing I've eaten since this morning."

"Do not fret, dear lady," Zagan said, "I understand. However, you must leave room for the main course."

The waitress approached the table dressed in her black vested uniform with a bow tie and introduced herself as Anna. Standing ramrod straight, arms behind her back, she waited patiently for Zagan to address her. She had waited on Zagan previously and knew the protocol he demanded: Always smile and only speak when spoken to. She also knew he was an excellent tipper which made his little idiosyncrasies tolerable.

"Anna, bring us a bottle of your finest pinot noir," Zagan ordered, "but before that I'd like to speak to you privately."

Why does everything about this man seem peculiar? She watched the two in a huddle, Zagan's arms gesturing to his whispered words. Anna listened, her mouth gaping.

"Right away, sir," Anna responded as she turned and scurried off to the kitchen.

Turning to Mandy he apologized, but he loved of surprises. "Sit back and finish your martini."

"What did you just order?" Mandy inquired.

"Something to your liking. Trust me."

What have I gotten myself into? Yes, this guy was beautiful, charming and generous, but she couldn't figure out his end game. She wanted to be sure he didn't get the wrong impression, but it was so nice to be pampered after the day she had. And fun, too. The encounter was pushing her pressing woes to the back for the time being.

Chapter 4

E VANGELINA TENDED TO HER CHORES. It had been a tough millennium being the smallest angel. Even though she had been relegated to menial chores in the Kingdom, she had aspirations to do bigger and better things. At present she'd been busy midwifing the birth of stars and coalescing dust clouds into meteors and planets. It was time consuming and boring, but as she had been told, someone had to do it. She had become quite proficient at her job and was exemplary in her work ethic and performance.

Evangelina wanted desperately to visit Earth and interact with God's creations. She had heard so much about the paradise called Earth and dreamed of one day becoming a messenger angel. She had watched other angels in her position move up the ladder, but when the calling came, she was always passed over. She refused to let herself get depressed about her situation and just doubled down and continued to work at her vocation.

Today's work centered on cleaning up after a star in a far galaxy that had melted down and blown up leaving a huge gassy mess that spanned many light-years. A task this big used to take Evangelina many millennia to clean up, but she had devised a method to significantly reduce the clean-up time. She called her new method the Ev Factor. Ev being short for Evangelina. She was quite proud of her innovation, but dared not to mention it to the others. She feared the others would consider it prideful and that was not an attribute that an angel should display.

Evangelina prepared to set out and tend to her daily mission. The hardest part was locating the wandering rogue planets that roamed the universe. Once she had located enough of them, she would give them a little nudge that changed their trajectory and send them hurtling toward the giant debris field of the nebula. Once the rogue planet was traveling through the fragments field its gravitational force would literally suck up billions of tons of refuse. Her favorite was the huge rogue gas giants. Their massiveness sucked in a hundred times the litter than your average rocky rogue planet. These little boosts, along with the inevitable black hole, pretty much cleaned up the debris field.

As Evangelina readied for her new task, a warm golden light enveloped her. She was startled by its intensity. The light coalesced and before her stood Vangelis, the messenger angel.

"The Lord be with you," greeted Vangelis.

"And also, with you," responded Evangelina.

"I come to you as directed by my audience with the Dominions and at Zadkiel's, the Archangel, request. Archangel Zadkiel requires your presence at this time," announced Vangelis.

Me? Why would he want to speak to a humble angel, such as I? mused Evangelina.

The Dominions are in the upper echelon of angels in Christianity who help keep the human world in order. The Dominion angels are best known for delivering God's justice into unjust situations. They show mercy toward human beings, and help angels in lower ranks stay on task and perform their work well.

Feeling like she had somehow, someway been inadequate in her vocation, Evangelina prepared for her audience with the Archangel Zadkiel. She thought back to all the tasks she had completed over the many millennia and tried to remember if she had left anything undone or did anything that would be considered negligent or subpar. She thought long and hard, but couldn't remember anything that might raise the wrath of the Archangel Zadkiel. Evagelina garnered her courage and started off to her audience with the Archangel Zadkiel and the Dominions. She hoped that Archangel Zadkiel adhered to his calling as being the angel of mercy and would give that when considering her performance. On the other hand, the Dominions are dedicated to doing what's truly best in difficult situations and she hoped what they deemed best did not include clipping her wings.

Evangelina traveled the vast expanse of the Kingdom as quickly as possible. She came upon the gates to the Choir of the Dominions and stood before the towering gold barrier. She touched the gate and it slowly opened. She stepped inside the gate and tread softly and slowly upon the path that wound through the clouds. In the distance she saw a glow of purple light emanating from the clouds. She knew she would find the Archangel Zadkiel there.

As she drew closer, she could hear trumpets in the distance announcing her arrival. She walked in awe of her surroundings. The closer she came to her destination the more intense the purple light became around her. As she broke through the last cloud, she was bathed in the intense purple light emitted from the orbs that adorned the swords and scepters of the choir of Dominions. There, standing in front of the Choir of Dominions stood Zadkiel, the Archangel in all his regalia.

"Welcome Evangelina. May the Lord be with you," Zadkiel smiled and opened his arms welcoming his guest.

"And also, with you," responded Evangelina.

"The Dominions and I have called you here, today, because we have spent a considerable amount of time observing you and your work," explained Zadkiel.

"I hope my performance has been satisfactory," replied Evangelina.

"Satisfactory," exclaimed Zadkiel, "it's been exemplary!"

"I am so pleased to hear that," Evangelina said humbly.

"We have been so pleased that we would like to give you an opportunity to prove your worthiness for an advancement in your angel status," said Zadkiel.

Evangelina's face lit up and said, "I would love the opportunity."

"Well, it is not an easy task and you will have to muster all your creativity and knowledge of demons to accomplish the mission," explained Zadkiel.

"Whatever the mission, I will always give my best," replied Evangelina.

"There is a soul that has earned her way to the Kingdom of Heaven who should be joining us momentarily, but the demons of Hell have decided to try to circumvent her arrival and steal her soul from Heaven. They are making a concerted effort to taint her soul and claim her as one of the minions of Lucifer," explained Zadkiel.

"That is despicable," interjected Evangelina.

"Yes, indeed. Your job, Evangelina, is to intercede on behalf of the Father and defend her soul from the onslaught of temptations that will beset this poor soul and bring her to the Kingdom of Heaven," Zadkiel explained. "Do you feel up for the job, Evangelina?"

"Must I use restraint in my efforts?" questioned Evangelina.

"Considering this situation is dire you may use any and all righteous and just methods necessary to save her soul from these despots, but you may never tell her who you really are," instructed Zadkiel.

"I accept the challenge," replied Evangelina.

"You need to leave quickly because the demon, Beelzebub, sits with her as we speak. You must intercede immediately and decisively or all hope is lost," commanded Zadkiel.

"Does this soul have a name?" questioned Evangelina.

"Her name is Amanda Abbessi."

CHAPTER 5

B LISDON PULLED THE BLACK LIMOUSINE to the mall entrance, and ran to the front door. Blisdon, known as "The Quick," knew when the Master said "with speed" he meant quickly, but when he said it twice in the same sentence Blisdon knew he had to fly to complete his mission. Inside the door he came to the mall directory and surveyed the long list of stores and boutiques that did business there. He knew his Master demanded only the best merchandise when he sent him on excursions and Blisdon understood the high importance the Master placed on this current endeavor.

Blisdon knew shoes because of his own foot fetish and relished the thought of slipping new footwear onto the Master's mark. That is, of course with the Master's permission. He ran down the list of shoe stores listed on the directory and discarded most out of hand as low rent. Giving up on the small-time shoe sellers, Blisdon perused the anchor stores. When he spotted Saks Fifth Avenue, he gave a proud, gratified smirk.

Pulling his vintage taxi hat down low over his pointy ears he scurried to the elevator as quickly as his short stubby legs could carry him. His black riding boots clacked loudly as he made his way through the crowd. A teenager stepped in front of his path and almost tripped him. Blisdon spun like a skilled football running back and continued on his path.

"Clumsy arse," Blisdon shouted.

He zigged and zagged through the mall crowd and made it to the glass elevator. He slipped into the elevator just as the doors were closing and squeezed into the packed car. As he stood watching the elevator numbers climb to the third floor, he felt a tug on the back of his black vest. Blisdon turned around and came eye to eye with an 8-year-old child holding his mother's hand.

"What grade are you in?" the young lad asked.

"Are you kidding me?" Blisdon growled, baring his shark-toothed teeth.

The wide-eyed boy grabbed his mother's waist and squeezed hard. Just then, the elevator chimed and the doors opened. Blisdon turned and was gone in the blink of an eye.

Blisdon hustled into the entrance of Saks and ran past the make-up and fine perfume counters to the directory next to the escalators. He scoured the directory and found the "Women's Shoe Fashion" entry and saw it was on the same floor. He turned around to spot its location, but unfortunately, he wasn't tall enough to see over the displays. Finally, spotting an older woman store associate, he asked "Clerk, where is the women's shoe department?" Blisdon said his words with urgency.

"Are you looking for your mother, young man?" the sales associate inquired.

Blisdon's rage boiled from his toes to the tip of his pointed ears. His faced reddened and his eyes glowed green. He grit a toothy frown and spoke slowly and deliberately. "Where . . . is . . . the . . . fucking . . . women's . . . shoe . . . department?"

The woman sale's associate gasped and staggered back to lean against the glass display for support, all while focusing on Blisdon's sharp toothy mouth. "Ba . . . Ba . . . Back in the corner," she stammered, pointing toward the area.

Blisdon was gone in a flash. Around the corner and down the aisle he dashed. Arriving at the shoe department, he surveyed the layout and spotted an associate at the front desk. He made his way quickly to the desk and addressed the cashier.

"I need a pair of Louis Vuitton New Patent Red Sole Pumps in size six and one half," blurted Blisdon.

"I'll get a sale's associate to assist you."

"I know exactly what I want, so go in the back and get them," Blisdon growled.

"I'm sorry, sir, but that's not how we do things in this department," the cashier explained.

"I don't care how you do business. I know exactly what I need. Go get them now," said Blisdon, slowly, enunciating his words.

"Let me get you a sale's associate," replied the cashier.

"Listen, you cretin, get me what I asked for now or I'll go back and get them myself."

The cashier waved frantically over his head and caught the eye of a young female salesperson rushing to his aid. She slowed at the sight of a small person burning his eyes into her.

"Sandra, can you help this . . . gentleman?" asked the cashier.

"It would be my pleasure." Sandra's lips quivered into a smile, "What can I show you sir?"

"Don't show me anything. Get me a pair of Louis Vuitton New Patent red sole pumps size six and a half and make it quick," Blisdon demanded.

"Well, I need to see if we have that in stock. I'll be right back," Sandra replied.

Blisdon paced back and forth in front of the desk mumbling to himself. With every passing minute he grew more agitated. He checked his pocket watch and uttered a low growl. Finally, he slammed his fist on the glass countertop and snapped at the cashier.

"I'm sure she'll be back shortly."

"I guarantee you that if she's not back here in the next thirty seconds you will rue the day you were born, you piece of excrement," Blisdon snarled.

The young man had dealt with difficult customers before, but none this abusive and scary. He thought about calling security, but knew if he did that would just incite this guy to riot. He hoped Sandra would return with the shoes soon and they could get him out of the store.

Sandra finally returned with a black shoebox with the large red "LV" initials on the box lid. She opened the box and showed Blisdon the shiny, new shoes. Blisdon smirked and shook his head approvingly. The cashier scanned the box and rang up the sale.

"That will be $736.70. Will that be debit or credit?"

"Cash."

"Well, all right then," said the cashier.

Blisdon pulled eight crisp new one hundred-dollar bills from his vest pocket and threw them in the cashier's face and turned to leave.

"Your change, your receipt," the cashier called.

"Keep the change," Blisdon called back.

Blisdon ran down the aisle toward the elevator. He zigged and zagged through the shoppers as they meandered down the aisle. Upon reaching the elevator he stopped and impatiently waited for the lift. He tapped his toe as he hugged the prized black shoebox, watching the numbers ascend.

The elevator doors opened to the exiting shoppers. Already annoyed, his anger began to boil over. Shoving a young girl aside, he pushed his way into the elevator. Once inside he began pounding the main floor button with his fist. Finally, the elevator door closed and began its descent. When the elevator stopped at the second floor to let passengers depart and new passengers enter, Blisdon almost lost his mind. He began ranting and raving about how humans didn't deserve to be alive. The elevator occupants stepped back and looked dumbfounded at the wild little man jumping and flapping his arms.

When the elevator door opened on the main floor Blisdon shoved an elderly woman out of the way and dashed down the wide aisle toward the main entrance. Carrying his precious cargo like a football, Blisdon made his way to the entrance. Before he could make his way out the door a hulking security guard stepped into his pathway.

"Whoa there, what's the big hurry there, little guy?" questioned the burly security guard.

"What business is it of yours fat guy?" asked Blisdon.

"Oh, it's definitely my business," replied the security guard.

"Fuck off, asshole," hissed Blisdon.

"Sir, can you show me the receipt for those very expensive pair of shoes you have there?"

"Receipt, I don't need a fucking receipt," raged Blisdon.

"Oh, I'm afraid you do. Would you mind coming with me to answer a few questions?"

"Sorry, no time," growled Blisdon.

"Oh, you're gonna make time," laughed the security guard, exerting his authority over the impudent little brat.

"Really . . . " Blisdon trailed off.

Blisdon snapped his fingers and the world stopped. Everything froze. Shoppers stood like statues. Cashiers remained motionless at checkout. The immobile security guard remained in front of him with a sarcastic smile frozen on his face.

"Like I said . . . I don't need a receipt, asshole," Blisdon smiled.

Blisdon walked around the security guard and out the doors. He dashed to the running limousine and tossed the box onto the passenger side seat. Looking back at the store entrance he snapped his fingers. The store came back to life along with the befuddled security guard. Blisdon jumped behind the wheel and roared off to The Capital.

CHAPTER 6

I N HIS RACE AGAINST TIME, the black limousine sideswiped the curb as it pulled up to the entrance of The Capital. With his precious cargo under his arm, Blisdon raced through the double doors, his short legs spinning like helicopter arms and beelined to Zagan's table.

Mandy sipped her now third chocolate martini as Zagan described his business ventures. Intrigued by the number and diversity of business holdings of B. Zagan Bubb, she contemplated how she could somehow get involved in the real estate end of his business, but the grim realization of her diagnosis demolished any hope for a future.

"I'm so sorry, I'm boring you to tears," Zagan apologized.

"No, no, it's not that," sniffled Mandy, "it's just I received some bad news today and I can't get it out of my mind."

"Well, maybe, if you share it with me, I can help," said Zagan.

"No, no, it's not like me to burden anyone, let alone a stranger, with my problems."

"I understand, but let me give you this. One of my favorite businesses I own is just down the street. I hope you've seen it. Bubb's Rejuvenating Rubs is a five-star massage and spa. My associate Asmo runs it. Just show him this card and he'll take care of you," Zagan said giving her a gold Bubb's Rubs card.

With that, an out-of-control body of motion landed at her feet.

"Mandy, meet Blisdon. My manservant. My crackerjack friend. He has a gift for you, don't you Blisdon?"

Blisdon bowed his head, and produced the box of shoes Zagan promised earlier. "Mandy, these shoes will complete you head to toe," Zagan said.

Opening the box of Louis Vuitton New Patent Red Sole Pumps prompted Mandy let out a hearty laugh. "Thank you, but if I wanted a pair of those shoes, I'd buy them. These are too, how shall I say it, over the top. Not my style, I don't wear status symbols. In other words, I can't accept them," said Mandy. "My father taught me long ago that if someone has to tell or show you they are important, they really aren't. If they were really important, you would already know," Mandy smiled. "I'm not sure what the "red sole" represents to hard workers like myself however, many people of wealth are wearing them. Thank you anyway."

She replaced the cover on the box choosing to ignore Zagan's disbelief and embarrassment and turned her attention to a team of busboys rushing from the kitchen to set up a small separate table adjoining Mandy and Zagan's.

With Mandy preoccupied, Zagan discretely motioned to Blisdon to return the shoes to their bag and mouthed, "Return them."

Peeved, Blisdon shrugged, but would follow his Master's order after he was dismissed. He stood submissively at attention behind Zagan's chair waiting for his master's next whim.

As one worker covered the table with a linen tablecloth, another finished the decor with a wreath of flowers surrounding a candle. With the table set up, a line of servers carrying steaming, dome-covered silver platters of food streamed out from the kitchen and stood behind their individual dish set on the table.

"There must be a mistake, this can't be what you ordered. All this for two people? What's under those lids?"

With a nod from Zagan, one by one the servers each lifted a lid and announced with flourish the name of their dish: Penne ai quattro formaggi. Martha Stewart's mac and cheese. Indian Desi Mac and Cheese. Pasta with cheese and maitake mushrooms. Macaroni Schotel from Indonesia. Truffle macaroni and asiago cream. Mac 'n' cheese Tolstoy style . . . all in all the table displayed a total of sixteen varieties of macaroni and cheese from traditional American to aristocratic recipes from around the world.

Mandy's awestruck silence was followed by a burst of uncontrollably giddy laughter, interrupted only by deep breaths.

"Oh, my, Zagan. How would you know mac and cheese is my comfort food? The food I first choose when I'm out of sorts. You must have a true spiritual insight granted by God."

Zagan would only nod in response and take that as a signal.

Waving a hand over the table of food, he chanted in a deep guttural voice:

"Post morde ne resistere," His words cursed the food with his incantation, activating the spell of gluttony by proclaiming food irresistible to any mortal. Only one bite and Mandy would be vulnerable to the curse and would not stop eating until she passed out. She would be guilty of gluttony and Beelzebub, (aka Zagan), would have captured her soul adding another notch to the hilt of his sword.

Zagan moved in close to Mandy. "Which one appeals to you most? I'm betting on the pasta with maitake mushrooms, direct from China. Or maybe the Macaroni from Indonesia. I'm sure you're familiar with Martha Stewart's version of mac and cheese. How about . . . ?"

"Stop. This is all too much. I've had too much to drink. The wine and martini aren't mixing well. However much every one of those dishes is appealing to me, I just can't . . . I really don't want any of this," Mandy protested. "Perhaps I could have a doggie bag?"

"Well, try *something*, Mandy. They worked so hard to bring you food you would like." Zagan's devil blood now boiled over. Not only had he misjudged his plan, but now he had mortified himself in front of the entire restaurant, including the rubbernecking patrons standing to watch "The Spectacle of Macaroni and Cheese" as it was later referred to in years to come. After all, he insisted she drink—loosen herself up to make her more amenable to suggestion and food. And now she dared ask for a doggie bag?

"I really don't want any of this," she said with a lingering eye on the good old-fashioned macaroni and cheese from Martha Stewart.

Zagan caught her fixed stare at the dish and commanded the waitress to "Scoop a healthy bowl of Stewart's macaroni and cheese for this young woman."

"Certainly, sir," she said, heaping the dish into a China bowl and placing the steaming aroma directly under her nose. Mandy hesitated before dipping her spoon into the mixture. Zagan watched with vulturous glee as she finally took the plunge and brought the spoon to her lips.

But his mood turned to outrage when Mandy's movement stopped midair, frozen in time, just as the spoon reached her mouth. Surveying the area, he saw an entire room of people frozen and motionless.

"Did you just freeze time, Beelzebub?" Blisdon asked.

"Not I. Didn't you?" responded Beelzebub.

"Nada."

Evangelina stepped out from behind Mandy's chair and stood defiantly to face her two nemeses. "You demons are pathetic," Evangelina said. "I'll put a stop to your charade."

Beelzebub looked and then looked again at the accuser and laughed.

"You're the best heaven has to intercede?" he questioned.

"Who is this puny excuse for an angel?" Blisdon asked, delighted to find she wasn't much bigger than him.

In the face of such insult, she jutted her gold breastplate out. With her hand clutching her sword of righteousness and clothed in full angelic battle regalia, she stood firm and faced them boldly. Folding her arms, she pronounced: "I am Evangelina. The Archangel Zadkiel has sent me to save this poor mortal from your feeble attempt to entrap her," Evangelina announced.

"Well, you're a little late, runt," Beelzebub laughed. "One bite from that spoon at her lips and the game's over."

"Your spell is a feeble attempt and no match for an angel worth her wings," Evangelina replied. "You realize it must be *her* choice, not through your incantation."

"Oh really?" said Beelzebub incredulously. "Look, little lady, she's about to exert her own free will and take a bite."

Evangelina turned toward Mandy, the spoon of macaroni and cheese precariously close to her open lips. Darting her eyes back to the two demons she smiled. In one brisk move she turned and swung her tiny fist, catching Mandy squarely in her stomach. Evangelina snapped her fingers and time resumed. Mandy dropped the spoon and doubled over in pain.

"Excuse me, but I don't feel well. Where's the rest room?" Mandy asked breathlessly.

The waitress pointed to the back corner of the restaurant. Mandy got up from her chair and gingerly walked toward the rest rooms. Beelzebub and Blisdon exchanged looks.

"That BITCH," they shouted simultaneously.

CHAPTER 7

S HE LEANED AGAINST the washbasin in the inner sanctum of the lady's lounge waiting for her charge to enter. Dressed in a billowy white tunic blouse cinched at the waste by a thin gold belt, her platinum hair flowed over her shoulders. She waited patiently drying her hands. The door to the ladies' room finally pushed open and Mandy staggered in, collapsing onto the lounge just inside and moaned softly in pain.

"Are you all right, dear?"

Mandy glanced briefly to see a young lady hovering over her.

"I'm fine," whispered Mandy.

"Mmm . . . You sound like you're in pain."

"Just some cramps." Mandy groaned.

"Was it something you ate?"

"Didn't have a chance to even get a spoonful." Oddly, Mandy's ache calmed with the woman's lulling, almost healing voice.

"Well, at least we know it's not food poisoning," the lady said with a smile. "Monthly cramps?"

"Um, no . . . shouldn't be."

Mandy sharply recoiled when the woman seated herself on the lounge and began rubbing her shoulders. But her touch offered a quick relief from the pain and she relaxed slightly.

"My name is Evangelina, but everyone calls me Ev. Is there something I can get you?"

Mandy looked up for the first time to face her benefactress. Threads of glistening platinum hair framed an angelic face. She had no choice but to ask this unknown person to help her leave the restaurant. "Could you get me out of here and to my car? . . . and by the way, I'm Amanda. Also known as Mandy."

"You certainly don't look like you're able to drive."

"I think I can make it," whispered Mandy.

"Should I call a taxi?"

"No, no . . . I can drive," Mandy explained.

"I'll tell you what. I'll drive you home and take a taxi back. It'll be the best for both of us," Ev proposed.

Mandy thought it odd that she trusted this woman so quickly. She hesitated to consider her proposal, but when a wave of cramps swept in, her decision was immediate.

"OK . . . OK. But there's a gentleman sitting at a table with a huge buffet set out next to the table. I have to say goodbye and thank him," Mandy explained.

"Don't worry, I'll take care of it for you," Ev promised. "I'll make sure he knows how grateful you are."

Ev stood and extended her hand to Mandy and helped ease her to her feet, then grabbed her shoulders to steady her wobbling legs. With great effort, Mandy put one foot in front of the other, finally reaching the ladies' room exit. She pushed it open with her elbow and the two ladies stepped out into the restaurant, staying along in the shadows of the back wall to avoid attention.

Nearly to the exit she was intercepted by the maître d'.

"Leaving so soon, miss?"

"She's not feeling well," answered Ev.

"Tell him to thank Zagan," Mandy whispered.

"Do us a favor and let Mr. Bubb know she's not feeling well and has left the restaurant with Evangelina," smiled Ev.

Once outside, the parking lot attendant walked up and was about to ask for the name of the car until he recognized Mandy's black boots.

"I know," he said with a smile. "Black Jag coming right up."

The attendant grabbed the keys and ran off into the parking lot. Mandy fumbled with her purse and pulled out a crumpled wad of bills and handed it to Ev.

"Give him something nice," Mandy whispered.

Upon his return Ev commandeered the car and drove off after handing the attendant a twenty-dollar bill.

"My, oh my, aren't we fancy," Ev smiled, "a black Jag, no less."

"It's a lease," said Mandy, "necessary for my business image."

"Well, I'm impressed. Where to?"

"Go east to Crooks Road and then south to 14 Mile Road. I live right there at the condos," Mandy directed.

"On our way," Ev said.

Ev pulled the Jag out of the parking lot and onto Big Beaver Road. She pulled into the Michigan turn-around to head East. It wasn't even a mile before she came to the corner of Crooks Road. She turned right and proceeded south toward 14 Mile Road. Nestled just north of 14 Mile Road and Crooks stood the Esplanade Condominiums Complex. It's reclaimed brick exterior and red tiled roof gave it a classic old-world feel. Mandy directed her to pull around the back to her reserved parking spot.

"We're here," Ev announced as she popped out and ran to the passenger's door to assist Mandy. "No tip necessary," she joked.

They walked along the brick paver path to Mandy's condo's door. Mandy fumbled with her purse and fished out her key.

"Please come in."

"I'd hate to impose on you," Ev replied.

"No, no, not at all. After all you've done for me it's the very least I can do for you," said Mandy.

"Thank you. It'll be much warmer waiting for my cab in here." "You know, I'm feeling a little better now that I'm home," Mandy said, "Can I make you a cup of coffee while you wait?"

"Coffee? Sure."

Mandy turned to Ev as an afterthought. "Ya know, tonight at the bistro was like a story out of Brothers Grimm. It had a fairy tale feel to it and I was the central figure waiting for a sinister end to befall me. Nothing made sense. Oh, well, too many martinis. Your coffee's coming up."

Standing in the vestibule Mandy's cat, Oscar, sidled up to Ev, rubbed against her leg, and purred loudly. She brought him into her arms and whispered, "We'll take care of her, won't we fella?"

Mandy stopped as she entered the room. "That's not like Oscar. Oscar doesn't like anyone. That's a first. Oscar barely likes me," she said in amazement.

"Animals seem to like me."

"That's an excellent endorsement in my book," Mandy smiled.

The black limousine rolled slowly through the Esplanade parking lot with its lights off. Blisdon pulled the limousine over and pointed to the black Jag. He looked back at his passenger.

"Master, I believe that is her car," announced Blisdon.

"Silence, peon," Beelzebub roared, "you're lucky I don't banish you to the seventh level right now after failing to deliver on my last command."

Wide-eyed, Blisdon slowly turned his head back and stared out the windshield. Master, as true to form, would blame him for his failure with the girl.

"Before you start whining, I have an alternative plan," Beelzebub confided. "I'm calling our friend." Beelzebub hit speed dial on his phone.

Blisdon knew not to be encouraged too early in the game.

"Greetings, old friend," said Beelzebub, speaking on the phone, "I have a mission for you I think you'll like. Yes, she's a beauty and no it can't wait. We need you tonight. I'll be waiting for you in my limousine. Use your tracker to my vehicle. Yes, hurry."

With a flash, a knock appeared at the driver's window and Blisdon immediately exited the limousine, ran around to the passenger side door and opened it. In stepped a dark figure.

"Incubus, old friend," greeted Beelzebub. "Master of lust, my favorite deadly sin.

CHAPTER 8

"How you feeling now, Mandy? You look better."

"Much better, thanks. Funny thing is that I feel like someone punched me in the gut."

Ev lowered her eyes and gave a silent chuckle. *If you only knew how close you are to what happened.* The two sat at the kitchen table sipping coffee while Mandy gave Ev a quick summary of the day's bizarre events.

"Last thing I remember is me sprawled out on a lounger in the ladies' room with your face hovering over me . . . but I can still picture that feast of mac and cheese. In fact, I haven't eaten since breakfast and I'm starving. What about you? Are you hungry, Ev? I make a mean toasted avocado and pico de gallo sandwich."

"No, no. I'm fine, but you go ahead." Ev smiled watching Mandy enthusiastically scurry about the kitchen to construct her sandwich.

Once the toast popped, Ev said, "That smells wonderful."

"I can still make you one."

"No, no, no, I've had enough for today," explained Ev.

"So, Ev are you from around here?" Mandy asked before her first bite.

"No, not really," Ev replied.

"Where are you from?"

"Uh, way north from here," Ev offered.

"The U.P.," Mandy clarified.

"Exactly, the U.P.," Ev smiled.

"Must be beautiful up there this time of year."

"More beautiful than you can imagine. Perhaps one day you can see it with me."

"Oh, I'd like that. I haven't been on a vacation since forever. I've been too busy with the business and my mother." Glumness took over after remembering the short time available to her to take that trip with Ev.

Ev pulled up her phone to answer its buzz. "Well, my ride is here," she said, pushing herself away from the table. A large warm smile played across her lips as she looked at Mandy—she liked her.

"Damn . . . I wish you could stay," said Mandy. "I feel so comfortable with you."

"Me, too, I feel the same. Thanks for the coffee."

Mandy and Oscar walked Ev to the door.

"Hold on," said Mandy, running back to the kitchen and returning with her business card. "Here, my cell number is on the card. Please call me, we can have lunch." She reluctantly opened the door.

"Oh, I'll be around. I'm sure we'll see each other very soon." Ev issued a knowing smile.

"And once again, thanks for your kindness. I truly appreciate what you did for me tonight. Not a lot of people in this world would get involved with a stranger."

"Good night, Mandy," Ev said.

"Good night."

Mandy lingered at the door and watched Ev disappear into the dark night before closing the door.

Once out of sight, Ev returned to her angel form in full battle regalia. She flapped her wings and flew to the roof of Mandy's condominium and crawled to the peak to survey the crystal-clear night sky. Ever vigilant, she remained there, cross-legged, guarding the grounds. Her ears perked at the sound of a running car. She rose, extending her neck to search the night until she spied a fog of light attached to a black limousine idling in the condominium's back parking lot. She shook her head.

"They're not going to give up easily," she spoke as she raised her eyes to the heavens and prayed. "Dear Almighty Father, I accept this challenge and ask you for the courage, strength and wisdom to defeat these abominations and defend this soul of your creation. Amen."

Mandy finished her avocado toast and cleaned up her mess. It wasn't until she was alone, shut up in her condo with only Oscar to keep her company that the weight of the day surfaced and brought up Dr. Fineman's image reminding her that her mother needed to be told. *After my shower,* she told herself. *Maybe.*

CHAPTER 8

After adjusting the water temperature, she disrobed and entered the stall blasting the high-pressure showerheads full force. The stomach pain subsided, but not fully. She felt better than she did just a few short hours ago. But, without invitation, Dr. Fineman's face haunted her daydream once again. She revisited his words, allowing a wave of acute anxiety overcome her. Sliding down into the tub, she choked on her tears. The warm water washed them away, but not the wretched fear of her diagnosis.

She remembered her silent resolve to not go out without a fight. Above all, she wanted no sympathy. Come what may, she was going to live in the moment and make a difference before leaving Earth. She was a winner with a new challenge; one she intended to beat and maintain her dignity through it all.

After drying herself, she slipped into her robe, and prepared to sit on the bed and make that dreaded call to her mother. But the lit numbers on her phone, gave her pause. *It's late. Too late.* That call would keep her mom up all night. Grateful for an excuse to put off what could be a long discussion into the late night, she collapsed back onto her bed, too tired to switch into her flannels, and kicked her legs under the comforter. She reached over and switched her small bedroom lamp off and nestled back into her pillow. Sleep came immediately.

Illuminated by the moon shining through Mandy's bedroom window, a black mist swirled into the room and manifested into the demon, Incubus, at the foot of her bed. He smiled his black toothy smile as he anticipated his nightly fun. Having enjoyed tempting many women, very few had Mandy's beauty.

Certain Mandy was in deep sleep, he approached the bed. Slowly and carefully, he slipped under the covers and lay next to her on his side. He stroked her cheek with his long nails and blew a warm breath into her ear. He stuck out his forked tongue and licked her lips. As he nibbled at her neck, Mandy sighed. The demon smiled and continued. Moving deeper under the comforter he reached to untie the robe and gingerly open it to begin his dastardly duty. When he nibbled down her neck to her chest, Mandy moaned. Incubus salivated.

"And what might you think you're going to do?" Evangelina asked rhetorically as she stood in the doorway holding Mandy's cat, Oscar.

A hissing Incubus popped up from under the covers, baffled by the mysterious voice interrupting his pleasure. He scrambled off the bed totally discombobulated and ready take up arms against the intruder. Evangelina laughed at him. "Go get him, Oscar." With that, she tossed a yowling and spitting angry Oscar into the open arms of Incubus. The cat dug his nails into the unclothed Incubus who quickly dissipated into the same mist he arrived. Oscar fell to the ground and landed on all four legs, looking a bit confused, but decided it wasn't worth his time. He glided out of the bedroom satisfied that he had defended his domain.

"Persistent buggers," Evangelina mumbled.

Evangelina pulled a small blue canister from her pocket and laid down a line of salt around Mandy's bed. She remembered learning that demons have a severe aversion to salt. "This perimeter will stop any repeat performances by the demon, Incubus." After completing the circle, Evangelina sighed and returned to her perch atop the condominium complex.

There was a tap at the limousine's window and Blisdon rushed around back to open the rear passenger side door. Incubus slipped into the back seat. He sat, arms tightly folded against his chest, and threw out a disgusted growl.

"Well?" questioned Beelzebub.

"That damned, puny little angel bitch got in the way and interfered with my work," Incubus complained.

"So, what did she do?" Beelzebub questioned.

"She threw a cat at me."

"A cat?" Beelzebub asked incredulously.

"Yes, a cat," replied Incubus.

"So, you let a little furry feline stop you from your mission?" Beelzebub enjoyed heckling this failed demon.

"Well, yes," said Incubus realizing how ridiculous he sounded.

"You sniveling little excuse for a demon . . . You let a puny angel throw a cat at you and you ran away like a cowering coward. How did you survive the millennia being such a pansy?" Beelzebub said with disgust.

"Well . . . I'm a lover, not a fighter," whispered Incubus.

"You're an idiot, Incubus," Beelzebub roared. "Incubus the Idiot."—it has a good ring, 'Incubus the Idiot.'"

"Anyway," Beelzebub continued, "we have another shot at the sin of lust. I gave her a gold card to Asmodeus' massage parlor. He and his team won't fail us. We may need your assistance getting her there, Incubus. She has an appointment that needs to be washed out her schedule. Something right up your alley."

Chapter 9

"Noooo," she screamed into the pillow, rolling over to cut off the cell phone alarm badgering her to get out of bed. She wanted to stay buried under the covers, but had a listing appointment at noon. She shuffled to her bathroom to make herself presentable for the long day. Her muddled mind slowly unwrapped the events of the previous day, and she laughed out loud. *Who was that little guy, Blisdon, with the pointy ears? Or Zagan, aka Mr. Bubb, Billy? Nothing made sense. The mac and cheese. The red sole shoes. Totally kinky.* But she admitted the diversion was fun.

She looked fixedly at her face in the mirror and recognized a subtle determination and off-kilter beauty she'd not seen before. Nothing she could explain. "Huh," she said to her reflection. "What's going on?"

Only after she addressed the helter-skelter of clothes she'd left abandoned to the floor, could she begin dressing for her appointment. She started with her wool blazer, checking her pockets for any reminder notes stuffed into them during the previous day. She pulled out a golden gift certificate for "Bubb's Rejuvenating Rubs," and a card which read "B. Zagan Bubb, Connecting You to Your Desires." Mandy smiled, remembering the interchange and set the card on her nightstand.

Facing her full-body mirror she checked each detail of her outfit. Her corporate blue suit, along with her city chic bow blouse always made a good first impression. A diamond-based tennis bracelet from her father added a sparkling punch. You only have one chance. She rummaged through her closet to find her blue pumps and slipped into them simultaneously looking down to laugh when she spotted her boots from yesterday. It was as if her brain was slowly unpacking the confusion from the day before and serving it to her as a balm for her to appreciate. *Always enjoy the uniqueness of each day.*

Finally, grabbing her black, full-length wool coat and fashionable scarf from the front closet to complete her look, she reached into her purse for her keys. When they weren't there, she checked the kitchen table. Nada. Same with her bedroom nightstand. Resigned they were hiding somewhere and time was running short, Mandy went to the kitchen drawer and grabbed her spare car fob.

Her cell phone chimed just as she reached the door. It was a text from her noon homeowner appointment. She checked the text to find that the homeowner's hot water heater had melted down and they were waiting for a plumber to come and replace it. They wanted to reschedule for Sunday.

"Well, that's just great," Mandy said aloud and texted the homeowner back saying she understood and would call Sunday morning to confirm a time. Mandy hung up her outerwear and returned to the bedroom to exchange her work uniform for yoga leggings, and a heavy cable knit sweater. She swapped her pumps for leather thigh high boots and proceeded to sit. And sit. And sit. Her thoughts returned to the night before again and how many emotional arrows hit their target: fear, surprise, sadness, confusion, and on and on. *What a wacky day,* she thought. *Hilarious.* With that thought she broke into nonstop laughter that included a cascade of cheerful tears. Every emotion in her repertoire lived at the surface, ready to be called.

Mom often lectured her on the physical benefits of laughter. "It washed out the ugly, honey." The relief she felt was sudden, but short-lived. She had to face her mom, tell her about the cancer, and discuss options. She'd spend the day comforting her. As much as she didn't want to face up to this, it was the right thing to do on this unplanned day off from work. She sat on the bed staring at nothing until her eyes lit on the gold Bubb's Rejuvenating Rubs card.

"Why not?" Mandy said aloud and stuffed the card in her pocket. She grabbed her burnished leather moto jacket and Burberry muffler scarf and made her way to the door. The idea of making the best out of a wasted day inspired her. She'd see Mom later. Maybe a massage would clear her thinking, prepare her for the discussion that had to come.

Mandy had a general idea where the spa might be, but didn't recall seeing it in her travels. Sitting at a light she punched the address into her GPS and a map appeared. The spa sat hidden behind one of the bigger skyscrapers on Big Beaver. She pulled into its parking lot, surprised to find the spa's parking lot packed.

The building, with its ancient Roman façade and marble columns, carved metope and frieze, presented an image of wealth. The sun peaked out from behind the clouds and shone brightly on a white marble building. Mandy knew this area well. She had sold many houses around here. How is it she had never seen this great edifice before?

She flipped down the sun visor and flipped up the vanity mirror to repair her weary eyes. Upon exiting the car, she was greeted by a large marble fountain, painstakingly detailed with two lovers in a sensual embrace at the center. Mandy asked herself: How did the tag line on Zagan's card read? "Connecting You to Your Desires?" or something like that. She reminded herself to be suspicious of strangers bearing gift cards to a spa. She walked through the plaza and up the white marble steps to reach a carved handle on the embellished heavy, wood doors. Once through the arched doorway, she stepped into an immense, elegant foyer with a tall arching ceiling. Behind a white marble counter stood a tall, beautiful Nigerian woman who greeted her with a huge smile.

"Welcome, madam, to Bubb's Rejuvenating Rubs," the receptionist said with a charming accent. "How may we serve you today?"

Mandy approached the counter and fumbled in her pocket to pull out the gold card Zagan had given her and presented it to the receptionist. One look at the card and the receptionist's demeanor perked up.

"Ah, you are a special young lady. Let me call my supervisor, Mr. Deus. He will take care of all your needs."

"Thank you," Mandy replied.

Mandy turned to survey the foyer. Astonishingly beautiful. Elaborate carvings adorned certain walls while classic oil artwork representing Italian Renaissance paintings of heaven and hell gave the space historical significance. Her real estate trained mind started to appraise the building's value, when she was interrupted by a warm hello.

"Let me introduce myself," the gentleman said, offering a slight bow. "I am Mr. Deus. I see you have a special friend. Zagan is my partner in this little endeavor."

Mr. Deus appeared to be in his early fifties with jet-black hair and carefully trimmed moustache. She stared at him through his smoke-tinted Cartier glasses which clouded his eyes. Impeccably dressed in a silk Italian three-piece suit, Empa gold tie with a ruby tiepin, and bearing a solid gold Rolex on his wrist—he made an imposing presence. But it was his smile revealing a gold front incisor that told her she stood in the aura of mega money.

"Yes, Mr. Deus, I recently met Zagan and he was kind enough to give me a gold card yesterday," Mandy said.

"No, no, no, please call me Asmo. Welcome, you are in for a special treat, my dear lady," Asmo replied.

"I could use a special something, that's for sure," Mandy half-heartedly joked, then blushing and wondering if joking in a place like this was inappropriate.

"Oh, I think your experience here will be totally satisfying for all your senses," Asmo said grinning. "Come with me, my dear."

She followed him through a hallway to the luxurious lounge area with gold leaf adorned couches and chairs upholstered in antique tapestry. Octagonal black marble-topped side chairs completed the area. A full bar spanned across one wall. Behind the bar stood a tall, beautiful young man dressed in a white toga waiting to serve them.

"Would you like anything from behind the bar?" Asmo offered.

"Thank you, but no, it's a little too early to drink," replied Mandy.

"How about a juice or smoothie just to invigorate?" offered Asmo.

"Thank you, but nothing for now."

"As you wish, Miss," said Asmo. "Come with me and we'll get you started on your day of luxury."

Asmo walked Mandy through the golden doors at the end of the lounge to the spa proper and, once again, she entered another meticulously decorated area with gilded appointments, exquisite furnishings and exotic tropical plants.

"Mandy, I'd like to introduce you to Lilith, our head attendant, who will be your chaperone throughout your experience here," announced Asmo.

"Please to meet you, Lilith."

"Welcome, Mandy. You're about to follow me into an enchanting experience. Come this way."

Lilith took Mandy's hand and walked her through the dressing room door and into the changing area. As Mandy would expect, the walls were lined with spacious, ornate wooden lockers. Lilith opened a locker to reveal personal brushes, toiletries and a full-length fluffy cotton robe. She stepped aside and began Mandy's introduction to everything in the locker and the services she was going to receive.

"On the top shelf you will find your toiletries and scents. The second shelf holds brushes, combs, dryers and curling irons. For your comfort throughout your experience here, this is your robe. Please exchange your outerwear for this robe and we will begin your experience with a nice sauna to purge the impurities from your body," Lilith explained.

"I don't know about using pre-used combs and brushes," Mandy said.

"Oh, no, each locker contains brand new equipment for each guest," Lilith clarified, shocked she would think otherwise.

"How nice."

Mandy proceeded to disrobe and hang her clothes on the wooden hangers in her locker. She slipped into the heated, luxurious robe that smelled of the subtle fragrance of lilacs. *What a glorious place.* She took the key attached to a wristband and locked the locker. She slipped her key onto her wrist and waited. Curiously, she stood alone in the locker room. One would think the place would be bustling on a Saturday, and the full parking lot also suggested that. *Odd,* she thought, but it wasn't her business. She intended to enjoy and relax after her tumultuous yesterday. This day is something she had promised herself to do for the last six months, but something always got in the way. She earned it, she deserved it, and now she was going to luxuriate in it.

Mandy smiled and said to a returning Lilith, "I'm ready,"

"We need to remove the toxins from your body; so, it's off to the sauna with you," Lilith replied.

CHAPTER 10

I N THE PARKING LOT of Bubb's Rejuvenating Rubs, Evangelina sat cross-legged atop the black Jag's roof dressed in full battle regalia, invisible to mortal eyes. An unexpected flurry of light October snow began to fall and Evangelina reveled in the beauty of nature. She watched as furry red squirrels scampered through the trees. A flock of red winged blackbirds circled and then lit upon the power lines along the street. She could feel the warm radiance of the sun upon her wings. It was amazing to watch the sun shining and yet it continued to snow at the same time, but then again, this was Michigan.

As Evangelina contemplated the wonders of the world, the black limousine pulled into the parking lot and came to a stop. It sat idling while grey clouds of exhaust billowed from its tail pipe. Evangelina shook her head and frowned. They weren't going to give up easily and this was a new battle she would have to defend against. Resigned to this fact, Evangelina morphed into her mortal form. The cold north wind blew and chilled her to the bone. She reached out and pulled a white wool coat out of thin air and wrapped it around her body and made her way to the entrance.

Blisdon was the first to spot Evangelina and called his Master's attention saying, "There's that damn angel again."

"I have faith in Asmodeus and his methods," said Beelzebub.

"I wouldn't be so sure," Incubus offered.

"Don't worry, I have Mammon coming in on Monday. If Asmodeus can't deliver I'm sure Mammon can persuade the mortal," smiled Beelzebub.

As Mandy had, Ev walked to the marble reception desk to face the beautiful Nigerian woman standing behind the desk, engrossed in her paperwork. Ev cleared her throat and the receptionist looked up; a bit taken aback by this young girl's sweet, unadorned face.

"I'm sorry, we have all the 'talent' we need for today." The receptionist continued sizing up Evangelina.

"Talent?" Ev questioned.

"Yes, dear, you know. You and your friends provide us with your services to accommodate our clients," explained the receptionist. "Come back tomorrow at 9 a.m. and I'm sure we'll have a gentleman who'll enjoy you. You have a purity about you we've never offered before. And please use the entrance at the rear."

"I'm here to talk to my friend . . . Mandy. I believe she is here using a gold card," Ev said sternly.

"I'm sorry, but our policy prohibits our clients from being disturbed for any and all reasons. You'll have to wait until she is finished with our services."

Ev turned around and folded her arms. She definitely wasn't going to argue with her. She hated to suspend time and tried to use it sparingly. She decided she had no other course of action. She'd be brief she promised herself, raising her hand above her head and snapping her fingers. Time suspended and she scurried past the receptionist to the inside doors of the spa. Without hesitation she snapped her fingers and time resumed. The receptionist stood befuddled. She looked around the foyer and couldn't find that little urchin. She even walked the half-circled front of the marble desk, just per chance the intruder was someplace, squatted down and hiding.

"Sometimes I think this job is playing with my head," the receptionist sighed.

Ev stepped through the doors and into the lounge area and instantly knew she was lost. The curly haired bartender, dressed in his toga, looked up and spied Ev. "Hey, you, where do you think you're going?"

"I'm supposed to meet someone here," Ev replied. "Where is everybody?"

"Well, you're late and you can't come through here. You must be new. Talent has to come through the service entrance," instructed the bartender.

"What?" said Ev. "I don't understand you."

"Here ya go," said the bartender, "go through the doors just past the bar, turn right and walk through my back room. You'll see a door. Go through that door into the kitchen. Walk straight through the kitchen to the end. You'll come to another door. Go out that door and turn right. The first door on your left are the dressing rooms, or as I call them, the undressing rooms."

"OK," said Ev, "I'll do that."

"I'm sure your client is waiting for you," he laughed.

Ev followed the bartender's instructions and made her way through the maze of bustling people. They didn't seem to notice her as they went about their business. She weaseled her way out of the kitchen door into the hallway. After walking in circles a bit she found the first door on the left and stepped into a dressing room of sorts. Much like a back stage dressing room at a theatre.

She looked around the room and was taken back. All shapes and sizes of women bustled about, naked, scantily clad or dressed in ornate costumes. At first Ev was confused, but it now all made sense. This was no spa. This was nothing more than a high-class brothel. *And these women are the "talent."*

"That clever demon," Ev said aloud. "I've gotta find Mandy."

Ev stopped a woman dressed as a lioness and asked, "Where would I find my friend, Mandy?"

"I don't know. Wha' she look like?" she asked, chomping her gum.

"Petite, mid-thirties, long blue-black hair and crystal blue eyes," Ev replied.

"Sweetie, with that description she could match nearly half the women in this place. Maybe ya should check peepholes on the doors to the suites. Ya might find her in one of those rooms. But don't let Lilith catch you if ya wanna live."

"Where are the suites," asked Ev.

"Go out those center doors. The suites line both sides of the hallway all around the building. Good luck," said the lioness.

Hurriedly, Ev rushed to the doors and blasted through into the hallway. Room by room she checked each peephole, zigzagging her way along the hall. She was disgusted by the carnal depravity she witnessed in some of the rooms. Women with men. Women with women. Men with men. What she saw occurring in the rooms made her question the thought processes of mortals, but she was not there to judge. That was up to higher authority. It was an excruciatingly slow process, but Ev couldn't find a faster way. There were so many rooms to check and so little time. She hoped and prayed she could find Mandy before anything foul besmirched her soul.

CHAPTER 11

I N THE MEANTIME, she closed her eyes and breathed deep to allow the healing steam from the eucalyptus do its almost sensual magic. *This is glorious,* Mandy thought as her sinuses opened and sweat exuded from her pores. Not only did she feel the toxins leaving her body, but she was certain she could see them as well.

After thirty minutes in the sauna, Lilith entered the room and whispered almost seductively that a warm bath awaits her.

She clasped Mandy's arm and lead her to an opulent adjoining room where candles lined the marble ledge of an oval tub, just large enough to encircle her body. Lilith offered a glass of champagne to Mandy, which she accepted. Lilith smiled her approval before leaving.

Mandy dropped her towel and slipped into the bath. She sipped the champagne, slowly savoring each sip, imagining being pampered like this regularly. Closing her eyes, the bath took an almost sensual possession of her and she drifted in and out of sleep.

"Mandy . . . Mandy," sang a quiet voice. "Come, you have much more that awaits you."

It was Lilith holding an open towel. Mandy wavered before stepping into the towel. It felt too personal. But Lilith pushed forward and wrapped the towel loosely around her and patted every part of her dry. With that finished, Lilith retrieved Mandy's robe off its hook and handed it to her then watched her exchange her towel for the robe and slip into it. Mandy followed Lilith to the next door. Upon opening it, she turned to Mandy and offered an unreadable smile.

"Come. This is the way to your next experience."

Mandy followed Lilith out the door, into a golden-lit hallway lined with doors. Her curiosity was piqued, she asked, "What do all these doors lead to?"

"They are private suites for our clients," answered Lilith.

"I haven't seen any other clients."

"Well, they're all engaged in their own private experiences," explained Lilith.

"I see," said Mandy, bringing to mind the Zagan's card: *Connecting You to Your Desires.*

At the end of the hall, Lilith opened a door to a salon to be greeted by two women.

"Meet Circe and her mother Hecate. They've been with us since leaving Greece many years ago. You'll be in experienced hands. They'll be giving you a manicure and pedicure. Now . . . can I get you another glass of champagne?"

"No, no, I'm fine," replied Mandy.

"Just relax and enjoy," Lilith said, giving her that same enigmatic, almost smug, smile before leaving the salon area.

Mandy smiled at the mother/daughter duo, both wearing interesting aprons over their black uniforms. Circe's bore an image of fat little pigs, while Hecate's apron was covered in pentagrams. Mandy wondered the significance of either design. Neither appeared to match the elegance of this establishment.

Once seated on the salon's chair, Hecate reclined her back slightly.

"First," said Hectate, "close your eyes and Circe will place chilled cucumber slices over them. You relax while I bathe and massage your feet in this warm basin of soaking solution. Circe will soak and massage your fingertips in soapy water. Enjoy the tingling sensation."

Mandy sighed in full relaxation.

Finally, after drying her nails, they were ready for the next step.

Circe removed the cucumber slices from Mandy's lids and asked, "What color would you like? With that beautiful black hair, I would suggest a warm red. Take a look at these and tell me which you prefer."

"There are so many, and they're all wonderful. How does anyone ever decide?" Her eyes flicked from one favorite to the next, each one replaced by a different shade. Eventually she settled on one. "That one," she said, pointing to the one called Marie-Marie, a bright red/orange. "Ironically it's the name of my mother, Momma Marie."

"A perfect choice," said Circe.

Circe applied the polish to Mandy's fingernails with complete precision while Hecate applied the polish to her toes. After they completed their artistry, Mandy laid back and waited for them to dry. Circe placed fresh cucumber slices on Mandy's eyes once more and asked her to enjoy a short wait. She listened to the two attendants pack their tools and leave the room. Immediately after, she heard the sound of the door opening.

"Hello, I am Gylou," said a voice in the room removing the cucumber slices, "and I will be giving you your facial."

Once her eyes adjusted to the light, Mandy looked up to a uniformed woman who appeared pregnant.

"I'll be using my special blend of avocados, honey, aloe vera, turmeric, lemon, coconut milk, yogurt and other secret inert ingredients. Are you allergic to any of those?"

"No, none of those," Mandy smiled.

"Very good."

Gylou carefully applied the nourishing mask to Mandy's face, outlining the fresh slices of cucumber over her eyes. She felt immediate tingling on her cheeks and forehead as the nutrients seeped into her pores.

"Now sit back and relax for about twenty minutes while the mask does its job."

Eyes closed, Mandy almost hypnotically attached a beat to the ticking timer, lulling her into a light sleep. It was the simple sound of a lighter being flicked that slid her from a dreamlike state into consciousness. She heard Gylou's long draw and smelled the smoke from a cigarette. What she couldn't see, however, was Gylou reaching into her pocket to remove a flask. Mandy, off put by the smell of smoke, removed the cucumber slices, opened her eyes and turned just in time to see Gylou swigging from a flask.

"Um, do they allow smoking in here?" Mandy questioned.

"Considering what they give me, I really don't care," Gylou laughed.

"Please excuse my boldness, but are you pregnant?"

"Let's just say that this is a side job and what I do is none of your business," Gylou snapped.

"Well, that's rude," Mandy replied. She sat back and endured the awkward silence until the timer finally rang. Unsettled by Gylou's impolite manner, she let out a relieved sigh once the mask had been gently removed. Her face tingled and felt alive. In spite of their last exchange, Mandy politely thanked Gylou for her services. Gylou nodded and packed up her supplies, apparently unfazed by their confrontation, and left the room.

Lilith returned to the room with a tall bald-headed gentleman carrying a black hair-styling bag. He walked confidently to his station and prepared to set up his equipment. Lilith took Mandy's hand and directed her to sit in the stylist's chair.

"I'd like you to meet Ptere Laus, an excellent hair stylist. He'll give you a trim or any hairstyle you can imagine. He's been with us a long, long time," said Lilith.

"I'm pleased to meet you, Ptere. I don't want anything radical, but you can trim my split ends," instructed Mandy.

"As you wish, madam," Ptere said with a smile.

Ptere combed through Mandy's hair, still damp from her bath. He picked appropriate scissors from his bag and began by snipping split ends.

"You have such beautiful thick hair. You know, I once had a beautiful golden hair," Ptere chatted.

"Your present look suits you fine," Mandy said. "You're a handsome man."

"Well, thank you. It killed me when I lost my hair, though," Ptere said. "Are you sure you won't try a new look? A shorter cut, perhaps?"

"Thank you for asking, but I'm fine. This cut serves my lifestyle."

He blew her hair using long brush strokes to add fullness and bring out the sheen. With a spritz of hair spray, he announced his artwork complete. He twirled her chair and used a mirror for her to see all the sides and back.

"You definitely have a flare. Thank you, so much," Mandy smiled wide.

"It was my pleasure. Enjoy the rest of your day," Ptere replied, quickly packing up his tools and exiting.

Right on schedule, the door opened and Lilith appeared with another gentleman. As she had with the other workers, Lilith introduced him.

"Mandy, I'd like you to meet Narciss, world famous makeup artist. He's going to do your make up today. I know you will be pleased with his work."

He was tall with sunken eyes and cheekbones that protruded. Mandy thought of those starving in third world countries. He looked emaciated. Perhaps ill. After shaking hands, Mandy avoided the inclination to step back, away from him. She questioned his credentials as a renowned artist.

"I need water. I'm sorry, Mandy is it?" Narciss said in a raspy voice.

"You'll get your water when you are finished," Lilith said sternly.

"But, but . . . " Narciss trailed off.

"Get to work. Stop wasting time and stay away from the mirror," Lilith instructed, "and with a little luck you may even get to see your nymph one day."

"As you wish, mistress," Narciss replied.

Narciss pulled a pallet from his bag and stood back. With a hand on his chin, he sized up Mandy's facial structure, features, and coloration. He fumbled back in his bag and extracted tubes of what he deemed the appropriate colors. Furiously, he worked the colors onto his pallet while explaining that "We use SpectraLights for near perfect color accuracy, much like sunlight." He reached again into his bag for his favorite brushes. He laid down a foundation on Mandy's face first, and then went to work. He was like a master painter dabbing, stroking, and blending the colors. He worked wildly, occasionally standing back to gain perspective.

"I like . . . " Mandy trailed off as Narciss shushed her.

"Do not talk and do not move unless I tell you," Narciss commanded.

He added a few more quick brush strokes and stood back to survey his work. He squinted at Mandy, then changed the angle of his view. Finally, he walked around her, looking with a critical eye.

"Well, I guess it will have to do," Narciss sighed, "you'll never be a beautiful as I."

Taken back by Narciss's comment, she asked, "May I see?"

"As you wish, young lady," Narciss said spinning her chair toward the salon mirror.

Mandy gasped. The face in the mirror belonged to her and yet it wasn't hers. Narciss created a lustrous glow that framed her face. Within that glow her eyes sparkled brilliantly. Through blending and shading he created a landscape where her cheekbones popped and her red, wet lips pulsated, both in contrast against her smoldering skin.

I'm beautiful she admitted to herself. Addressing Narciss she said, "You are truly a genius at what you do, Narciss."

"Well, thank you, but I already know that," he said smugly.

Mandy, now humored by his conceit, smiled and said, "Of course you do; how could you not."

The salon door swung open and Lilith stood holding out a glass of water. Narciss, gasping, hurriedly packed up his equipment, and literally sprinted to the glass of water.

"Try not to stare at it, Narciss," Lilith quipped. "Drink it with your eyes closed." Narciss grabbed the glass and swallowed the water in one gulp.

His transformation was immediate. Just one glass of water replenished his withering skin. His eyes fell neatly into their sockets; his cheeks filled out to meld with his restored lips. Mandy looked at him and saw the most beautiful man she had ever seen.

"What was that all about?" questioned Mandy.

"Don't concern yourself with him. He is a very strange fellow. Brilliant artists are generally a little weird," explained Lilith. "You look amazing. Are you ready for your final service for today?"

"And what that might be?"

Lilith extended her hand to help Mandy out of the chair and said, "Your next and final treatment is a massage executed by one of the world's most talented artist of body manipulation."

"Fantastic," said Mandy.

"I hope your time at Bubb's Rejuvenating Rubs has been pleasurable. You are welcome to return at any time for any or all the services we provide. It has been a pleasure to serve you."

"Well, it's been an extraordinary experience," Mandy smiled.

"Our goal has been to pamper and indulge you for a day in your life, unlike one you've ever experienced before. We want you to return. I'll be taking you to your final room. After that, you'll be escorted to the locker room to dress and take leave of the property."

Lilith led Mandy down the door-lined corridor to her room.

CHAPTER 12

LILITH OPENED THE DOOR to Mandy's suite and ushered her to the center of the room, where a massage table, covered with a towel awaited her. Ornate white wainscoting paneled the lower walls. Marble statues of Cupid sat in recessed alcoves around the room. One for each of the four walls. Lilith helped Mandy remove her robe covering the towel underneath. But Mandy resisted when Lilith reached for the towel.

"No! I want to keep the towel on. I don't feel comfortable being naked while getting a massage."

"I understand. I'm sure you'll work it out with your attendant," said Lilith. "Just lay face down on the table and your attendant will be in shortly."

As she left the room, Lilith turned on the signature smile that continued to annoy Mandy. Now alone, Mandy crawled up on the table and propped her chin on the little pillow at her head to wait for her masseuse. She reviewed the day and thought how fortunate she was that her listing clients rescheduled for the following day. She had thoroughly enjoyed all this pampering and preening at Bubb's Rejuvenating Rubs.

After a soft knock, the door opened slowly. In walked a handsome young man wearing a white toga fastened with an elegant, fiery gold broach at the shoulder.

"Hello, my name is Dolos and I will provide your service today," smiled Dolos.

"And I'm Mandy."

"I'm pleased to meet you, Mandy."

"I must tell you that I want to keep my towel on during the massage," Mandy informed him.

"I understand, but if you change your mind, please let me know."

Dolos set up his stand with the lotions he intended to use and arranged them neatly on the tray. Once ready, he raised his head to address Mandy.

"So which scents do you like?"

"Well, I really love lavender, but I'm open to something new. Oh, and by the way, I hope you're not using oils because I feel fresh and clean right now and want to leave it like that."

"No, no, I'm only using lotions that will absorb into your skin and make it soft and silken," Dolos replied. "Does this scent meet your approval?" he asked, running the scent of garden peonies under her nose.

"Mmm, uniquely wonderful. Does it have a name?"

"It's a new mixture, as yet unnamed. We shall use it, but first I need you to relax your face into the pillow."

As Mandy complied, Dolos took a quick four steps to the thermostat and moved the temperature up to 90 degrees. He returned to immediately apply warmed lotion to his hands before plunging them deep into her back. He felt her body relax and waited for her to expel a soft sigh, prompting him she was ready. He worked his thumbs up her neck to the base of her skull rubbing in a circular motion.

"Can we loosen your towel just a bit so I can hit the pressure points between your shoulder blades?"

"I guess so," Mandy offered reluctantly. "You know, I've had a knot on my right side for so long."

"Let's see if we can work that thing out." Dolos began working his magic on the muscles between her shoulder blades. Locating the knot, he gently used his elbow to press deep into the tissue and rotate it to encourage blood flow back to the heart. Mandy exhaled a sigh as his elbow eased the knotted muscle.

"I think we've worked that mean old knot out of there," said Dolos.

"Your hands are incredible."

"How's your lower back?" he asked.

"I do a lot of sitting at a computer so it tends to stiffen up."

"May I work on it?"

"Well . . . yes," said Mandy, looking up to detect a lustful glaze in his eyes.

"Can we pull your towel down so I can access the area?" he asked.

"I suppose . . ."

Dolos heard her hesitancy and proceeded slowly drawing the towel lower. *She will be a challenge* he told himself as he watched her pull her elbows in tight to not expose the sides of her breasts. As Dolos worked his magic she began to revel in the experience in spite of tiny droplets of sweat forming on her forehead.

"Is it getting warm in here or is it just me," asked Mandy.

"I feel fine, but let me check. I can turn it down slightly," said Dolos, returning to the thermostat if only to crank the heat up even more.

Dolos moved to the head of the table and began running his knuckles in a slow "S" pattern from Mandy's lower back to her shoulders. Mandy glanced up at the fiery pin worn on his toga.

"That's an interesting broach you have," she said. "It looks quite old."

"Yes, I wear it to remember my father," explained Dolos.

"So, it's sentimental," suggested Mandy.

"Yes, it reminds me of him and the pain and struggles he endured to make the world a warmer place," Dolos continued to explain.

"I see," said Mandy.

"Would you like a closer look?" asked Dolos, removing the pin from his shoulder and handing it to her. Without support from the broach the toga loosened and slowly slipped off his body and fell to the floor. Dolos stood naked before Mandy, his chiseled body glistening with a light sweat. Her eyes grew wide. She struggled to roll off the massage table and still maintain a clutch on her towel.

"What the hell are you doing?" she shouted, continuing to wrestle with her towel and maintain her dignity.

"I'm showing you my broach," Dolos laughed.

She ran to the hook where her robe hung and held it in front of her naked body, almost hysterical with fear and anger. "Get the fuck away from me, you pervert."

"You know you want it," Dolos chuckled.

"I want you to get the fuck out of this room," she shouted.

"Hey, we do this the easy way or the hard way. Either way our viewers will like it." Dolos sent out a wicked smile as he walked toward her, one arm reaching for her robe.

"Viewers!? What viewers?"

Dolos indicated to the four Cupids located in the alcoves along the wall. Little red LED lights glowed at the base of each statue's neck. Dolos sniggered, still moving closer.

"I'm going to make you are a star one way or another," Dolos said. "Well, at least on Bubb's closed circuit TV."

"What the fuck," said Mandy, refusing to cry.

The door to the suite blasted open and there, standing with her hands on her hips, stood Ev. She scowled as she surveyed the room and saw a naked Dolos had Mandy trapped in the corner.

"Wow, what an upgrade. I must have done something right to rate a threesome," exclaimed Dolos.

"Threesome," Ev repeated, "I'll give you a threesome."

Ev grabbed the end of the massage cart and rammed it into Dolos's midsection and drove him into the wall. He lay sprawled atop the cart, doubled over in pain and trying to catch his breath. Meanwhile, Ev grabbed Mandy's hand and yanked her out of the room into the hall.

"Quickly, put on that robe," Ev instructed.

Mandy put on her robe while Ev surveyed the corridor. Once Mandy secured the sash around her robe, Ev gripped her hand again and the two began running down the hallway. They had distanced themselves from the room by just a few doors, when Dolos staggered out.

"Stop! Wait!" yelled the naked Dolos as he began to chase them down.

"Don't look back," Ev said to Mandy as they ran along the passageway.

Dolos stumbled along clutching his gut, calling after the two. Ev and Mandy widened their lead. Finally, Dolos doubled over holding his gut and leaned against the wall. The ladies picked up speed and increased their distance from the naked Dolos. At the end of the hall, they came to a set of wooden double doors. They stopped and Ev peeked into the room. Shutting the door quickly, she shook her head. "Won't work," she uttered, more to herself than her trembling partner. Scanning the surrounding area, she gave a second peek into the room as her only hope.

"This is not going to be easy, but do exactly as I say and we'll get through this together," Ev instructed. "Keep your head down and hold onto my hand tight. Do not let go for any reason. Do not respond to anyone. It's going to get dicey, but we want to get through the room and out the back as quickly as possible. Do you understand?"

"Got it," stuttered Mandy.

"We're going to move quickly, so please keep up," Ev said. It was only then Ev's eyes landed on Mandy's feet. "Good gracious, Mandy, you're only in thin spa slippers. It'll be rocky outside."

"Don't worry, I'm used to pain. Nothing can stop me."

"We've no choice. I wish I could carry you," she said, privately imagining her wings carrying them both.

Ev took one last inspection of the room to identify the nearest exit, then looked back at Mandy and said, "Let's roll."

The ladies entered a room that appeared to be a sports bar. The walls were lined with flat screen TVs. Men and a spattering of women sat at tables imbibing beer, mixed drinks, and eating finger food. There were men standing holding beers, chanting and waving their fists at one TV screen and others clapping and pounding on tables. You would have thought they were watching the Super Bowl or some other huge sporting event, but the multiple screens showed the closed-circuit feeds from all the rooms Mandy and Ev had passed along the corridor.

"Do not look up," Ev said pulling Mandy along the aisle.

"Hey, aren't they the girls from the threesome that didn't happen," yelled one of the drunks in the crowd.

"Where? Where?" responded another patron.

"Over there . . . toward the door," responded the drunk.

"Yeah, that's them," said the patron.

"Somebody should grab 'em and send them back," said the drunk.

"Hey, somebody grab those sluts. They're trying to get away," called out another patron.

Luckily, the ladies made it to the exit before anyone could block their passage.

Barefoot and nearly naked, Mandy ran out into the frosty October afternoon to the parking lot. Ev led the way back to Mandy's Jag and pulled up key fob to unlock it. Mandy scrambled into the passenger seat and prepared to push the heat up once the car started. Ev wasted no time revving the engine and peeling out of the parking lot and onto Big Beaver Road.

Blisdon was the first to spot the women escaping out the back exit of the spa. He tried to alert the two demons in the soundproof back of the limousine, but they were too busy reveling in their apparent victory, ready to congratulate Asmos and Dolos for their achievement.

"Lust is her ticket to our world. Once again we won."

Finally, in a desperate attempt, Blisdon honked the limousine's horn.

"Damn it Blisdon, you imbecile, we are talking here," roared Beelzebub.

"They're getting away," Blisdon said.

"What's that you say?" Beelzebub queried.

"They're getting away," Blisdon repeated.

"What? Did Dolos fail?"

"Look," Blisdon said pointing to the women getting into the car.

"It's that damn angel again," Beelzebub said sternly. "We must do away with her . . . rip her wings off and cast her back from whence she came."

"Should I follow them, Master?" Blisdon asked.

"No, no, no," Beelzebub growled, "it would be too obvious."

"I could try again tonight," offered Incubus.

"Really? We wouldn't want a common house cat to beat you up, pansy-ass," jeered Beelzebub.

"I'll have to call in Mammon," said Beelzebub, "and we'll appeal to her business side. I'm sure we can make her an offer she can't refuse.

CHAPTER 13

M ANDY RODE ALONG IN the passenger seat, her eyes following the twists and curves of the road. She was finding it impossible to put clarity into the events of a day that started with so much promise—a reprieve from the problems she faced in her everyday life—but in the end became so distorted that she ended up a potential victim of rape. What happened? Reality broke in, forcing her to face her tomorrows: cancer, chemo, dependent clients, and the overarching fear of telling her mother about her cancer. It took only a mental image of her mother that pushed her to surrender her inner control and dissolve in tears.

Ev, intent on keeping her eyes on the road, reached into her sleeve and pulled out a handkerchief. "Here, wipe your eyes."

Mandy lowered her face into it and continued to sob.

"It's OK. You're safe now," Ev reassured, pulling into Mandy's reserved parking spot.

"You're home."

"Thank God you were there, Ev. How did you find me?"

"Well, I came to your condo to return your car key. I forgot to give it back to you before I left last night. When you weren't home, I just took a chance that you were at the spa. I knew you had that gold card . . . "

"I never told you about the gold card," Mandy interrupted.

"You must have. How else would I have known?"

"I feel lucky you guessed right," sniffled Mandy. "I want to file a police report against that animal. Take me to the police department."

"That's an exercise in futility," responded Ev. "I'm sure that an operation like Bubb's has already shipped that monster out and any record of him has been destroyed. You'll end up looking like a crazy person."

"Son of a bitch," Mandy said in frustration, "that bastard deserves to die."

"I think he already has," Ev replied. "Com'on, let's get you inside."

"Wait, all my stuff is in that locker at the spa," Mandy realized, "in my gym bag. My house key was in there."

"Don't you have a spare house key hidden or doesn't a neighbor have a key?"

"That's right," said Mandy, "Mrs. DiDia has my spare. I hope she's home," Mandy said.

"Well, let's find out." Ev lent a lilt to her voice, hoping to change the mood.

The pair walked along the paver brick path to Mrs. DiDia's condo and knocked. When no answer came, Mandy rang the doorbell. They were about to walk away when Mrs. DiDia answered the door.

"Hello Mandy. So nice to see you. Aren't you a bit underdressed for this time of year?" asked Mrs. DiDia.

"Well, I guess so, Mrs. DiDia. I . . . ," said Mandy.

"No, no, no, dear, please call me Grace," said Mrs. DiDia.

"OK, Grace, do you have my spare key?" Mandy asked urgently.

"I'm pretty sure I do. Com'on in before you catch your death of cold."

Mandy introduced Ev as they moved into the small vestibule. "Come this way girls," Grace said, leading them into the living room. "I'd like you to meet my sisters, Eva, Rose and Katie . . . Ladies, this is my neighbor Mandy and her friend . . . "

The three older women sat around a coffee table smiling sweetly.

"Please keep these young ladies company while I fetch Mandy's key," instructed Grace.

"So, Mandy, did you lock yourself out answering your door?" asked Eva, her eyes referring to the robe loosely closed by a sash.

"Yeah, something like that."

"It looks like you've been crying. Is it some boy?" asked Rose.

"Um, you can say that was a part of it."

"Oh, my. You're too pretty to be crying over some boy. Some boy should be crying about you, dear," said Katie.

"Well, thank you," Mandy said sheepishly.

"Here you go," said Grace cheerfully as she returned with the house key in hand.

"Thank you, Grace," said Mandy, "and it's been nice meeting you ladies."

"Oh, you're welcome, sweetie," Grace said, accompanying the two to the front door. She stood and watched for them until they crossed back to Mandy's door.

"She's such a nice girl," said Grace to her sisters, "Single, though."

"Oh . . . Bless her heart," chimed the sisters.

Mandy unlocked the condo and placed the key on the kitchen counter, telling herself to return it to Grace once she had the original.

"Ev, if you hadn't shown up, I would have gone nuclear on his ass. He had no idea who he was dealing with."

Ev laughed. "Oh, yeah, he didn't know who he was dealing with, huh?"

"You don't know what I'm capable of, Ev."

Ev laughed a little harder. "OK, whatever you believe. But the way I look at it now, seeing you standing in that full length, luxurious robe, I figure you got the best deal."

"I guess you're right. Let me go upstairs and get some clothes on. Make yourself at home," said Mandy. Turning around on the way up the stairs she said emphatically, "And I could have beaten him up."

Ev took in the condo, looking for anything that spoke of Mandy's personal life. Judging from her choice of décor, there wasn't much to learn about this girl. There was a sofa, a coffee table and cushy side chair. A small, healthy fica tree sat by the window. It added a little life to the place. But that was it.

Walking further, Ev found Mandy's story told in all the framed photographs hanging on the walls. She absorbed the stories they told. An arrangement of family photos filled one wall. Pictures from trips and other significant events lined another. Another collection of colorful photos caught her attention. Upon inspection it was obvious that Mandy was a soccer player and a very good one at that. Off to the side of the collection of Mandy's sport photos, she came upon a framed letter from the head coach of the Women's Italian Football Team inviting her to try out for the Italian Olympic Team.

Mandy returned to the main floor wearing her jeans and a sweatshirt. She joined Ev in front of her team pictures. "All that was a lifetime ago," she said wistfully.

"Looks like you were pretty good back then."

"Yeah, I was OK," replied Mandy.

"You were more than OK," Ev disagreed.

"Well, we did rack up some championships," laughed Mandy

"Looks like you were the MVP on your team according to the trophy in this photo," said Ev.

"Yeah," she acknowledged, overcoming her modesty. "But there were others who deserved it as much as me."

"What was your team's name? asked Ev.

"I played for The Courage," replied Mandy.

"Yes, I know you're brave," smiled Ev.

"No, no, no, the name of the team was The Courage," corrected Mandy.

"I know . . . just kidding," chuckled Ev. "What's this letter here from Italy?"

"Yeah, that was quite flattering, but it didn't work out," said Mandy.

"What happened?" questioned Ev.

"Blew out my knee . . . Career over," sighed Mandy.

"I'm so sorry," said Ev sincerely.

"Don't be. It was probably the best thing that ever happened to me. Since that time, I have built a business and a career. I'm satisfied with that chapter in my past and it's over," explained Mandy.

"Do you ever dream about what could have been?"

"Marching into the Olympic Stadium would have been really cool," confessed Mandy, "but playing in the gold medal game would have been a dream come true. Anyway, that ship has long sailed."

"I understand . . . and duly noted," smiled Ev. "You must have tons of friends from your years in soccer."

"Not really, most of my friends are sadly down South and many married. I talk to them occasionally, but really, I don't have friends to hang with. With all the hours I put in, my business is my life. How about you, Ev? You're from the U.P. Do you have any family or friends here?"

"Well, no, I haven't been here long."

"So, where do you work?"

"I freelance in security and do a little caregiving," said Ev.

"For anybody I know?" asked Mandy.

"Well, let's just say my employer is private and leave it at that."

Mandy jumped up, and with a quick change of conversation exclaimed, "Oh, Ev, My gym bag. I can afford to leave my clothes behind, but

I just remembered my watch. It's a diamond studded Cartier, awarded to me for highest sales for last year. I need that back."

"Oh, wow, what about your purse and ID?"

"I didn't bring that stuff into the gym or . . . spa, or whatever you want to call that place. I kept my ID and stuff in the Jag," explained Mandy.

"Don't worry, we'll find a way to sneak back in and get your stuff," said Ev.

"I still have the key to the locker," said Mandy, raising her wrist to show the dangling key.

"Good, hang onto it. I'll look into it and get back to you. Don't do anything crazy without me."

"Seems I only do crazy things when I'm with you," laughed Mandy.

Chapter 14

"WHAT A CREEPY, CRAZY WEEKEND," Mandy said to herself, gathering paperwork off the kitchen counter where she'd left it, tossing it into her briefcase along with her laptop. Standing in the glare of sunshine beaming through the window, she felt hopefulness in the air.

She slipped into her suit jacket and grabbed her bags and computer. She was within a few steps of the door, when a thrusting pain forced her to her knees. Waiting on all fours, panting and hoping the pain would subside; she eventually rolled to her side and then flat on her back with her knees drawn to her chest. She stayed there taking deep breaths, just as she was taught during her years in sports.

Slowly her pain eased, but she continued to lie staring at the ceiling, thinking she needed to call Dr. Fineman. It took time, but she finally gathered herself together, enough to sit up on the floor. With a whimper she flexed her muscles and heaved herself to stand and claim her belongings. A quick glance at the hallway mirror satisfied her that she was presentable.

Within twenty minutes, Mandy clicked her spiked heels across the marble floored lobby to the elevators, her mind listing the tasks needing her attention: turn in the paperwork on her new listing; order pictures, a sign, and a drone flyover video; there was also the Multiple Listing Service search to find properties she discussed with her new clients at the listing presentation; and then there were the follow-up phone calls to make; and multitudes of last week's leads to sift through. On her list of top priorities was that dreaded call to Dr. Fineman, but even worse, the phone call to her mother.

The brass elevator doors opened and Mandy scrambled in, joining and jostling with the usual host of business people. "Fourth floor, please." She felt the first twinge of pain at the first stop. By the fourth floor, anxiety rose after experiencing erratic breathing and increased pressure in her chest. By the time the fourth-floor door opened, a cluster of people sensing her distress, moved to open a pathway for her to exit.

"You, OK?" "You need a doctor?"

"I'm fine, thank you. I just need air. Yes, I'm fine."

This was new to her. An elevator ride never posed this problem. She continued to take deep breaths and repeat to herself that this would pass. It's just fatigue from the weekend, she assured herself. "Just need one more day to get my priorities organized and a good night's sleep will do the trick," she muttered aloud.

To enter the brokerage firm, Mandy needed to brace her shoulder against door, and push using whatever strength she had left. She stopped at the front desk where Sam sat with his perpetual smile. *His smile is making me angry,* she thought for no particular reason other than she brought her bad mood into the office. Her briefcase automatically popped open with a hard slam onto the counter. She pulled out the listing paperwork and handed them to Sam.

"Morning Sam," she said.

"Morning, Boss," Sam replied.

"Please input this into the MLS for me. I'll order the sign and pics," instructed Mandy.

"Sure thing, Boss," replied Sam smiling widely.

"What's going on, Sam? What's with the grin?"

"Uh, well, there's another delivery for you," Sam said, grinning widely.

"Sam, your grinning is starting to annoy me."

"Sorry, Boss."

"Oh, good grief, don't apologize for smiling. I'm a jerk this morning. NOW, what delivery? I didn't order anything."

Sam reached under his desk and extracted a long, white box decorated with a pink satin ribbon and placed it for her to open. Smiling, Sam handed her the letter opener. "These came for you this morning," Sam said, offering her the letter opener.

"Again?" said Mandy, incredulously. "Why don't you open it for me?" Mandy said, feigning indifference. She wouldn't allow him to know she lacked the energy to do it herself.

"Sure thing." He sliced through the taped sides and looked down to find another two dozen roses. She snatched the little envelope and tore it open. "Guess who, Sam," Mandy laughed.

"Your secret admirer?"

"Bingo!

"Whodda thunk it?" Sam laughed.

"This time he says 'When you stop and smell the roses, I'll be waiting.' . . . Please put these in water for me."

"Sure thing, Boss."

"Thanks," Mandy said. "I'll be in my office, and Sam . . . go ahead and smile. It's OK."

"Where's the hustle-bustle? I need the hustle-bustle," she said out loud. With so many people working from home, only the diehard agents made it to the office on a regular basis. She opened her personal office to the exploding fragrance of roses and saw Friday's flowers standing tall and fully opened on her desk. Stunning.

Sitting back into her plush, leather desk chair (her first purchase after moving into this office), she rested to regain her equilibrium. Spotting the two messages from her anonymous admirer, she brought them together, hoping to recognize their penmanship. Nothin'. She hoped it was no one in the office because it was against company policy to have a relationship within. She had seen others in previous offices fall into that trap and it always ended badly.

"Oh, well," she said aloud, firing up her laptop. She checked her emails first. Fifty-seven emails over the weekend were par for the course.

She had pressing business with her new listing, so she put them aside to make her phone calls. Mandy ordered the FOR SALE sign and then called her photographer to find out his availability. Next, she called the "drone guy" to see if he could get everything filmed by the end of the week. He didn't pick up so she left a message. Sam walked into her office with the roses in a coffee thermos.

"Sorry Boss, it's all I could find," apologized Sam.

"It's OK, Sam. You're quite resourceful," Mandy laughed.

"Anything else, Boss?"

"A coffee would be nice. Whenever you get a chance. And while you're out there could you stop off at the dollar store and pick up a few cheap vases? You can never tell. Or is that below your pay grade?"

When he realized she wasn't joking, he said, "I'm here to please you."

She glanced up, waiting for a smile, or chuckle. Had she stomped on his sweet disposition? *I'll address that again later,* she thought.

Back to work. She opened her MLS site and put in the parameters specified by a couple that listed their home with her last Friday. The MLS produced 27 listings that would meet the specs expressed by the couple. Mandy clicked on each potential listing and shuffled through the online pictures. She settled on three that met all the couple's expectations. She emailed them to the couple with a note asking them which times and days would best suit them to tour the homes.

"There's that attorney guy waiting at the front desk to see you, Boss," said Sam returning with her coffee.

"Thanks," said Mandy. "You mean Brent?"

"Yeah, Brent's at the front desk. What should I do?" asked Sam.

"Send him back here."

"Will do."

Brent stopped to examine his reflection in the mirrored wall, intent on presenting an appealing image to Mandy. Sam snickered as Brent straightened his tie, smoothed his vest and finally tugged on his suit jacket to smooth away wrinkles before approaching her door. He knocked.

"Door's open."

"Well, hello, Mandy," he said, coming to a halt. "Wow . . . just wow. Are you starting a floral business in here?"

"Ah, no," Mandy laughed quietly, "seems I have a secret admirer."

"Well, I can understand his infatuation," Brent said warmly.

"That's nice, but I can't. Who wants a relationship with someone who works 24/7? I certainly wouldn't."

"Maybe it's time to slow down and smell the roses," suggested Brent, "No pun intended."

Mandy squinted at Brent and considered what he had just said. That was what was written in the note from the second delivery. It seemed odd, but Mandy dismissed it as a common cliché and a coincidence.

"I have a new one for you," Brent said. "What's the difference between the Godfather and an attorney?"

Mandy rolled her eyes and said, "What Brent?"

"Well, the Godfather will make you an offer you can't refuse, but an attorney will make you an offer you can't understand," Brent quipped.

"Really?" said Mandy shaking her head. "Really?"

"I thought you liked Italian jokes," said Brent.

"I do . . . when they're funny," deadpanned Mandy. "Did you come all the way up here to tell me a joke?"

"Well, no," said Brent, "I have a function tonight at the Brazilian Steakhouse down the street and I'd like you to accompany me. I know how you love a good steak. What do ya think?"

"I'm kinda busy . . . but I love that steakhouse. What time and what do I wear," asked Mandy.

"I'll pick you up at 8 p.m. and a cocktail dress." He drew his lips in, but nothing could hide his elation.

"Ah, one thing, Brent," said Mandy.

"Yes?" Brent replied.

"No more attorney jokes for today."

"You got it . . . See you then."

Evangelina sat floating in the corner of Mandy's office. She giggled to herself watching the whole exchange. Mandy may not have seen it, but Evangelina recognized love in the air.

Mandy went back to work setting appointments to service her new listing. She organized the photos she took at the listing appointment and emailed them to Sam. She checked her watch and felt tempted to cradle her head in her arms on the desk and take a short nap. But the thought of being caught with her head down forced her to sit up and place her call to Dr. Fineman. Just do it. *Pick up the damn phone and make the call.* She knew if she chose chemotherapy her time on this Earth would be extended, but questioned by how much more and the quality of that extra time. She dreaded the thought of the regular appointments, the nausea, the wasting of her body, and the loss of her hair. The worst of it all was she didn't have health insurance. She considered just letting the disease take its course and come what may.

Evangelina floated in the corner of Mandy's office taking in the ambience of Mandy's space. She floated down and marveled at the desk with three separate computer screens along with Mandy's laptop. She floated to the far wall to admire the numerous awards she had earned in real estate over the years, and read the titles on her bookshelf. She turned back to see Mandy at her desk, with four dozen roses acting like bookends, framing her face with a black poster behind spelling the word, "GRIT" emblazoned across it. Evangelina smiled and thought Mandy would need every ounce of grit she could muster. Quickly her smile turned to a look of concern as she felt an evil presence approaching. The feeling was intense. It disturbed Evangelina and she pondered what she would have to do next.

CHAPTER 15

A SOFT KNOCK INTERRUPTED HER dialing and she hung up. Dr. Fineman could wait. "Hold on for a sec," she said, scrambling in her desk drawer for her compact mirror. *It'll have to do*, she thought, despite her red-rimmed eyes. "Come in."

"Hey, you, OK?" said Sam, peeking around the door.

"I'm fine, what do you want?" she asked curtly, obviously not open to conversation.

"You have people here for you."

"I don't have any appointments scheduled for now," said Mandy.

"Well, they specifically asked for you. What should I do?"

"Who are they?" asked Mandy.

"I don't know . . . four guys. One's really short and another in a tux. The other two look like money."

"Put them in the conference room and I'll be in there shortly."

"OK," said Sam, quietly shutting the door, distracted by Mandy's annoyed tone. He approached the men huddled together, speaking in hushed voices. They abruptly stopped talking and turned their attention to Sam.

"Ms. Abbessi will be with you shortly. Let me show you to the conference room," Sam said, nodding for the men to follow. An open arm waved them to the conference table and they pushed past him, brusquely delivering their coats to empty chairs, before seating themselves. The short one with the briefcase was directed to stand at the back corner.

"Can I get anyone coffee or bottled water?" Sam asked.

The men just glared at him. He took that as his cue to leave. "I guess not," he said and awkwardly backed out the doorway. Thankfully the phone rang calling him back to his station. It was Mandy on the other end.

"Are they in there?" asked Mandy through her phone.

"Yeah, Mandy, but they're an odd lot. Let me sit in there with you; you shouldn't be alone with them. I could take notes or something," he said, covering the mouthpiece on the phone.

"Sam," she laughed, "are you serious?"

"I am." He looked up to see her standing in front of him, constraining laughter.

"Hang up," she said in a hushed voice. She took a deep breath before marching into the conference room and immediately recognizing three of the characters out of her nightmare.

"You must have some real balls showing up at my work," Mandy seethed.

"We've come to apologize," Asmodeus said.

"Apologize?"

"Yes, apologize. Things got a little out of hand Saturday," Asmodeus tried to explain.

"A little out of hand?" Mandy said incredulously.

"Rest assured that Dolos no longer works at our establishment. We fired him on the spot." He actually spoke the truth. In demon world, recruiting a mortal by means of force is against policy. Dolos had to be remanded to a lower level for retraining.

"Fired? Fired! I'm contemplating filing a police report."

"That would not benefit either one of us," Zagan said, "but we have an offer that might make it up to you."

"I'm afraid any offer from you would be attached to something criminal. But, I'm listening," said Mandy.

"I'd like to introduce you to Mr. Mammon. He's the majority owner of Bubb's Rejuvenating Rubs and we have agreed to make an offer to you," said Asmo.

"I'm very pleased to meet you," said Mr. Mammon standing. "We have a business proposition to make."

"I'm listening."

Mammon couldn't miss Mandy's lips curled into a sneer.

"We'd like to sell Bubb's Rejuvenating Rubs and we want you to list it."

"You mean put it on the market?"

Mammon ignored the question and continued. "Our asking price is two million dollars and would agree to give you any amount you receive above our asking price as your commission. And to show you how serious we are, we'll pay you a non-refundable portion of your commission up front," said Mr. Mammon. He motioned to the short man in the corner. "Blisdon," he said.

With no response from the dark corner, Mr. Mammon issued a stern "BLISDON!

It seems Blisdon had dozed off while standing.

"Um, huh, um," Blisdon snorted, "Sorry. Yes, Mr. Mammon."

Blisdon walked forward lugging the oversized briefcase. He strained hoisting it onto the conference table. Unlocking and opening the lid, he swiveled it to face Mandy. The briefcase brimmed with packs of one hundred-dollar bills. Blisdon returned to his corner.

"There is one million dollars in that briefcase and it is all yours if you take the listing," smiled Mr. Mammon.

"Let's see," Mandy said thoughtfully, "number one, . . . considering the building alone is worth twice the asking price and the business is worth as much, the type of listing you have proposed would be considered a net listing. Net listings are illegal in the State of Michigan. Number two, accepting a briefcase of cash as "prepayment" of my commission could be considered money laundering in a court of law. Number three, I don't sell whorehouses. Gentlemen, you need to leave."

"Please, reconsider Mandy," said Zagan, "considering your condition you need this money."

"What do you know about my condition?" Mandy said in angry indignation.

"Well . . . Ah . . . Mmm." Zagan hemmed and hawed fearing he disclosed his knowledge of her medical condition, "You know . . . ah, poor."

"Poor. Poor? Are you kidding me? I do very well for myself. My business is thriving," Mandy said in defiance.

"Well, you must admit, you're not a millionaire," said Zagan, "and this deal would make you a multimillionaire."

"So, your answer is firm? No room for reconsideration?" Mammon intruded.

She made it a point to claim his attention by flashing her finger in his face. He usually controlled conversations, but her determination to push him off his game presented him with an unexpected challenge. She took charge and set about directing him.

"Mr. Millionaire, you greedy vulture . . . Take you, your briefcase, and your friends and get the fuck out of here before I call security," Mandy seethed. "I'm going to go back to my office and get my coffee. When I return you will be gone. If not, I will call security immediately and the police. I'd love to hear your explanation to the police explaining why you have a million dollars in cash in your briefcase . . . and where it came from."

Mandy stomped out from the conference room, passing Evangelina's invisible angel form at the door next to the conference room.

"That's my girl," Evangelina said, proud of Mandy's performance.

"Make sure they leave," Mandy said, remarkably calm.

"Sure thing, Boss," He wanted to confront her, ask her about the raised voices through the door. He found himself in an unfamiliar position, one that overstepped his role as "gopher" as he saw it. To see her charging out the room spewing slang, would have given him the opportunity to engage her. But her almost placid demeanor told him she didn't want questions or comments from him. He knew to keep boundaries.

She dropped her head to the desk and told herself: *I'll never have the stamina to deflect the shooting arrows pointed at me.*

Her cell phone ringing brought her out from her muddled, dreamlike state. Ev.

"Ev, they're here," Mandy said hurriedly.

"Who?" asked Ev in mock surprise.

"Those perverts from Bubb's."

"Why would they come to where you work?"

"They want me to do some illegal stuff and sell that whorehouse," said Mandy.

"What did you say?"

"I threw them out."

"Good . . . good."

"Listen, I wanna go back to the conference room . . . be sure they're gone. Lemme call you back."

"Sure thing," said Ev.

Mandy hurried through the office back to the front desk. Sam, his face deep into an important conversation, didn't see her at first, so she waited, impatiently strumming her nails on the counter.

He noticed her impatience, and mouthed the word "What?"

She raised her brows as in question and pointed to the conference room door and then to the front door. Sam shook his head, "no."

"No?" she mouthed.

He again rolled his head in the negative and returned to his conversation.

She sluffed her shoulders, rolled her eyes, and took a deep breath to prepare herself for a brawl in the conference room. Swinging the door open with bravado, she entered. Empty. She twirled around, looked under the table, even checked the restroom. They were gone.

"Are you asleep at the wheel, Sam?" Mandy yelled down the hall.

"What?" said Sam.

"There's no one in the conference room. How did you miss four people and a suitcase exit?"

"I swear to you I have been right here the entire time."

"You didn't drift off and take a nap, did you?"

"Honest, I've been here and awake," said Sam.

"That's too strange. Did they vanish into thin air, Sam? You must have been distracted."

"I must have been," resigned Sam.

She redialed Ev.

"Are they gone?" questioned Ev.

"Yep, seems they vanished. Poof."

"Strange. Anyway, I was calling to see if you'd like to have lunch with me," Ev invited.

"You know, it's only 10:30 and I'm exhausted . . . Brent came to my office and wanted a date for tonight, then those kooks showed up here offering me a bribe, I need to place a personal call and . . . Ah, hell. Tell you what. Can we meet at 11:30?" asked Mandy.

"Perfect. We'll discuss strategy to recover your gym bag, especially your watch," explained Ev.

"All right, where?" asked Mandy, happy for a reason not to place that call to the good doctor.

"How about The Capital," suggested Ev.

"That'll work. It gives me time to make a few phone calls here and tie up loose ends," agreed Mandy. "See ya then."

Mandy replaced her phone in her pocket and returned to her office. She sat in her chair and leaned back and questioned whether to divulge the state of her health to Ev. *After all, I really don't know her. Why would I take her into my confidence?* Truthfully, she needed a friend. Her busy schedule didn't allow for that special camaraderie only girl on girl conversations could offer. Besides, as an unrelated third party she could bounce her decisions off her and get an honest response . . . What harm could a few more hours or another day hurt? Once again, she postponed that call to her mother.

Mandy rehearsed again and again the various words and ways to open the topic with her mother. Not over the phone, though. It was going to be so painful, but her mother had to know. Mandy dialed her mother's number.

"Hello, Mandy, is that you?"

"Yes, Mom, it's me," replied Mandy, cringing at the distress in her mother's voice.

"Thank God, I was so worried something happened to you. Why didn't you answer my calls?"

"Mom, I was swamped on Sunday. I had a listing appointment I had to prepare, then go to Lake Orion, have a two-hour conversation with the seller and then do all the things I must do to list their home. By the time I got back I was exhausted," explained Mandy. "In fact, it makes me exhausted just telling you all this."

"Tsk, tsk . . . you couldn't find five minutes to call your own mother?" scolded her mom. "I'm not fallin' for all this 'I'm too tired bit.' You know how I worry. You're all I got."

Mom's last four words struck a deep chord, making it nearly impossible to continue their conversation without her voice cracking. "You're right, Mom, I should have called you, but I'm calling you now,"

"I called because I wanted to know how your meeting with Dr. Fineman went."

"Well, things went as well as could be expected. I'll tell you all about it tomorrow when I come to see you," said Mandy.

"You're coming over tomorrow?" Mandy's mom said excitedly.

"Yes, for dinner, if that's all right with you, Mom."

"Oh, that's wonderful. I'll make your favorite, homemade macaroni and cheese and for good measure, I'll buy you a steak."

"No need for anything elaborate, Mom," said Mandy, "but I do look forward to your macaroni and cheese."

"What time, sweetie?"

"How about 6 p.m.?" suggested Mandy.

"Perfect. Now, don't be late."

"I love you, Mom," said Mandy, a sense of dread building.

"I love you, too."

There was not an easy way to reveal her condition and prognosis without creating an emotional explosion. She loved her mother so much and they had grown close after her father died. They walked each other daily, step by step, through the grim days after his death, until one day they saw themselves on the other side of the tunnel. And now this.

He had gone so suddenly and too young. It was them against the world and they survived. Her father was not a "saver" and had no life insurance, nor savings. They were thankful that the house was paid off, but there was no income and her mother was a stay-at-home wife. The whole situation inspired Mandy to get into real estate. She thought it was the best way to take care of her mom and build a future.

Mandy had savings, a stock portfolio and a 401K and hated to see it all go to medical expenses. It would leave her mother penniless with no other income, but a small Social Security check each month. This situation was one of the reasons she agreed to her "date" with Brent. She wanted to pick his brain about how she could leave her mother in a better situation. She felt guilty about her underlying motivation, but Brent was a good guy and she knew he'd understand.

CHAPTER 16

"TABLE FOR ONE?" the hostess questioned.

"No, I'm meeting someone here. Young lady, about thirty, white blonde hair . . . " Mandy trailed off.

"Oh, yes, she's already here waiting for you. Please follow me," instructed the hostess.

Mandy followed along into the main candlelit room, greeted by happy chatter, the fragrance of fresh flowers and light classical music. She spotted Ev seated in a small, discreet booth in an intimate back corner, perfect for the discussion she hoped she could have. Mandy slid in before either greeted the other with words. Their wide smiles said it all.

"Been waiting long?"

"No, just got here."

"I know we just saw each other, Ev, but seeing you again cheers me. It's been a long, complex three days and somehow your smile comforts me."

"Oh, Mandy, I think we're going to have a long, fulfilling friendship. At least I hope so."

"So, I figured I'd never get my items back from Bubbs. I gave them up for lost. Do you think you have a plan to retrieve them?"

"No, not really. That's why I wanted lunch . . . so we can plan a strategy to get them back," explained Ev.

The waitress approached their table, her notepad at ready. She was dressed in standard Capital waitress uniform: black pants, white shirt, black vest, black bow tie and the specially made name tag. Her hair was slicked back in a tight ponytail and her bronze nametag was on her left lapel.

"Can I get you ladies anything from the bar?"

"I'll have an ice tea," said Mandy.

"I'll have water with a lemon slice," requested Ev.

"Coming right up," said the waitress, walking away.

"What color were the waitress's eyes, Mandy?" Ev asked abruptly.

"Well, I don't know."

"What was her name?

"She had a name tag on? Uh, I don't know."

"Exactly," said Ev.

"And your point?" asked Mandy.

"I'm getting there. When I came to Bubbs I came in the front door and slipped by the receptionist. But when I got to the lounge, the bartender mistook me for "talent." Their policy is that "talent" and their employees must come through the back entrance. He made me go through the back room of the bar and through the kitchen. I saw the kitchen help and their uniform. I have acquired the same blouse, pants and necktie they were wearing for you and I to wear this Friday night," explained Ev.

"And your point?" Mandy asked again.

"Just like you couldn't pick our waitress out of a police line-up, they won't even notice us if we dress exactly like them. The locker room is just down the hall from the kitchen, so once we're in, we just sneak into the locker room, get your stuff and hightail it out of there. The front door is right there," Ev explained.

"Great, but why Friday?" asked Mandy.

"By my estimations, Friday is their busiest night. They will be so preoccupied with their guests; they won't have time to bother with us."

"What time?" Mandy asked.

"My guesstimate is they will be at their busiest at 10 p.m.," Ev smiled.

"It sounds reasonable," said Mandy.

"I even acquired a bag of potatoes and a bag of onions to carry in on our shoulders," said Ev proudly.

"Uh, why?" questioned Mandy.

"Well, if we carry them in on our shoulders it will obscure our faces and nobody will see either one of us as trespassers. Plus, who is going to interfere with two hard working ladies hauling kitchen supplies?"

"You know, it might even work. I'm putting my faith in the fact you know what you're doing."

"Of course, it's going to work. You just need a little faith," said Ev.

"You'll have to excuse me, but after recent events my faith is more than little tattered," frowned Mandy.

"You must keep the faith, Mandy. There are powers greater than you and I that are looking out for you. You will prevail. I'm betting on you," Ev said with conviction.

With that said, Mandy slid close to Ev and drew her into a huge hug. "Your words give me encouragement to face other battles in my life."

The waitress returned with the ladies' drinks. Retrieving two straws and her order pad from her apron pocket.

"So, have you made your choices?"

"I'll have the chicken Caesar salad with the dressing on the side," Mandy spoke up.

"I'm good for now," Ev said.

"Are you sure? We have wonderful appetizers if you're not hungry for a whole meal."

"No, I'm good, thank you anyway," said Ev. "Now," turning to Mandy, asked, "What 'other battles' are you facing, kiddo?"

Mandy's eyes flicked the room, assuring they had privacy. "I have something I must tell you, Ev. It's a lot and I don't want to burden you with it, but I have to tell someone before I tell my mother. I have to work it out in my mind so when I tell her it won't be so, how do I say it . . . blunt,"

"What is it?" said Ev, knowing what was coming. "You can tell me anything."

"Well, where do I begin," Mandy started slowly, "I recently have not been feeling very well. I went to my doctor, Dr. Fineman, and he ordered some tests."

"You're OK, right?" said Ev.

"No, not really," said Mandy choking back tears.

"What's wrong?"

"I've been diagnosed with ovarian cancer and it has metastasized," Mandy began to cry.

"Oh, my God," said Ev, "what are you going to do?"

"I don't know," said Mandy, her eyes red, waiting for tears to be shed.

"Well, what does your doctor say you should do?" asked Ev.

"He wants me to start chemo immediately, but the prognosis is not good. I don't have medical insurance and for me to go through all that will cost tons of money. It's just my mom and me and she doesn't have much.

I have some money, but medical costs could take it all. If I pass in spite of chemo, I won't have money to leave her. She won't survive without it."

"Wow," said Ev.

"I'm sorry for unloading on you, but I really don't have anyone to turn to right now." Finally, the tears fell fast and hard.

Ev put her arms around her. "It's my turn to offer a hug and a shoulder to cry on . . . It's OK, it's OK. Let it out, Mandy."

"You're amazing. It's unbelievable that someone I met days ago would be my rock. I guess fate works in mysterious ways," Mandy sniffed.

She felt an incredible goodness emanating from Ev. "I'm glad I'm here to help you," Ev smiled.

"What are the odds that you would have been in that bathroom when I was hurting?" Mandy asked rhetorically.

"Divine intervention," Ev laughed.

Was it her imagination that Ev gave off a sprightly buoyancy, bordering on exhilaration in situations that required anything but? Mandy had that sense that whatever Ev set her mind to, she'd get it done and enjoy doing it. She first felt it when they were skipping/running off from Bubs. And now, as they planned their "dangerous" mission, she didn't question they'd accomplish it with Ev directing. And it was contagious. Mandy, too, felt a charged energy with Ev that was both enervating and calming simultaneously. Like a storm surge that hits her and releases her from stress.

Mandy grabbed her napkin and dried her eyes with Ev's arms still comforting her. "Thank God you were there," sighed Mandy. "I have to admit that Dolos looked like a deranged, serial rapist chasing his next victim."

"That was funny, wasn't it?" Ev said.

The two women sat back in their seats and fell into nonstop stream of laughter.

"You are a godsend," Mandy smiled.

Ev smiled and nodded her head in agreement.

Chapter 17

H ER HOME HAD ALWAYS been a sanctuary from work. She could open her door and feel it a place of tranquility and rest away from her workday pressures. But now, even in this refuge she felt vulnerable to nightmares, phone calls, knocks at the door. Even the air had a certain heaviness that pressed down on her. Until she faced Dr. Fineman with her decision and talked with her mom, she couldn't be at peace.

Mandy purposely took her time to change into comfortable clothes, hang up her suit jacket, toss her leftover salad from lunch in the refrigerator, water her neglected plants, make a fresh coffee . . . do anything to postpone the inevitable.

She paced back and forth at her kitchen island mumbling to herself, rehearsing a dry run for her phone call to Dr. Fineman. Unfortunately, she had two storylines. On one hand, she wanted to extend her life as long as possible; on the other hand, the financial costs would leave her penniless. She agonized over the choices, but finally came to her decision. She dialed Dr. Fineman's number and listened to the phone ring. The receptionist picked up.

"Hello, Dr. Fineman's office. How can I help you," asked the receptionist?

"Good afternoon," said Mandy, "I'd like to talk with Dr. Fineman, please."

"I'm sorry, Dr. Fineman is out. Can I take a message and have the doctor call you back?" said the receptionist.

"I guess so," said Mandy, "this is Amanda Abbessi. I suspect he is waiting for my call."

"Certainly, I'll let him know you called. Give him about a half hour, maybe a little more," said the receptionist.

"Thank you," said Mandy and she hung up.

Mandy lay on her couch with her phone clutched in her hand. She thought about what she would say to the good doctor. She knew he would disagree with her decision. Her mind wandered a bit and then she focused on the event she had promised Brent she would attend with him. *How could I have let myself agree to it?* She felt like a mess and would be dismal company. On top of it, her acceptance was based on deceit. She knew she would tell him about her situation and ask for his advice and help. While he expected a sunny, animated Amanda, she would be a real downer—a terrible date.

Date Mandy thought to herself. She never thought of Brent as anything other than a friend and business associate. He was a very nice man. Handsome and in great shape for being in his forties, she considered him attractive, but she never considered dating him. Mandy hoped he wouldn't misread her agreement to accompany him to his event. Considering her state of mind, she didn't want to lead him on.

The shrill sound of the phone startled her out of her daydream. She closed her eyes against the sound. She knew she had to talk to Dr. Fineman and give him her decision.

"Hello," said Mandy.

"Hello, this is Dr. Fineman," said the doctor.

"This is Amanda Abbessi."

"Yes, yes," said Dr. Fineman, "I've been expecting your call."

"Dr. Fineman, I've done a lot of soul searching and consideration of my personal situation," said Mandy.

"And what have you decided my dear girl?"

"Well, it was a tough, tough decision," she said, "but I don't want to go through chemo therapy," said Mandy.

"I don't understand," said Dr. Fineman. "Why wouldn't you want to take advantage of the latest treatments? Treatment that could extend your life?"

"Considering the prognosis you gave me, I would gain how much time . . . six months, a year? I don't have health insurance and I have an elderly mother that lives exclusively on a small Social Security check each month. Instead of spending my money on a futile cause, I prefer to leave it to my mother," explained Mandy.

"I understand your concern and, yes, the chemo regimen is costly, but you could apply for a grant. It's possible they would pay a substantial amount of the cost," explained Dr. Fineman.

"I've done my research, Doctor Fineman, and I know my prognosis. My odds are quite small even with chemo. I think a person who could really benefit from a grant should get it instead of me," said Mandy.

"My dear, miracles do happen," said Dr. Fineman.

"Well, if there's going to be a miracle it will happen whether I'm receiving chemo or not."

"I respect your decision, but I wish you would reconsider."

Mandy heard his heavy sigh at the other end of the line. "If I do, you will be the first to know," she said

"Please call me next week," requested Dr. Fineman.

"I will. I just have one request," Mandy said, "I went through a really painful episode over the weekend. Can you prescribe something for the pain?"

"Of course, young lady," said Dr. Fineman, "I'll have my nurse contact your pharmacy. Perhaps you should make an appointment to have it checked out."

"I will," she lied. "Thank you for everything, Doctor," Mandy said, determined to restrain the emotion creeping into her voice.

"Follow the directions for the prescription to the letter, Amanda. What I'm prescribing for you is a powerful painkiller," directed Dr. Fineman. "And call me next week."

"Certainly, goodbye Doctor," said Mandy.

"Goodbye, Amanda."

Mandy dismissed the call and closed her eyes. Bitter tears fell uncontrollably. Why was this happening to her? She contemplated what she might have done in her life to deserve this. She set her phone alarm for forty-five minutes and she drifted into a light sleep.

Evangelina sat guard atop the peak of Mandy's condo. It saddened her as she listened in on her conversation with Dr. Fineman. She understood how Mandy could feel all this was so unfair. This world Mandy lives in burns with resplendent beauty she thought. To leave all this for some place you've only heard about and don't even know exists takes real strength and faith. Evangelina wished she could assure Mandy all would be all right.

"Sleep, sleep, sleep . . . sleep," whispered Evagelina and Mandy drifted off into a deep dreamless sleep.

CHAPTER 18

MANDY'S PHONE ALARM JOLTED her awake from her cat nap to the tune of her favorite song, "Miss Independent." The song spoke to her heart because she felt she was a strong independent woman. She had fought many battles and had won most. She always tried to learn from her losses as her father had taught her. Mandy swiped the alarm away.

Mandy's father was her coach and biggest fan. Through his guidance and support, she rose through the ranks at a mercurial rate. She held so many awards and records proclaiming her a legend in the world of amateur soccer. Her college career was star-studded and she began playing professional soccer at the ripe age of nineteen. Then her life and career came to a crashing halt.

In a regional playoff game, Mandy went down in a horrific crash with an opponent and the goal post that devastated her right leg. She suffered a spiral compound fracture and a torn ACL, MCL and patellar tendon.

It took a long time to heal from that injury that mangled her leg, but through the long and painful rehab her father walked with her, always working to restore optimism about her bleak future. Her mom brought treats and her favorite foods during her extended stay in the hospital. Her teammates also visited when they were in town and not on the road playing. As time went on, it became apparent that Mandy's soccer days were over.

Once released from the hospital, a team official visited her home. Apologetically, he offered her a small buyout from her pro soccer contract. She graciously accepted, considering the team had paid all of her medical costs. It was a sad day for Mandy. The team official also brought a letter postmarked from Italy addressed to Mandy. The official explained to her that the Italian coach had called the team recently and, sadly, they related the story of her injury and the final prognosis. He thought that Mandy might want the letter as memorabilia.

Mandy remembered opening the letter and feeling a sense of pride and sadness. The letter offered her a fully paid trip to Italy to try out for the Italian Olympic Team. Mandy smiled at the bittersweet memory and thought to herself what could have been.

Not long after that visit, her father passed away. They say it was a massive heart attack. It devastated Mandy and her mother. There was an insurance policy that, along with her buyout check, provided enough to bury her father and move them back to their home in Michigan. Other than that, there were no extras. Mom was old enough to collect Social Security, but it wasn't much. It spurred Mandy to get her real estate license and begin her career in real estate.

With the work ethic and determination her father instilled in her, Mandy was the Rookie of the Year in her real estate office. She built her business one client at a time. She focused solely on real estate and the fruits of her hard work paid handsomely. Within a few years she was able to support her mother and buy her own condominium. She was happy with her accomplishment and thanked her father for her resolve to never give in.

Mandy checked the clock. *Time to hustle.* She groaned, not for the fact that she was spending the evening with Brent, but for the discussion she would have with him, disclosing her condition and asking for his help. She cringed at what she had to do, but time dictated it.

She flexed her muscles and hauled herself to the standing position and sighed. Remembering her father's words "when the going gets tough, the tough get going" and she raised an imaginary wine glass above her head. "Thanks, Dad." It was time to get going. Tonight, would be a major first step toward getting ready for the inevitable.

Applying her makeup at the vanity mirror, her mind drifted again to the memory of her father and how he had inspired her throughout the years of competition. His words often came back to her like it was yesterday. He had always told her it wasn't whether you won or lost, but how you played the game. She was down in this medical game with no hope of coming back. She vowed to play the rest of this game with strength and dignity. There was no time for self-pity. She would take it one day at a time and never look back.

Mandy slipped on her black cocktail dress and looked in the mirror. It seemed baggier since the last time she wore it, so she knew she had lost more weight. She told herself there was no need to be judicious in what she ate tonight because she certainly could afford a few pounds. She turned to her jewelry box sitting open on the vanity. Almost involuntarily, the gold chain with the golden star, inlaid with a diamond, caught her eye. Her father had given her the necklace after she and her team won their first national championship. She took it from the box and clasped the necklace around her neck, admiring its perfect placement, vowing to never take it off again. A shudder of warmth spread through her listless body, almost energizing her. Her mind's eye brought up a picture of her father broadly grinning approvingly at her and applauding. He'll be with me through this.

She slid into her black heels and checked the contents of her little velvet dress purse then declared herself ready for the evening. Her watch told her she had fifteen minutes to spare before Brent arrived. She hoped he'd be on time and, based upon the past business experience she had with him, he was very punctual. The idea of sitting around waiting gave her mind the opportunity to wander and obsess over her condition, so she grabbed a feather duster and began brushing down pictures on the mantle. She stopped at the picture of her with her mom and dad standing behind a championship trophy. She remembered the love and pride of that moment. Mandy smiled affectionately and uttered: "Do you two know how much I love you both and how grateful I am for your support over the years?" Her eyes fogged up just as the doorbell rang.

She blinked away her misty eyes before opening the door to Brent, decked out in a tuxedo, smirking at her in a black dress and feather duster.

"I didn't know I was taking a French maid with me tonight, but it's fine with me," Brent chuckled.

"Oh, right," said Mandy tossing the duster into the corner, "I just need to get my coat."

"Please let me assist you," Brent said helping Mandy slip into her coat. "This is a very special night for me."

"How so?" asked Mandy.

"Well, first of all, I'm taking my all-time favorite real estate lady out and number two, I expect to . . . " Brent trailed off.

"Expect to what?" she quizzed.

"I don't want to jinx myself," said Brent.

"So, what's this event tonight?" asked Mandy.

"It's our firm's award dinner."

"Are you nominated for something special?" asked Mandy.

"Sorta," said Brent.

"You should have told me. Well, I'll be rooting for you, Brent."

"How can I lose with such a beautiful woman on my side?"

The two walked arm in arm to a waiting limousine where a bottle of champagne chilled on ice.

"Wow, Brent, you really went all out," said Mandy.

Brent popped the cork on the champagne and poured a glass for Mandy and himself. Mandy clinked her glass with his.

"To, hopefully, a very, very special night," said Brent.

"To victory," smiled Mandy.

As the limousine drove off, they sipped their champagne and fell into easy, good-humored conversation. Evangelina watched from the rooftop and smiled upon them and proceeded to trail at a distance. She watched the limousine pull into the posh Brazilian restaurant's valet parking.

"Let the night begin and hopefully it will be one to remember," said Brent.

"Here, here!" Mandy laughed.

CHAPTER 19

"GOOD EVENING, MR. BRENT, nice to see you again," greeted the maître d'. "Are you here for tonight's festivities with Great Lakes, P.C.?"

"Yes, we are, Carlos," said Brent.

"You will be in the Barra Grande Room tonight," said Carlos. "Right this way."

Carlos led them through the restaurant to a private room in back. He opened the door to the Barra Grande Room, festively decorated with candles and arrangements of poinsettias. A soft choro number played in the background as he took Mandy's wrap and gave her a claim ticket. At the front of the room was a small stage equipped with a microphone, a podium and a "Great Lakes and Associates, P.C." banner behind it. Most of the early arrivals congregated at the private bar. The men were dressed in tuxes and the women in sequined gowns.

"Brent," whispered Mandy loudly, "I'm under-dressed for this."

"No, you're not. You're perfect," said Brent. "I wouldn't want you to change a thing."

"The ladies are dressed in full length gowns," Mandy whispered.

"Don't worry, you're with me. I love understated elegance," Brent snickered.

They found their place cards and before sitting, Brent turned to Mandy and asked how he looked. Mandy reached up and straightened his bow tie. She stood back and smiled.

"Dashing Brent, you look just dashing."

"What can I get you to drink?" he asked.

"I really love their cucumber mint smash," said Mandy.

"Coming right up," Brent said.

They snaked through the tables and made it to the bar. Brent ordered Mandy's cucumber mint smash and a Lagavulin Scotch for himself.

"Looks like a healthy drink," said Brent handing her the tall glass decorated with cucumber slices and basil leaves.

"It's lovely," she said, immediately taking a long draw from her drink. "Thanks, I needed that."

"Don't be nervous. I know all these people and they are lucky to have you as company."

"Well, I just don't want to embarrass you," Mandy said.

"Embarrass? You make me look good."

"Flattery will get you everywhere."

A young man, pulling a young woman by the hand, snaked his way to Brent and Mandy. The young man appeared flustered.

"Hello, I mean good evening Mr. Maxwell," stuttered the young man.

"Hello, Pauli. I'm glad to see you could make it tonight. And, who is your lovely guest?"

"Ah, like, ah, this is my girlfriend, Cherylann," said Pauli.

"Well, pleased to meet you, Miss Cherylann. I'd like you both to meet a dear friend of mine. Mandy."

"Nice to meet you," Pauli and Cherylann said in unison.

"Are you nervous, Mr. Maxwell?"

"Not a bit," said Brent, "it is what it is."

"Wow, to think they may announce you as their newest partner tonight," gushed Pauli.

"We shall see," Brent said coolly.

"Well, I just wanted to wish you luck, you know."

"I appreciate it," said Brent.

"We're going back to our table. We're rooting for you," said Pauli.

"Once again, thank you."

Pauli and Cherylann turned and made their way back through the crowd, which had grown considerably over the last twenty minutes. Brent turned to face Mandy standing with a hand on her hip and shaking her head in disbelief. She took a sip from her drink, looking amused.

"And . . . when were you going to fill me in on this?"

"Ah," stammered Brent, "I didn't want to build up any expectations, you know."

"Who were those people?" asked Mandy.

"That was Pauli, my intern. He's been with me for about a year. Good kid and a hard worker."

"Looks like a little hero worship there," said Mandy.

"Stop it," said Brent.

Cyril, one of the Great Lakes partners stepped up to the mic and fumbled with the on/off switch. It turned on, startling him with screeching feedback. He stepped back and shook his head, then cautiously returned to the mic.

"Test, test, test," Cyril said. "This thing is dangerous. I told my beautiful wife, Annette, I would make this short, so please return to your seats because dinner will be served shortly."

The crowd milled about a bit and then a mass migration from the bar to the tables began. Brent and Mandy moved with the crowd toward their table placement up front near the podium. Brent pulled out Mandy's chair and she smiled up at him as a thank you. He then sat himself down awkwardly close to her.

"By the way, I ordered the filet for you tonight," said Brent.

"Perfect . . . medium rare, I hope."

"But, of course! If I recall, that's the only way you like your steak."

The dinner began with a generous shrimp cocktail followed by a fresh garden salad. The steaks arrived hot off the grill with sides of asparagus and garlic-mashed potatoes. Mandy was famished and wanted to clean her plate, but she knew etiquette required her to leave a portion—grudgingly she chose to leave a smidgen of potatoes and a stick of asparagus. Nothing could persuade her into leaving any of the mouth-watering filet. When the dessert cart came by, Mandy debated between the key lime pie and the tre leches cake. Since Brent wasn't a dessert sort of guy, he made the decision easy for her and asked for both.

As the guests finished their meals, Cyril took the podium to begin the after-dinner awards ceremony. Once again, he fumbled with the mic, but more efficiently this time. He cleared his throat and began.

"Welcome partners, associates and distinguished guests," he began. "We are grateful for another fantastic year at Great Lakes and Associates, P.C. This year we have experienced explosive growth at our firm and it was accomplished with the hard work and perseverance of everyone involved. We are thankful for each and every one of you who work with us at Great Lakes and Associates. It is only through a team effort that we could accomplish all we have this year."

Cyril paused as the crowd politely applauded. He marveled at how big the Great Lakes family had grown over the ten years he had been a partner. A wave of thankfulness made him smile.

"It's time to acknowledge the people who made this all possible. First and foremost, our founding partners, Robert, his wife Darlene, and Bruce and his wife Deborah."

The crowd loudly applauded as the couples stood and waved to the crowd, sitting down as the applause subsided. The attention returned to the master of ceremony.

"I'd like the following persons to stand and remain standing while I introduce those who run the day-to-day operations at Great Lakes and Associates. Our fearless office manager, Daryl; paralegals Allison, Olivia and Megan; our research and investigation unit, Evan and Ross and finally our receptionist and gatekeeper, Mya. Please give them a rousing round of applause for all the hard work they do for us."

The crowd roared with applause. They knew these were the people who made everything tick. They were a solid no-nonsense group who always managed to get the job done. They were the backbone of a finely tuned machine. The group smiled and waved as they returned to their seats.

"It's time to get to the awards for tonight," said Cyril putting on his reading glasses. "Cyril pulled a piece of paper from his vest pocket and opened it saying, "Let's recognize the people who have shown great potential, fantastic growth and consistent excellence in their work for Great Lakes and Associates. Let's start with Rookie of the Year. She joined us last January and won her very first case in April of this year. She set the record for billable hours for a year-one associate. Put your hands together for Rachel Rackel."

Rachel stood, covering her mouth in disbelief. The people at her table applauded wildly for her as she made her way to the stage. Upon reaching the stage, Cyril handed her the plaque and shook her hand. Teary eyed she made her way back to her table.

"Next up, Associate of the year . . . " Cyril announced. "This young man is a tireless worker who is truly a tremendous producer for Great Lakes and Associates. I can recall returning to the office late at night to retrieve some things and found him working. I told him to go home, but of course, he remained until the job was done. Please give him a rousing round of applause. Come up to the stage Ryan Russell."

Ryan proudly stood up and shook hands with his colleagues at the table, then leaned over and kissed his wife, Lisa. He straightened his tie and walked to the stage.

The crowd clapped furiously because they knew, even though he was the busiest guy at the office, he would always take time to help. He took the trophy from Cyril, shook his hand and raised the trophy above his head. The crowd cheered.

"We have another award to give tonight. It's a first-time award and hopefully it will become an annual recognition. For her tireless work for Children's Hospital of Michigan, we'd like to recognize Chelsea Miles with this Humanitarian of the Year award," Cyril announced.

Quite surprised, Chelsea stood to a roar of applause and quickly made her way to the stage. She proudly displayed the plaque to the audience and smiled widely. She almost forgot to shake Cyril's hand. She danced on the way back to her seat.

"Finally, tonight we are going to announce something we haven't done in a decade," Cyril began. "This man is a tireless worker, a consistent top-notch litigator and man of integrity. He has produced over a half million dollars in new clients and institutional representations in each of the last three years. I'd like to introduce the newest partner of Great Lakes and Associates, Mr. Brent Maxwell."

A round of applause rose from the crowd as Brent stood. He looked down at Mandy who was beaming ear to ear. She squeezed his hand with tenderness. With a quick flick of her eyes to his tie, he instinctively reached up and straightened it. He walked slowly, taking in the moment. Upon reaching the stage, Cyril stepped forward to shake his hand and then pointed him towards the microphone, inviting him to say a few words.

"Thank you, Cyril," said Brent, taking the mic. "I'm proud and thankful to have this opportunity to become a partner in this exceptional organization. I want to recognize the fantastic support of the staff and their willingness to go above and beyond. You are the best. Thank you, Mom and Dad. I know you're watching from above."

Completing his acceptance speech, Brent reached out again and shook Cyril's hand. He stepped down from the stage and walked to the partners' table to shake each of their hands. He proceeded to his table amid a standing ovation. Mandy, too, clapped enthusiastically along with the others. He thought he saw something more than just pride on her beaming face. Did he detect real affection for him? He walked up to her and gave her a kiss on the cheek and sat down in his place.

"This concludes our little program," said Cyril at the mic. "Please enjoy the rest of your evening. Most importantly, please drink responsibly."

"Wow, partner," Mandy exclaimed.

"Yes, indeed," said Brent.

"Well, Mr. Maxwell, I'm impressed," laughed Mandy.

"Don't be. I'm the same guy with the lame attorney jokes," chuckled Brent. "Did you hear the one . . . "

"Stop! You promised," Mandy interrupted.

"You're right, you're right, but I want to say one more thing . . . ," laughed Brent. "Not a joke." He paused and waited for her complete attention. "You know receiving an honor, like becoming a partner, is a wonderful honor, but not as wonderful as having someone to share it with. I'm so happy you agreed to come tonight. It made all of this so much more special," Brent began. "Mandy, I sent you those flowers. I'm your secret admirer."

"YOU?"

Until that moment, Mandy was enjoying a reprieve from her problems, lost in the gaiety of the night, so proud for her friend. Once he received that promotion on stage, and she saw how deeply he was loved and admired by his fellow employees, she determined not to interfere in his moment. This was his night.

With his admission to her, emotions took a radical turn from joy and admiration to agitation. She could feel tears welling in her eyes, and breathed in to keep them at bay. Her reaction took him by surprise.

"What happened? What did I say? Was it my admission? Did it come too fast?" When she didn't answer, he could only think to ask, "You want another drink?"

"Yes, I'd like another, but can we go somewhere more private? There's something I need to talk to you about." Her expression turned serious.

"Of course. How about we get one of those little booths in the back?"

"Perfect."

Mandy gathered her things and walked with Brent through the banquet room. They pushed through the doors into the main restaurant and found a secluded corner booth. Since it was late there weren't many patrons left in the restaurant. As Mandy slid into the booth Brent waved and caught the eye of a waitress.

"What can I bring you?" the smiling waitress asked.

"Please bring me a Lagavulin and the lady will have . . . "

"A cucumber mint smash," Mandy filled in.

As the waitress quickly departed, Brent and Mandy settled into the booth. At an empty table, cloaked in invisibility, Evangelina gazed at the couple, so matched for one another. Brent was tall, athletic and distinguished. Mandy was stunning with her jet-black hair and crystal blue eyes. *If only I could change the shape of things to come.*

CHAPTER 20

T HE WAITRESS RETURNED TO the table with Brent and Mandy's drinks, and when she asked if there would be anything else, Brent shook his head no, but asked her to check back. He picked up his glass and proposed a toast.

"It's a wonderful life," Brent said lifting his glass.

"It certainly was," Mandy said forcing a look of high spirit to her face. "I need to talk to you, Brent."

Mandy reached down for her glass and chugged the remainder of her drink.

"Whatever it is, it must be serious."

"Damn," Mandy shook her head.

"What's wrong?"

Despite her best efforts to choke back her tears, she trembled and reflexively gave in when she looked into Brent's face and saw his discomfort. She covered her face with her hands and let the tears run freely.

Brent fidgeted in the booth, searching for words to make her understand he was here to help. He pulled up his handkerchief and offered it, but she turned away. Finally, Brent got up from his seat and sat close to her and grabbed her shoulder with two hands and forced her to face him.

"Look, I can't help you unless I know what it is. Help me out. Was it something I said? Was it my bold admission? Maybe it came too fast."

Mandy slowly regained her composure and took the handkerchief from his hand to wipe her tears. She forced a smile and looked into his eyes.

"I was hoping it wasn't you."

"Why?"

"Because I think too much of you."

"You're not making sense. Listen, I can handle rejection. I'm a lawyer. It's a way of life for me."

"Oh, I'm not rejecting you. I'm sure you'll be rejecting me. I don't know if even the toughest lawyer in the land could handle me with my problems."

"What? Are you being sued? I'm at your service, Miss Mandy," said Brent boldly.

"Seriously, Brent, it's better I wait for another time," Mandy said patting dry her eyes with Brent's handkerchief again.

"No. The time is now. Trust me. I can handle it," Brent assured her.

"I wish it could be that easy," Mandy said. "Before I say anything, I want to apologize for ruining your day. It's not just any day that you become a partner in a prestigious law firm," Mandy began. "I just want you to know that you can say no to my request if you feel too burdened by it."

"Never," said Brent with conviction.

"Well . . . here goes," Mandy said, "Uh, recently I went to the doctor and he ordered some tests. I got the results back and, well, the results were not good. I need to get my house in order quickly."

Brent stared off, and tried to wrap his head around what she was telling him, and whispered, "What are you saying?"

"I'm dying, Brent," Mandy said.

"What?" gasped Brent. "Can't they do something?"

"The treatment wouldn't give me much more time and the cost would wipe me out. I need to take care of my mother after I go. Brent, she's given me so much and she has so little. I need you to help me set that up."

"Of course. Have you told anyone yet?" Brent questioned.

"Only a girlfriend of mine . . . I'm going to tell my mother tomorrow. I truly dread that," said Mandy.

"I understand," said Brent.

After an uncomfortable wordless pause, Brent pulled back and looked fixedly into space, his mind racing through the different alternatives available. Mandy took his hand and held it with both hers. She looked directly into his eyes and saw the light fading.

"I want you to know those flowers you sent lifted my spirit. To think that someone thought so special of me. Learning it was you made it all the better. You are a good man, a fighter for right and protector of the wronged. I want you to know that I have always admired you and I am honored to have you feel so much for me. If only . . . " Mandy trailed off.

He blinked away a mist of tears. "We were dealt a terrible hand, but I will stand by your side. From now until whatever comes, I will be your champion. I'll hover over you like a papa hen. And, God willing, we will beat this thing together."

Mandy looked up and met his steady gaze, tears of gratitude shining in her eyes, then hugged his neck and said, "I'm so scared."

"I know, I know . . . Let me be strong for you."

Evangelina was touched by the love and compassion from this man. If only Mandy knew the beauty and love that awaited her. Evangelina was puzzled why mortals held on so dearly for life here when greater things awaited them in the next life. Here, there were struggles and pain. There, all things were good and wonderful. The beauty of this world was intoxicating, but no match for what awaited her.

CHAPTER 21

Asmodeus sidled up to Bubb's Relaxing Rubs reception desk and fidgeted while the receptionist finished her phone call. He strummed his fingers impatiently on the marble counter indicating for her to hurry. The receptionist hung up the phone and turned to Asmodeus.

"How can I help you, Mr. Deus?" asked the receptionist. She took note of his blotchy skin and pinched face indicating stress of some sort.

"The Crown Prince, Satan, is coming today," said Asmodeus.

"The Prince is coming?" The receptionist repeated with concern in her voice. She now understood the anxiety Asmodeus was feeling.

"Everything must be perfect for his arrival," said Asmodeus.

"What time can we expect him?" asked the receptionist.

"Sometime this afternoon," Asmodeus replied.

"Have you told his wife?"

"I didn't tell her, but I'm sure she knows. You know Lilith, she learns things by osmosis. I think she's somewhere in back whipping the staff into shape," laughed Asmodeus. "As for me, I'm going to the kitchen to give them the heads up and make sure things are spick and span. You know how tough he is when he does an inspection."

Lilith stood in the middle of the spa, hands on her hips with a bullwhip in one hand. It was her savage eyes crisscrossing the area that forced everyone to cower back, away from her in fright. The scowl on her face told she was upset with what she saw.

"Listen up, peons," she yelled, "stand in formation."

In quick military fashion the staff dropped what they were doing and lined up to stand at attention. One mortal girl fell into line late and caught the attention and ire of Lilith.

"Do you not like working here little girl?" Lilith addressed the young lady.

"Oh, no, ma'am, I love working here," the girl replied.

"Well, it doesn't appear that you want to be working here, you lump of pond scum. Step forward so everyone can see how pathetic you are and what happens to those who come late."

With eyes lowered, the girl stepped forward out of line, weak-kneed in fright. The staff could see tears streaming down her cheeks.

"Look at you, you ugly troll. You are a poster child for abortion," Lilith screamed.

Was it the bitter cruelty in Lilith's words or the embarrassment in front of her peers that caused the girl to snap? "Bitch," she said, loud enough for the room to hear, including Lilith.

"What did you say?" screamed Lilith with fire in her eyes.

"Nothing, ma'am," the girl hurriedly replied.

Lilith uncoiled the bullwhip, swung it above her head and lashed it toward the girl. The whip coiled around her neck. No tugging or grasping could release its hold to provide her breath. Lilith hesitated, laughed and then jerked hard on the whip's handle. A loud snap echoed through the spa and the girl fell to the ground. Lilith walked up to the girl's body lying on the tiled floor, her lifeless eyes staring up at her. Her neck was disjointed and bruised. Lilith used her toe to roll the inert mass onto its stomach and gave it one last brutal kick.

"Does anybody else have something to say?" Lilith addressed the staff.

The staff snapped to attention and stared at the floor. No one dared to look Lilith in the eye. A mortal woman sniffled, but stopped immediately when Lilith gave her a stern look.

"My husband, the Crown Prince, is coming here today and he may want to do an inspection of the premises. You will clean this place floor to ceiling and if he finds a hair, a fingernail, or even a smudge . . . heads will roll!"

CHAPTER 21

Lilith looked down at the dead girl's body and cackled a laugh as she kicked her in the ribs. One more for good luck. Lilith put her foot on the body's buttocks and rolled them back and forward as a final humiliation.

"Dolos, front and center," Lilith commanded.

Dolos ran from the back of the room to stand facing Lilith. He looked down averting his eyes. The last thing he wanted to do was provoke her anger.

"Dolos, grab an attendant and take this piece of whore meat to the kitchen and tell the chef that I want him to butcher this cow. Tell him to prepare a feast for my husband using this prime rump meat. He likes his meat rare," instructed Lilith. "Use the rest for the patrons."

"Right away, ma'am," Dolos choked.

Dolos pointed to an attendant standing close to the body. Both men grabbed the body under the arms and dragged it out of the spa. The staff turned and began to work furiously on their stations. Lilith strutted out of the spa into the hallway where she encountered Asmodeus leaning against the wall, his head down in deep thought.

"What troubles you, Sire?" questioned Lilith.

"Your husband, the Crown Prince, is not pleased with the current state of affairs here," informed Asmodeus.

"You're referring to that wench and her angel?" inquired Lilith.

"Exactly," replied Asmodeus.

"He abhors incompetence," Lilith said.

"He ordered our legion of demons to meet him in the Ceremony Room at the witching hour tonight. He is not pleased. Spread the word to all," instructed Asmodeus.

"This is going to be a blood bath," cautioned Lilith.

"Probably," sighed Asmodeus.

Lilith continued down the hallway to the Ceremony Room. She arrived at the ornately carved door and reached into her pocket to retrieve an oversized golden key to insert into the screaming skull mouth that comprised the lock's keyhole. Turning the key, the dead bolt tumbled open and Lilith pushed through. Black candles lining the walls burst into flames at her entry into the inner sanctum, their fiery light revealing ebony granite walls and floor. At the center of the room, a coal black altar, with a jeweled dagger stuck in the middle, jutted from the floor. To the left of the altar stood a golden pulpit where their bible lay open. Elevated behind the altar rose a throne of gold shimmering in the candlelight. Not far from the altar, twelve chairs made of human bones were strategically spaced around a granite table—a golden pentagram etched into the center.

She walked the room inspecting every inch for vulnerabilities that could weaken them. Everything must be in order and to the specifications laid down by the book. She demanded that everything be perfect; any irregularity would reflect poorly on her and set her husband off. If he lost his temper tonight, she was certain that blood would be let and heads would roll. Exiles and banishments to the farthest reaches of the netherworld would be in order and she didn't want to be included in either lot.

Upon checking the conditions of the Ceremony Room, Lilith concluded that everything was in order. She made her way to the door and took one more assessment; making certain all details were in place and her work complete. She backed out, pulling the door shut after her. All that remained was to use the gold key and lock the door tight.

Throughout the day and evening the staff of Bubb's Rejuvenating Rubs scurried to and fro cleaning this and polishing that. The gold sparkled and the marble gleamed. Everyone kept one eye on the clock in anticipation of the Crown Prince's arrival. After twelve hours of continuous cleaning a call came over the speakers requiring the staff to report to their stations.

Lilith, followed by her entourage of demon handmaidens, entered the reception area where Asmodeus and his color guard of warrior demons waited. Asmodeus, in his regal robes, sported his crown and scepter. Lilith walked directly to him. A handmaiden demon assisted her by pulling back the hood on her robe. Asmodeus gazed into Lilith's sultry dark eyes. Blood red lips punctuated her pale white face framed by her braided locks of black hair. A golden tiara studded with black diamonds crowned her head.

"You look lovely, Lilith."

"What, or rather who, are we waiting for?" questioned Lilith.

"We're waiting for Beelzebub, Leviathan, Mammon, and Belphegor to arrive," replied Asmodeus.

"Let us do our inspection and by the time we finish they all should have arrived," said Asmodeus.

Asmodeus and Lilith, with their separate entourages in tow, began to move from the marbled entrance to the inner sanctum of the facility. They stopped at the reception desk and addressed the Nigerian woman.

"Shadé, let us know when the others arrive."

The Nigerian nodded and the demons proceeded on their way. Shadé had worked a millennium for Asmodeus, after he snatched her away from the Nigerian demon, Yoruba. She was a loyal and trusted servant.

The limousine pulled up in front of Bubb's Rejuvenating Rubs. Blisdon jumped out and promptly opened the door to let his passengers exit. Out stepped Beelzebub, Leviathan, Mammon and Incubus all slowly ascending the marble steps to the doors of the spa. Beelzebub, dressed in his tuxedo, waved his hand and the entry doors opened. Mammon, dressed in his three-piece Italian silk suit, Leviathan, dressed in a low-cut formal gown, and Incubus in his naked blacked out shadow form entered the foyer and approached Shadé at the front desk.

"Greetings, Princes of Darkness," said Shadé bowing as she greeted them.

"Shadé, always nice to see you, said Beelzebub.

"I'm sorry, but I recognize you, Beelzebub, Mammon and Incubus. But who is this beautiful lady that accompanies you," asked Shadé?

"It's Leviathan," laughed Beelzebub. "He's exploring his feminine side."

"I'm so sorry, Master, I did not recognize you," Shadé apologized.

"That's quite all right, Shadé," said Leviathan, "I like my new look. I feel liberated."

"Liberated?" Beelzebub scoffed. "You look ridiculous. How can any revered demon look like that?"

"How can any revered demon look like a penguin," retorted Leviathan.

"Enough," said Beelzebub. "Where are we meeting, Shadé?"

"In the Ceremonial Room," she said, "and you need to hurry. The witching hour is upon us."

The group of demons walked through the entrance, down the hallway to the Ceremonial Room. Beelzebub opened the door and the group entered the candle lit room, noting that Narcis, Hecate, Circe, and Pterlaus had already arrived. With a nod from Lilith, each demon took his place at the pentagon inscribed table. Lilith and Asmodeus sat at their places. Two seats remained. One for the guest of honor, the Crown Prince; the other for a demon noticeably absent. Asmodeus inquired about the missing demon Belphegor.

"He was invited," replied Beelzebub.

"He said he just wasn't into it and wasn't motivated enough to make the trip," laughed Leviathan.

"Typical," said Asmodeus sternly. "He's afflicted by his own venom."

The clock struck twelve and chimed twelve rumbling bongs. A hush grew over the attendees as they watched the center of the table's pentagon swirl with fire. The swirl grew larger and larger until a pillar of fire shot to the ceiling. As the final bong faded, the Crown Prince stepped from the pillar of fire and stood before them, bearing a pitchfork in his right hand and a menacing scowl on his face. The attendees bowed their heads.

"All hail, Satan," they said in unison.

"I bring greetings from the Emperor, Lucifer," boomed Satan, "and he is quite concerned why his top lieutenants cannot convert one lonely, little lady's soul and deliver her to him."

"Well, you see . . . " Beelzebub trailed off.

"Silence! I do not want to hear any of your excuses. The problem is staring me right in face. Look at you. You dare to attend this ceremonial meeting looking like this? How dare you sit in this chamber in the guise of mortals. You have become fat cats accustomed to the luxuries of the mortal world. Show yourselves as I know you."

Slowly and uneasily, each individual demon reverted to his grotesque demon form. The process took but a few minutes. When finished, the demons exchanged looks of obvious discomfort, hardly recognizing the others true form. They had grown to know each demon only in his mortal form.

"Since you are all incompetent fools, I will show you how it is done," bellowed Satan. "No mortal is any match for me."

"All hail Satan," they said in unison.

"Wait! Wait!" Leviathan stepped forward. "I, Leviathan, demon of envy, will bring you the young woman named Amanda. It is only I who knows the intimate nature of the mortal woman and her envious nature. I understand the status of Versace, Yves Saint Laurent, Chanel, Lagerfeld, Vuitton and all the top fashion designers that women covet to wear."

"All hail Leviathan," cheered the easily persuadable demons.

"Silence, if have to tell you how to dress, you don't stand a chance with this mortal. As I said, I, the master will show you how it's done," roared Satan into the room. He then motioned to his color guard and two of his top aides left the room.

Minutes later they returned with the mortal woman who cried when the spa attendant was whipped to death. The woman's bellows against the guards went unheard. They hoisted her onto the sacrificial altar and strapped her down. Unable to move, the woman begged for her life. One of the guards handed the bejeweled dagger to Lilith.

Lilith arose from her seat and walked to the altar. She stood before the mortal woman and recited an incantation. Then, in one swift move, she plunged the dagger into the woman's chest. With a few quick slices, Lilith cut the woman's heart from her chest and held it high. Lilith walked to Satan and handed him the heart. He eyed it greedily, opened his saber-toothed mouth and swallowed it whole.

Chapter 22

I T WAS THE END of Tuesday and Mandy sat in her office contemplating how to approach her mother. Before she did that, though, she had to take care of her real estate business. She didn't know how long she could service the clients she had under contract, so she had to inform her broker of her intentions to put her license in the Holding Company.

She gathered her files for the clients she was currently working with and marched to the broker's office. Sadly, she thought about her clients and regretted she could not see each deal to fruition. That she would leave her clients with highly trained and ethical agents who worked at her office gave solace. They would still get top-notch service. She knocked softly on her broker's door.

"Enter," he called.

She peeked her head into the room to see Michael, the broker, on the telephone negotiating a problem resolution with another broker. This was not an unusual occurrence in the real estate business as there were always conflicts and misunderstandings to resolve. He looked up and, with a wide smile, waved her to the chair opposite him. She laid her files on his desk and fidgeted nervously in her seat until his call ended.

"Mandy, my star agent," Michael greeted her.

"Hi, Mike," said Mandy.

"What brings you to my office today?" queried Michael.

"It's a sad day, Mike," Mandy began. "I must put my license in the Holding Company and deactivate my Real Estate Board account."

"Wow, what's going on?" asked Michael.

"Well, without going into much detail, I have a medical situation I must attend to and it wouldn't be fair to my clients if I didn't put them in good hands while I'm still available. If I wait, I won't be able to assist the agents."

"Oh my God, Mandy, are you OK? This is so sudden. I don't know how to react."

"My decision to deactivate came suddenly. But once you know my state, you'll agree it's the right thing," replied Mandy. "I'm not in a position to talk about it just yet. Bear with me."

"Is it temporary? When will you return?" She heard panic in his question.

"If I get through this thing, I will be back here with you," Mandy assured.

"Is there anything I can do?"

"Here are all my current files. Please give them to someone who values clients as much as I do," said Mandy.

"I will do that for you and I will give you your commission on each," said Michael.

"I truly appreciate that, Mike. You've always been the greatest broker," she said, extending her hand . . .

"None of that," he said, taking seconds to reach her for a hug. Mandy squeezed him tight, fighting back tears.

"I consider you more than just a broker, Mike. I consider you a friend," she said and quickly faced the door.

"If you ever need anything, Mandy, please call me," said Michael. The sincerity in his voice brought her to the threat of tears.

"I will. Take care, Mike," Mandy said, her voice breaking.

She returned to her office for the last time. There were a lot of memories, mostly good, that scrambled through her thoughts. She was going to miss her place at the brokerage, but circumstances dictated her departure. Mandy took one last look and closed the door.

Mandy met Sam at her car loading the last of the boxes into her backseat. His uncustomary quietness told her he was hoping for an explanation. After all, it was just yesterday when the two of them bantered about her anonymous admirers. What, so dramatic, happened to bring her to folding up on a day's notice? It was so like her to hide away her problems from the eyes of others.

"Sam . . . " she started. But the sadness in his eyes prevented her from going further. "Sam, sometime I'll explain all this to you. I promise."

"I understand," he said, but he really didn't.

"Thank You, Sam." Her voice began to crack.

"No problem, Boss," said Sam. "I'll miss you. There's no one here like you."

"That could be either good or bad." Her attempt at humor fell flat.

"You're the best."

"Thanks, Boss," said Sam. "You always treated me well and I appreciate that."

"I know it's not much, but I want you to have this," Mandy said pressing a folded one-hundred-dollar bill into his hand.

"Ah, you didn't have to do that."

"It's the least I can do for all the help you've been to me," said Mandy.

"You don't pay friends for doing their job." Sam blushed when she grabbed him into a hug and squeezed out a quiet sob.

"I'd better go, Sam," she said, afraid of this turning into a cry fest.

Finally in the car, her composure close to breaking, she rolled down the window and gave a hearty wave, put the car into gear and sped off.

———

Mandy was on the road to see her mother, but had to stop at the pharmacy to pick up the prescription Dr. Fineman had prescribed. She slipped her hand into her purse and grabbed a tissue to wipe her eyes. *God, forbid I break down before I get to Mom's place.* She cruised the lot looking for a spot in the crowded pharmacy parking lot, finally turning into one near the rear of the building. She raced around to the entrance to the pharmacy.

Slowly, the black limousine rolled into the pharmacy parking lot, pulling around to the back of the building and parked. It sat at the building's rear idling in the nippy October afternoon. Inside the limo, the demons sat listening to the Crown Prince.

"When we return to Hell, I will deal with each and every one of you. I will bring you in front of Emperor Lucifer and he will determine your fate. Enjoy yourselves now while you walk this Earth. Your time is limited," scolded Satan.

Beelzebub, Mammon and Incubus stared out the window. They dared not look Satan in the eye or confront him. He embodied his specialty. He was the demon of anger and had perfected his craft.

"Now, I'm going to show you how it's done. Watch carefully and learn," Satan said sternly.

It took just moments for Satan to morph from his grotesque demon self into a mortal-looking being. Pleased with his exchange, he turned to the other demons for approval. While privately none agreed his choice of body-change, especially his choice of the Fu Manchu mustache, they nodded approval. They told him they thought the jean jacket and ripped jeans combined well with the backwards ball cap and flannel shirt.

"Smart outfit," said Beelzebub wondering which segment of society Satan represented. Only time will tell. After all, Satan knows best.

Satan's black eyes glowed under his bushy brows. He smiled showing a gold incisor. He was pleased with his morphed mortal-looking body.

"It's showtime, peons. Let me show you how it's done," crowed Satan. "Blisdon! The door!"

Blisdon popped out of the limousine and ran to open the passenger door. Satan emerged and inhaled deeply into the fresh air, disappearing to the front door of the pharmacy. He pulled a cigarette as a clever prop from his pocket, lit it and waited for his mark.

Mandy stood at the pharmacy counter waiting to be served. The pharmacy was busy and the techs scurried about counting pills, packaging orders and taking phone orders. Finally, a pharmacy tech approached the counter.

"Hi, may I help you?"

"I had a prescription called in for me by Dr. Fineman," said Mandy.

"Name?"

"Amanda Abbessi."

The tech turned and shuffled through the "A" box looking for Mandy's prescription, eventually pulling a bag from the box. After examining it carefully, she returned to the counter.

"There's a note here saying the pharmacist wants to go over a couple of things with you before I give you your prescription," said the tech. "Let me get her for you."

Mandy watched her walk back to the pharmacist and whisper in her ear. The pharmacist was on the phone, but still nodded to the tech that she understood. Mandy waited, getting edgier with each minute. It took time before the pharmacist completed her phone conversation to finally address Mandy.

"Hello, I'm Dr. Rachel," said the pharmacist, "and I need to go over a few things about your prescription. I saw from your records that this is the first time you are receiving this medication and I thought it prudent to go over its use and the side effects with you."

"Thank you, I appreciate it," said Mandy, still showing signs of consternation as a result of the wait.

"First of all, this is a powerful narcotic. It's an opioid and very potent. You should take this only when you are in severe pain. Never take more than the prescribed dose and when you take this, you most certainly should not drive. This drug will affect your perception and state of mind. Some people even experience hallucinations. Please understand this. It also has some other less serious side effects that you should read about in the literature contained inside the bag. If you have any other questions, please ask now, or if you have questions later, feel free to call the pharmacy . . . and needless to say, no alcohol.

"I understand," said Mandy.

"I need you to sign this form required by the federal government. Your total will be $245.05," said the pharmacist.

Mandy handed Dr. Rachel her card and electronically signed the federally required form. She then signed the credit card charge electronically, bemoaning the frightful fee. Finally, she was handed the bag containing her prescription.

"Be sure to read all the literature prior to taking the medication," Dr. Rachel once again cautioned.

"I will," said Mandy forcing a smile.

Mandy turned and made a fast clip through the aisles to the front door of the pharmacy, still edgy from the long wait, the price of the pills, and the time she lost when she could have been with her mom. Exiting the door, she came face to face with Satan in his human form.

"Hey, don't I know you," said Satan flicking his cigarette into the parking lot.

"Excuse me?" said Mandy, taken off guard.

"You look real familiar," said Satan.

"I'm sure your wrong," replied Mandy.

"Yeah, I remember you," said Satan, "you're that whore from Bubb's Rubs."

"You must be mistaken."

"No, no, you were part of that threesome that didn't happen," Satan said.

"I don't know what you're talking about," Mandy said picking up her pace.

"Yeah, remember that other broad came into your massage room and screwed everything up," said Satan following along.

Mandy's walk became a slow trot. In one of the trees that overhung Mandy's car Evangelina sat cloaked in invisibility. She observed Mandy's interaction with Satan and prayed she would not have to intercede.

Mandy reached her car door and fumbled with her purse, looking for her keys. Satan stood there at her car and continued his mission. He had her exactly where he wanted.

"Yeah, you're definitely her," Satan laughed. "I'd know that fine ass anywhere."

"Fuck off, asshole," Mandy hissed.

"Hey, I can give you what you missed out on last weekend," said Satan grabbing his crotch, "I got what you need, Baby."

Mandy could feel her anger welling up inside. Her ears began to burn hot. She took a deep breath. She had been here before, but on the soccer field. Opponents have always tried to take her off her game by verbally attacking her. In her early years she would succumb to her opponent's verbal attacks, but with the help of her father she learned to control her temper. Even now, with her psyche in a fragile state, she relied on those coping techniques.

Her stoic, almost blank, face was bringing him to a slow boil. After all, his task included bringing her to intense rage. But her calm demeanor worked against him and his own rage spewed out.

"Com'on baby, do me in your car," he screamed, his words nearly flaming the air. His voice grew high-pitched and his words poured out like a spray of pellets.

"Com'on baby do me in your car. I got twenty bucks for you. I want to push that bush. Com'on slut, YOU KNOW YOU WANT IT." He pumped his legs up and down and thrashed his arms in the air. His words unintelligible.

"My, my young man, I see you haven't outgrown your temper tantrums."

Meanwhile, Evangelina continued to watch the interaction, and admired Mandy for holding her own against this demon. But for fun, she decided to intervene anyway. Her eye caught a flock of sea gulls feasting on garbage rotting on the ground around the dumpster at the rear of the pharmacy. *Aha!* She knew exactly what she would do.

Evangelina left her perch and flew to the dumpster. She picked the fattest and most engorged sea gull and seized it from behind. She flew back to her perch in the tree with the sea gull in her grasp and sat on a limb directly above Satan.

It's time for action. Time for a little fun. Evangelina squeezed the fat sea gull with all her might and watched a glop of white, grey and green goo spurt out from the rear of the bird and land directly on Satan's forehead, gushing down into his eyes, nose and into his mouth.

"What the . . . ?" screamed Satan. He spit and sputtered the fowl slop onto his costume.

Finally, Mandy managed to scoot into her car and avoid the shit spray before slamming the door on Satan's foot.

"Justice," she called out. "Thanks for the entertainment." She discharged a cringeworthy laugh, releasing endorphins that triggered a well-received sense of elation, making her wait at the pharmaceutical counter worth it.

She barely missed Satan flopping around as she fired the engine, put the car in reverse and squealed out the parking lot.

With Mandy out of sight, Evangelina left her perch and flew to the ground to confront Satan.

"You are a miserable excuse for a demon," laughed Evangelina.

"It was you," said Satan still sputtering trying to get the taste of goo from his mouth.

"You're on notice. Stay away from her. If you think this was bad, I haven't even begun. You and your slimy friends will never steal her soul," declared Evangelina.

"You and your feeble parlor tricks don't stand a chance," said Satan, fuming with vicious anger and embarrassment. "I look forward to the challenge."

She let her engaging smile speak for itself.

Evangelina spread her wings and slowly ascended into the air. She flapped her wings and flew off toward the direction Mandy had driven.

Chapter 23

B LISDON HEARD A MUTED RAP at the limousine window and cautiously let it slide down until he came face to face with a fuming, red-faced Satan. Blisdon's eyes grew wide and his mouth gaped open when he recognized the bird goo sliding down his master's face.

"Get me a towel," Satan growled, low but with menace.

"Um . . . yeah . . . ah." Without hesitation Blisdon ripped open the center console and rummaged furiously through the contents. He found a small tissue pack and, keeping his distance, tossed it to Satan. Satan stared down at the small package and looked to Blisdon.

"These sheets are no bigger than square toilet sheets. Does this look like a towel to you, imbecile?" This time Satan screamed with such ferocity Blisdon scrambled to the opposite side of the vehicle.

"Ah, ah, no . . . but wait, wait." Blisdon ducked down and rummaged under his seat and popped back up with an old rag used to dry off the limousine. Sheepishly he handed it over to Satan. Satan snatched it from his outstretched hand.

"Now get the door," Satan demanded.

Blisdon popped out of the limo and ran to the rear passenger side door and opened it quickly. Wiping his face, Satan moved slowly toward the door, and slithered into the back seat to confront the abject horror on the faces of the other passengers mingled with their attempt to restrain laughter.

"Say one word and you'll be shoveling shit on the seventh level of Hell," Satan growled at his fellow occupants.

Beelzebub, Mammon and Incubus sat in silence, pretending to be distracted by something outside the window. When Satan finished wiping his face, he tossed the soiled towel at them.

Stroking his Fu Manchu, he took a moment to assess his predicament. "Blisdon, take us back to Bubb's Rubs," Satan commanded.

"Yes, Master," Blisdon said and quickly pulled out into traffic.

———

Satan sat alone, brooding in the ceremonial chamber at Bubb's Rubs, forced to stare at Lucifer's golden throne directly in front of him. He dreaded returning to the underworld, having to face Lucifer as a failure. Lucifer was the beautiful one and may have been the bringer of light, but he was darker and more deplorable than the rest of the demons combined. Throughout the annals of time, Satan was relegated to doing all the heavy work. He tempted Adam and Eve in the garden. He sparked Caligula's desires. He lit Nero's fires. He inspired Attila the Hun. He whispered in Hitler's ear. He directed Stalin's hand, but since he failed to tempt Jesus in the desert, he had been berated and ridiculed ever since. Hell's Emperor had no patience for failure and this excuse for an angel was not going to stymie his effort.

Deep in thought, Satan didn't notice that his wife, Lilith, had entered the ceremonial chamber carrying a covered silver platter. Quietly she walked to Satan's side and placed the platter before him. She put an arm around his scaly back and rubbed his shoulder to comfort his broken ego.

"Do not fret, my love," Lilith soothed. "You will prevail."

"Of course, I will woman," Satan snapped.

"I brought you your favorite, mortal rump roast," offered Lilith removing the cover.

"I need something to take this taste from my mouth," snarled Satan.

Satan cut the roast into two with a quick slice of his claw, skewered it with his index finger and ravaged it whole. He wiped his mouth with the back of his hand.

"Tender," he commented.

"A young Peruvian girl who was impertinent," said Lilith.

"Still, it does not remove the taste of defeat," Satan said sadly.

"You might have lost a battle, but it's the war you will win," said Lilith.

"Yes, but how?" said Satan.

"Well, the mortal knows death is coming, so I'm sure there will be important things she won't really care to do or even address. I'm sure she will become apathetic and not care about anything, but herself. We just have to give her the opportunity," suggested Lilith.

"Ah, yes," said Satan stroking his chin, "Where is Belphegor?"

"I checked and he's currently possessing a young girl in Puerto Rico," said Lilith.

"Summon him here now," exclaimed Satan.

"As you wish, sire," said Lilith.

Satan looked down at the remaining roast, stabbed it with his index claw and popped it into his mouth. After swallowing it whole, he licked his fingers and smiled. He knew the best was yet to come.

CHAPTER 24

M ANDY ENJOYED THE DRIVE to her mother's home in the city of Royal Oak. It was a quaint community of beautiful brick homes and variations of classic architecture. Its downtown area offered an upscale, safe nightlife. She had lived there with her parents until she was eighteen, but left to join the professional ranks of soccer. Her parents joined her down south during the season and set up in a condominium the team rented for her use.

Mandy and her mother moved back after her soccer team released her. Between rehabbing her knee injury and her father's untimely death, the two committed to living in Michigan.

By smart planning, her mother's house was paid off. Mandy paid the yearly taxes and the company that did outside maintenance, while her mom's small Social Security check took care of food and utilities. Her mother now lived in the house alone. Fortunately, many of the same people from the block were still there, but many were widows. She filled her days playing pinochle, shopping at the mall, and talking with the others about their grown children. So, when Mandy chose to move out and live closer to her job, she felt secure knowing there were those around to fill her mom's days. She lived alone, except for Hope, her aging dog, but she was not lonely. Mandy's major concern was to be sure her mother's financial status remained stable.

After pulling into the driveway of the small brick colonial, she turned off the engine and sat for a moment to absorb the fullness of the area with its big oak trees lining the street, safeguarding the neighborhood's quaint-ness. She studied her family home wistfully. Every fall Mom decorated the front stoop with one large pumpkin and six gourds arranged exactly the same, year after year. And of course, the copper mums in the two planter's boxes under the windows—always the same color. *Enough* she told herself, reaching into the backseat for the bottle of wine she bought the night before. Her mom loved her wine and Mandy knew she would need a glass or two to swallow the bad news she was bringing. She could see her mother peeking out the window, sporting a big smile. She could hear the barking Hope. *Brace yourself, girl.*

As Mandy walked up the paver brick walk, her mom was at the door in her usual flowered apron, grinning ear to ear, struggling to hold a jumping Hope away from the storm door. After subduing Hope with a bear hug and pat on the head, Mandy maneuvered her way into the house, and with a few quick steps release her purse and bottle of wine to an end table. She turned and opened her arms wide.

"Oh, Amanda, I've missed you so much."

The two fell into a prolonged embrace.

"Mom, Mom . . . I saw you two weeks ago, remember?" said Mandy, breaking the hug. "Come on, let's sit."

Settling on the couch she motioned to Hope to join her for some petting time. She stroked the dog's ears while Hope licked her arm furiously.

"You're just as cute as ever, Hope." Mandy glanced to her mother's serious eyes firmly fixed on her face. "Now," she said, hoping to distract and bring levity to the moment, "tell me what's going on in the neighborhood."

"Two weeks . . . that's a long time."

"Yes, I guess you're right," said Mandy, concluding her mother wouldn't be distracted.

"How did your appointment with Dr. Fineman go?"

"I'll tell you after we eat."

"Sweetie, dinner won't be ready for a while. Let's talk. Was everything OK? At the doctors?" asked Mom.

"Mom," whined Mandy, "after dinner, OK? I didn't have lunch and I'm too hungry to get into a discussion of my health on an empty stomach."

"Oh, all right," Mom said in resignation.

"Come on, let's open the wine," said Mandy already moving to the kitchen, looking for any diversion.

Mandy poured the Pinot Noir and the two clinked glasses. Her mother offered a toast: "To a good wine, good food, and good health."

The aroma of Mom's mac-n-cheese filled the kitchen. "That's such a good smell, so reminiscent of our ritual Friday night dinners in front of the TV watching "Everybody Loves Raymond." How many different types of cheese do you use, Mom?"

"Well, let's see. I use sharp cheddar, Parmesan, Asiago, and creamy Provolone. So, that's four."

The two women broke out in laughter after hearing Mandy's stomach grumble.

"Listen, you can hear that train rumbling to a stop in my stomach, waiting to be stoked with your mac and cheese. I told you I hadn't eaten since breakfast in anticipation of your creamy goodness."

Mom scurried around setting the table, bringing out the Caesar salad, sliced bread and other fixin's all while reciting the ingredients in tonight's dinner. Now, you just sit at the table and it'll be ready shortly."

Mandy sat propped with one leg crossed, watching her mom bring a small plate to the table and pour extra virgin olive oil into the center.

"So, what's that? Something new?"

Ignoring her, Mom went to the counter and brought back a container of Parmesan-Reggiano cheese and heaped a handful into a bowl of olive oil. She salted and peppered the mixture and announced, "There," Mom said smiling, "so you can dip your bread. This should quiet your stomach until I bring out the big guns."

Mandy dunked a chunk of bread into the mixture. "MMmmm . . . " she moaned over and over, while Mom added Caesar salads to the table.

Finally, as if unveiling a magic trick, Mom swung around and planted the entree on the waiting trivet, warning her daughter it's hot. The steamy aroma gave her little choice but to dig in for a full bite, only to let out a whoop afterwards.

"I told you so," scolded Mom.

Small chit-chat ceased once Mandy set about filling her stomach, letting out an occasional "this is so good, Ma." Hope sat guard watching for any morsel of human food to hit the floor. Once, as Mom stood to bring more napkins to the table, Mandy looked down and sighed to see Hope in the classic "beg pose." "OK, girl," she whispered, and surreptitiously slipped her a piece of bread dipped in the olive oil.

"Don't feed the dog from the table. You'll give her bad habits," said Mom. "Now sweetie, I want you to go in the other room while I clean the kitchen."

"No. Let me help."

"It's much faster if I clean it myself. Now scoot."

Mandy refilled her wine glass and ambled into the living room. *I'm bushed* she told herself kicking off her shoes and flopping herself heavily on the sofa. Between the wine and a stomach of carbs, she wondered if she had the energy for the discussion about to take place, let alone play the upbeat, positive daughter. Mandy concluded there really wasn't a good way to do it. Just be realistic yet optimistic. She dreaded what lay ahead.

"Ready for dessert?" Mom asked, returning to the living room with two plates of tiramisu.

"Who's that for?"

"Don't be silly, it's for you, of course."

"Maybe later. Here," she patted the couch, "Come sit with me."

"Do you mind if we watch 'Wheel'"? asked Mom.

Mandy met her request with silence.

"What are you doing, Ma? You asked me here to discuss my visit with Dr. Fineman, but you're doing everything to avoid it. *Please*, take the tiramisu back to the kitchen then sit with me."

"You're right, honey. Who knows, maybe I wasn't ready for this, even though I kept bugging you for answers. Deep down I know that whatever you tell me about your visit is not good news."

Mom took her time returning the dessert to the kitchen. When she did return, she seated herself next to her daughter as ordered. "OK. I'm ready."

It took moments for Mandy to open the discussion.

"Do you remember Aunt Virgie?"

"Oh, of course I do, my poor, poor sister," Mom said shaking her head. How could she forget her baby sister's protracted illness? Mom shifted on the sofa recalling how the family suffered along with her sister's husband and two-year-old for more than three years. They watched her slow decline. "Taken before her time."

"Mom, look at me." Mandy moved closer. "Mom, it's serious. Dr. Fineman said I have the same thing she had, only worse." She blurted it out, her words blunt, almost to the point of cruelty.

"What are you saying? . . . " Her mother paused to process her daughter's words. "What are you telling me?"

"Mamma, I have stage four ovarian cancer that's metastasized."

"No! No, no, no," screamed Mom.

"Oh, Mom, I'm sorry."

"Figlia mia, figlia mia," cried Mom over and over, "No, no, no."

"I love you, Mama," Mandy cried, "I love you so much."

Mandy held her mother as she gasped for air.

"It's OK, Mom. I got you. Just take deep breaths."

After an endless wait, Mom folded her hands and bent her head while noiseless tears fell into her lap. She strained for composure, eventually pulling away from her daughter to stand and face her. In a voice, low and melancholy, she said, "You can talk to me, honey. Tell me what I need to know. I promise to listen without my dramatics."

Her wringing hands, her rapid breathing spoke otherwise—Mandy could sense an inner storm brewing. She credited herself for knowing her mother so well that she could predict that her mother could not keep her promise and would eventually revert to form. This was just a silence before the storm.

"I'll always be straight with you. We'll have differences, but we'll work through them and . . . "

"Enough . . . just tell me."

"OK. Here goes." After a deep intake of breath, she spelled it out. "I don't have a lot of time left to spend with you." Mandy allowed tears to well in her eyes.

"What are you saying? Your aunt had more than three years after her chemo."

"They said my cancer is too far advanced and anything they do won't help much, including chemo," explained Mandy. "With chemo I'd have maybe a year, without it, give or take three months. And what do you think that year would be like? I'd waste away. I think of Aunt Virgie's prolonged pain and you'd have to watch that all over again with me. I fear that pain for myself and I don't especially want that for you. Please, for me, let this be my decision."

"You'll need to take time off from work to begin your treatment. I'll be with you for that."

Mandy's mouth dropped. She was certain she was lecturing to the air.

"You're not hearing me. Listen to me, you don't understand. I'm not going through treatment."

"They must have something they can give you to fight this," questioned Mom. There have to be new treatments since Virgie.

"Mom, all the new or traditional stuff might help me for a few months, but I still wouldn't make a year with you," said Mandy, her voice weakening as she strained to hold back unshed tears.

"No, no, no," Mom cried out, "That can't be. There must be something."

Her mom looked small and vulnerable. "I wish . . . " sniffled Mandy. "There is so much more to life than simply surviving it, Mom. I know you'll always miss me, but I want to leave you with good memories. Not me struggling to live without success. We can build new memories. Let's use these last days to prepare you. Get your finances in order. Maybe we can even find time to laugh together. I remember the days after my soccer injury and how gallantly you and Dad fought to bring order to our lives. You'll do that again if you know that if you did otherwise, it would break my heart. Please Mom. It's important you remember me with the joy I hope I gave you during my life." Inwardly she cursed the cancer. "Remember, I'm not leaving because I want to. Each day before I die, I want to show you courage. I will have the strength to die at peace if I know you'll be prepared for life without me. Give me the power to share my last days with you."

Exhausted from raw emotion, they cried themselves out into the wee hours of the night until they fell asleep in each other's arms. Hope reclined at their feet, whimpering from time to time.

Evangelina sat atop Mom's house and could hear the cries of grief. Their sorrow tugged at her heart. If only there was some way or somehow, she could change Mandy's fate. All she could do was to pray for her soul.

CHAPTER 25

E v KNOCKED ON MRS. ABBESSI's door and waited patiently. She admired the arrangement of pumpkins and gourds on the porch and imagined Mandy as a little girl playing on the stoop. Ev could hear movement behind the door and continued to wait. Mrs. Abbessi eventually opened the door a crack, hiding her face in the shadow of the door.

Mom cleared her throat, then asked "Can I help you?"

"Is Mandy here?" asked Ev with a smile.

"And who are you?" questioned Mrs. Abbassi.

"I'm her friend, Ev. Could you tell her I'm here?"

"We had a rough night. She's still in bed." A crumpled tissue fell through the narrow door opening.

"I'm sorry to hear that," said Ev. "Could you see if she's awake? I know she'll want to see me."

"I suppose," Mrs. Abbassi said without enthusiasm, suddenly aware that Hope wasn't jumping at the door as was her trademark greeting for anyone who came to visit. "Come in and I'll see if she's up to having visitors."

Ev stepped in the door and Hope backed up, studying Ev.

"Hi, girl." Ev stooped to scratch Hope's ears and whispered, "Be strong, girl. In time things will be OK."

Mom stepped back befuddled by Hope's reaction to this person she had never met. "I've never seen *that* before."

"What's that?" asked Ev.

"Hope should be jumping up and down on you, barking and being a general nuisance," said Mom.

"Animals generally trust me, Mrs. Abbessi," smiled Ev. "We kinda read each other."

"I guess there's a first for everything," said Mom. "I'll check on Mandy. Oh, and call me Mama Marie. Most people do."

She tiptoed to the top of the stairs, to Mandy's room and knocked softly. Sliding her head into a crack in the door she saw Mandy sitting up reading a magazine.

"You're up?"

"Morning, Ma," said Mandy motioning for her to sit on the side of the bed.

"It's not morning anymore. It's three o'clock in the afternoon."

"Oh, my God, I had no idea."

"It's OK, you needed your rest," said Mom. "Your friend Ev is downstairs."

"Ev? Wow, how'd she know I was here?" Mandy said rhetorically. "Let me get dressed and I'll be right down."

"I'll let her know. She seems like a nice girl."

"She is, Mom. I'll let her know you said that," Mandy smirked.

Mandy sat on the edge of the bed and yawned. She slipped out of her sleeping attire and went to her closet. Her clothes still hung from when she was eighteen. She figured none would fit, *but it's worth a try.* She grabbed an old faded pair of ragtag jeans and wiggled them on. Surprisingly they fit. She then scrounged to find an old "Comets on Fire" t-shirt and slipped it on. To complete her outfit reminiscent of her high school days, slipped into her old tattered slippers. She ran her fingers though her tangled hair and fluffed it with her fingers. Looking in the mirror she thought, *It's only Ev . . . she'll understand.*

Ev grinned upon seeing Mandy. "Mandy, you look . . . interesting," jested Ev.

"I wore my finest when I heard you were here," joked Mandy. "How'd you know I was here? And how did you find this place?"

"Well, I stopped by your condo and you weren't there and your neighbor, Grace, told me you didn't come home last night. That's when I remembered you telling me you were visiting your mom on Tuesday, so I figured you had spent the night," said Ev. "Grace gave me vague directions and I put the rest together. Oh, and besides the directions, she tried to feed me some of her eggplant parmesan."

"Lucky you. She loves to garden and brings me fresh veggies during the summer. I love her baking. You know, she's such a good person. If she's a bit nosey, well, it comes with the territory."

"I didn't come to talk about Grace," said Ev. "I just wanted to quickly go over the details for Friday."

Mama Marie entered the room with tiramisu on dessert plates. "Have something to eat, girls. You need to keep your strength up."

"That's so sweet of you, Mrs. Abbessi, but I can't stay. I just wanted to return Mandy her scarf." Proud of her quick thinking she pulled her own scarf from her pocket and handed it over, with a wink, to Mandy.

"Remember, it's Mama Marie," she said tsk, tsking her way back to the kitchen.

"This is not going to work," whispered Ev.

"You're right. This isn't the right time to discuss Friday. What if I meet you at The Capital at six tonight?"

"Perfect."

"Oh my, is that the right time?" Ev said looking at her watch, as Mama Marie returned. "I've gotta go." And with a wink to Mandy, added "I can't miss my six o'clock appointment. Thank you so much for the hospitality, Mama Marie."

"You have to leave so soon? Oh my, uh, you know Saturday is Halloween. I'd love it if both of you were here. I want to be with my daughter as much as I can. You could help by handing out candy."

"I'll be there," said Ev.

"Mom, please," said Mandy.

"It's OK. It'll be fun seeing all those little ghosts and goblins," said Ev walking to the door. Hope followed along wagging her tail. "Never seen Hope take to a stranger so quickly."

"My cat loves her, too," said Mandy.

"Animals know good souls," said Mom.

"Wow, it's after four o'clock," said Mandy, "I have to get going, too. I gotta go to the condo and get ready for an after-hours meeting. I'll probably stay there tonight, so don't wait up."

"Well, if you change your mind, I'll be up," said Mom.

"Oh, Mom," resigned Mandy.

Mandy walked up the stairs to grab her belongings. She was only gone a short time before returning to the living room and finding Mom had switched seats to her rocking chair and sat reading her Bible.

"Gotta go, Mom," said Mandy.

"I'll be praying for you."

The two exchanged a tight embrace.

"I hate leaving you, but I'll see you Saturday. I love you," said Mandy.

"I'll make chili and hot mulled cider just like when you were little," said Mom tearing up.

"Oh, that sounds good. See ya 'round four o'clock. I'll bring the wine."

———

Pulling into the parking lot of her condo, Mandy saw flashing red and blue lights reflecting off the walls of the buildings. She parked in her spot and saw an EMS truck at the entrance to the courtyard. She grabbed her purse and clothes and hurried up the walk. She turned the corner to her condo just in time to see the EMS techs wheeling Grace out on a gurney. She ran to the techs.

"What happened?" asked Mandy urgently.

"Ma'am we can't answer that question," said the EMS tech.

"Where are you taking her?" asked Mandy.

"Royal Oak Beaumont," responded the tech.

"All right then," said Mandy as she watched them wheel her down the path to the ambulance.

Chapter 26

M ANDY THREW HER COAT and bag on the couch and sprinted up the stairs, two at a time, disrobing on the way for a quick shower. She had little time to spare. Afterwards, wrapped in her terry robe, she stood face to face before the bathroom mirror to blow dry her hair. It was then she took a second look at her image and stopped to stare. Turning her head to and fro she assessed her face, noting her cheekbones appeared more prominent against the darkening circles around her eyes. *Do they appear sunken?* she asked herself. *Is this part of my illness? So soon?*

She had that appointment with Ev she couldn't miss. *I'll worry about my looks later*, she told herself. As she began to dash from the bathroom, stabbing pain grabbed her midsection, forcing her to double over and sink to her knees. A coughing spasm drove her to all fours.

Her heart throbbed in unison with deep rasping and uneven breaths of air. Shuddering at the sight of deep red splotches of blood on the floor. She began to cry and crumbled. With her face buried in her hands she broke down, sobbing, but dismissed the idea of going to emergency. She knew if she went, they wouldn't let her leave before demanding a CAT scan or MRI or blood work. She had things to do. Important things.

Mandy gathered every ounce of strength in her body and stood, holding onto the vanity until she gained equilibrium. She clung to the walls and followed them to her bedroom, then to her nightstand where she had left her prescription bottle. She picked up the bottle and read the directions. It read: no driving, nor use of machinery while taking the drug. Mandy wanted to take one immediately, but she had to drive. Besides, she felt the pain beginning to ease. She decided to take the bottle with her just in case the pain worsened.

By the time Mandy finished getting ready and made her way downstairs, she felt even more relief. Grabbing her coat and purse she hurried her way out the door. Walking briskly to her car, she breathed in the earthy autumn air, and tried to bring her thoughts together. Once in the car, she took off in a flash, minutes later pulling into The Capital's parking lot and entering the restaurant. It took only seconds to bypass the hostess after spotting Ev in a booth at the rear of the restaurant.

"Hi, Ev," said Mandy, removing her coat. "Long time no see," she joked

"Hi. So glad you upped your wardrobe," laughed Ev.

"Now, now," Mandy deadpanned, "that was vintage attire. You can't buy that stylish ensemble today."

"And we're all better off because of that," laughed Ev.

"I agree."

"I see you also went with the clean brushed hair look. Very becoming," poked Ev.

"It's not quite as stylish as my crazed woman hair from this afternoon, but more appropriate for this more dignified setting, don't you think?" Mandy replied faking an English accent.

Both ladies enjoyed the repartee.

Pointing at Ev's glass of sparkling clear liquid garnished with a lime, Mandy inquired, "Gin and tonic?"

"No, just sparkling water with lime."

"Well, you're no fun . . . and the package? What's in it?" nodding to a neatly wrapped parcel tied with string.

Ev leaned closely and said in a hushed voice, "Your costume for Friday night. It's an exact duplicate of what the kitchen help wear at Bubbs."

"Ah, my ninja wear," said Mandy.

"Do you still have the key to the locker?" questioned Ev.

"Yes, right here," Mandy said, pulling it from her purse.

"Excellent," said Ev, "don't lose it."

"The only thing I'm losing right now is my mind," said Mandy.

"What do you mean?" asked Ev.

"Remember Grace?" asked Mandy. "They were taking her away in an ambulance when I got to the condo this afternoon. I'm worried sick about her."

"What happened to her?" asked Ev.

"I don't know. I'm going to try to see her Friday morning at the hospital; I have scattered meetings tomorrow." said Mandy.

"I'll come with you if you need moral support," said Ev.

"That would be nice," Mandy said with an appreciative smile.

Distracted by her ringing cell, Mandy read a text from Brent.

"It's from Brent," Mandy said with a broad smile. "He wants to take me out to dinner tomorrow night. What should I do?"

"If you have feelings for whoever he is, you should go," said Ev.

"But I don't want to lead him on or anything . . . you know. My situation is depressing."

"If you've explained what you're going through, enjoy yourself while you have time."

"Yeah, you're right, Ev," said Mandy, "I'll text him "Yes.""

"SOOO, who's Brent? Is he your boyfriend?" finally getting to ask the question.

"What? I thought I told you about Brent," said Mandy.

"No, you haven't mentioned anything about a Brent," said Ev feigning ignorance.

"Oh," said Mandy sheepishly.

"So, give me the scoop."

"Well, it's complicated."

"I would think nothing less coming from you," laughed Ev.

"I've known Brent for a few years. He's an attorney at the firm below my office," began Mandy. "We consulted on a few real estate deals. He's very nice . . . and very handsome."

"Ooh! Tell me more," said Ev leaning in.

"The other day he invited me to a company "party" at The Brazilian Steakhouse. I agreed to go only because I needed his advice on the best way to set Mom's future after my death. But he hadn't explained that we were going to an awards' ceremony. And he would be named partner," said Mandy. "Pretty big stuff, huh?"

"I'd say," said Ev.

"The entire event impressed me and I started to see Brent as I'd not seen him before. To say he is liked by his coworkers is an understatement. They adore him. So, I needed to take a second look and as the night drew on, I found myself blushing when he smiled at me and wanting to hold his hand, or kiss him on the cheek . . . you know, silly, girly stuff like that. He has this warm, wonderful way about him."

"That's fantastic," said Ev.

"After the ceremony I couldn't break into his special night. It'd be mean. You know, 'Hey Brent, nice party, but I'm dying and need your help.' I guess my face gave me away, though, and he saw my distress. He walked me to a private area of the room and I broke. Honestly, I didn't want to cry and embarrass him in front of his co-workers, but truth is, I did. Discretely, at first. I told him everything. And felt pathetic doing it to him."

"How did he take the news?" asked Ev.

"Well, he was very comforting. I asked him to help me set up my mother so after I'm gone, she won't have to worry about money," explained Mandy.

"Is tomorrow a meeting or a date?" asked Ev.

"I'm not sure," said Mandy.

"Ooh," said Ev.

"Stop it. Would you be interested in someone who's here today and gone tomorrow?" asked Mandy.

"The heart wants what the heart wants," said Ev.

"Why would anyone invest time and energy into me, knowing that I couldn't be there for them?" said Mandy.

"Well, I am," said Ev.

"I truly appreciate what you're doing for me, Ev. You are the sweetest person in the whole world. There's a place in heaven for you," said Mandy.

Ev just laughed.

CHAPTER 27

S HE CUDDLED DEEPER UNDER the comforter, languidly lost in thought about her evening out with Brent, careful not to allow a vision of her future with him get carried away. Her future lived in days, not months or years.

She mentally inspected her closet for the perfect dress to wear, but only came up with the black sheath she'd worn to the company dinner. Was it ridiculous to shop for something new? Never one to stay up with fashion trends, more precisely, her daring wardrobe lagged behind. She blushed trying to remember her last purchase of bras and panties.

She recalled frequent Saks ads in the *Detroit Free Press*. Perhaps a quick jaunt to Somerset Mall was in order. Find a sale dress. Red, if possible.

It didn't take long to apply makeup, slip into casual slacks and a loose turtleneck and be on her way. The Saks store in Troy wasn't far, just a quick swing to the Somerset Collection mall off Big Beaver Road. If she hurried, she would be back for lunch.

The store smelled of class and wealth. The aisles seemed short of salespeople; those she saw were women dressed like fashion models. It was early in the day, most of their richer customers were probably still in bed, she thought sarcastically. Passing a mirror on every wall convinced her she looked like a beggar from a different planet.

She tootled along, visiting different boutique departments, admiring the collections from Marc Jacobs, Yves Saint Laurent, Versace and a long list of others. Now and then she'd hit upon a red dress to her liking, but turn away after flipping over the price tag. On one such occasion her eyes lit upon an Oscar de la Renta, off-the-shoulder, red dress at $5,590. *Sure.* At that point she considered turning an about face and settle with her black dress back home. That is until she found herself in the "Big Sale" department. She picked various tags and found the clothes more in her price range. She stopped at a tight fitting, red, knit dress on the sale rack and imagined herself wearing it for Brent. She held it to her body in front of a full-length mirror and felt a wave of relief. How easy. Serendipitous. Crazy. The price at $105 was slightly high, but, *What the hell.*

She looked up for a dressing room when a voice popped up from behind.

"Ah, dahling, that dress would be nice on you, but not awe-inspiring. Is there a special occasion?"

Mandy turned to put a face to the smooth voice with a low, almost guttural undertone. A tall, well above five foot nine, darkly stunning, but overdressed saleslady stood addressing her.

"Nothing special," Mandy said, purposely not offering more.

"I'm Levia, here to help. Flag me if you need assistance." With that she disappeared to Mandy's relief; she preferred shopping without a trailing employee.

Stepping into the dressing room, thankful to be concealed from her sketchy saleslady, she shed her slacks, but struggled to slip her turtleneck over her head, all the while cussing herself for not wearing a simple button-down blouse. As she prepared to slide into the tailored, red dress a furious whirl of feathers and sparkles blew into her dressing room

"Stop! Don't go any further. No, no, no. Can't you see that dress is too . . . too 'off the rack'? Here, try this Dolce & Gabbana, only $9,4450. Feathers and metallic sequins. A showstopper. When you go out, sweetheart, you should always want to be seen as a woman of influence, power, and good taste."

Mandy drew back to the wall and tried to speak. "Who are you? Get out of here."

But Levia rammed her words together, leaving little room for Mandy to interject. "If that one is not to your liking, here's another, slightly less costly than the Gabbana but equally powerful. It's perfect for you. A

Valentino must have. Made for you my little peach kin. It's marked down to only $8,000. Other women will be jealous and men will know you're prosperous, a woman to watch."

"What the hell? Get your face out of here. If you don't leave, I'll call management and security." Mandy had no time for politeness. She let her commanding words pour out of the dressing room into the store proper.

Something about the stranger's distinctive features reminded her of Narcis and his ability to paint a beautiful face—a false face—by simply laying few dabs and splashes of color. She recognized his imprint played out on the face before her. But how was it possible?

"And, look," continued Levia, "if you insist on red, here's a tailored Alexander McQueen with a plunging neckline at only $2,100. It's nicely tailored, so people will know you're rich and important and treat you with respect. You'll be the envy of all your female friends." She held out a Mc-Queen cherry red dress.

"You're pathetic as a saleswoman." Mandy spit out her words like rocks aimed to target Levia's vanity, then crouched low to the ground and scooched out the door like a cowering animal, into the aisle, into a gathering crowd interested in the chaos growing around the dressing room.

Levia gave chase only to be halted when Mandy made an abrupt stop in the center of the crowd protecting her and turned to face her nemesis.

"The only power I need right now is power to stop you."

To her shock, the words took effect. Levia threw her head back as if injured by the words. And with that her wig shifted to the side, exposing a bald head, broad shoulders and an enlarged Adam's apple.

Levia's exposure created fear and sweat to blend with her makeup. Everyone watched the colors of deep blue and black and red wash down her face, leaving her vulnerable to what was to follow.

It was Mandy's strident words booming out that stopped the crowd. "Or is it really a salesMAN?"

The audience of customers pulled back and spewed out an expanded collective "Ohhhhhhh."

Unbeknownst to Mandy, Ev had joined the fray. Proud to be watching her protégé handle this situation without her help.

"I don't understand your goal, but know this, I have jealously of no one. I covet no one for what they have and I have no need to be coveted by anyone by the likes of you. You're a contemptible demon born of envy, right out the playbook on the seven deadly sins.

Once the gathering spotted Levia's weakness, they surrounded him like vultures circling for a kill. But he managed to elbow his way through the crowd of elegantly dressed patrons and disappear.

Once the crowd dispersed, Mandy returned to rescue the red dress left behind. At the entrance to the dressing room, she stumbled over a pair of red Louis Vuitton shoes, sole side up.

———

Blisdon, Incubus, Mammon, Beelzebub, and Satan weighed down the limo while waiting for Leviathan. While he was not their last hope to capture Mandy's soul, he was certainly their most manipulative, cunning, and creative demon.

They saw a figure exit the mall in a quick run, braying like a frightened donkey, followed by an angry mob of women, fists raised, shouting: Scoundrel, weirdo, charlatan, con-artist. As the figure closed the gap to the limo, it was clear to the demons that it was a wigless Leviathan in a Chanel gown being whipped around by the wind. His arms flailed in the air.

As he neared the car, they could see fat raindrops exploding from his eyes. He dropped to the hood of the car and pounded. "Open up, damn you."

"Leave him, Blisdon. Get out of here before the riffraff arrives." With that Blisdon backed the car up, but Leviathan held on as they swerved in and out and around other limos, Mercedes, Teslas, BMWs in the parking lot . . .

Finally, out of danger Blisdon pulled off to a side street to open the door to Leviathan. "Put him in the front seat so we don't have to look at him/her," said Satan, which brought Leviathan to howling in tears.

Each demon, their arms folded, avoided eye contact with him.

Finally, Beelzebub spoke up. "Stop bawling like a baby; you've embarrassed us all."

CHAPTER 28

M ANDY TWIRLED IN FRONT of her bedroom mirror. Thrilled by her purchase of the red dress that caused such ruckus at Saks. It was feminine, but not frilly. Classy, without being stuffy. Best yet, she felt comfortable in it, though it was a touch too big. With another twenty minutes to spare before Brent arrived, she sat down at the edge of her bed and switched on the small TV on her dresser to check out the evening news.

"Good God!" she hollered catching the tail end of the sales person from Saks running out into the parking lot like a crazy person. She, unfortunately, missed the storyline, but it would be in the morning paper. *What a crazy adventure*. Thankfully she got a red dress out of it. She added the morning's adventure to a growing list of bizarre incidents, but something rancored her, niggled into her subconscious. Were Zagan, Blisdon, Dolos, Narciss a mere coincident? And what about the red shoes left at the entrance to her dressing room? Did all this connect in some way?

She put these ridiculous thoughts aside when the doorbell rang and made her way down the stairs, checking her watch on the way. Right on time. She opened the door to a grinning Brent holding a delicate bouquet of southern peach and pink roses, and baby's breath. "These are for you," said Brent.

" Oh, my, they're exquisite, Brent. You're making some florist happy and rich. Come in a moment while I put them in water."

"Pretty flowers for an even prettier woman," smiled Brent.

"Oh, Lawdy, that's one thing I'd never guess about you . . . "

"What's that?"

"That you could be so corny."

They both laughed, enjoying the playful banter. Mandy's best relationships always included easy, light-hearted poking in good fun.

"Truly, you're so sweet," said Mandy, "you brought me flowers and a reason to laugh. It feels good to find a little comedy, even through a crisis."

"Well, I thought they'd bring you a smile, certainly not a laugh at my expense, however. I'll do my best to give you reason to poke at me . . . how 'bout I become your personal jester. Let's face it, you haven't had much to smile about . . . Oh, and I have a little something else for you," said Brent reaching into his pocket. "I saw it and thought you'd like it and definitely need it."

He pulled out a small box wrapped in silver paper and tied with a silver bow. He tried to hand it to Mandy, but she put her hand up and backed away, shaking her head saying, "No, Brent . . . I can't."

"Hey, I'm celebrating being made a partner. What fun is it if I can't share my success," Brent asked rhetorically. "Just open it. If you don't like it, I'll take it back."

Reluctantly Mandy took the package and untied the bow. She carefully peeled the wrapping, revealing a silver Tiffany's box. From the box, she pulled out a velvet jewelry case. She opened the top and touched a gold Celtic knot heart on a gold chain.

"Oh, it's beautiful, Brent," Mandy exclaimed, bringing out the chain and holding it up to her neck.

"I thought a little Scottish luck wouldn't hurt. I made sure the chain was longer than the diamond studded star you're wearing so you could wear both," smiled Brent. "Here, let me put it on you."

Brent took the Celtic knot from Mandy's hand and she turned around to lift her hair in the back as Brent latched the chain. She clutched the Celtic Knot and turned to face him. "It's perfect on you, Mandy. It hangs just as I'd planned, right below your father's gold star.

"Oh my, it's beautiful, Brent," said Mandy, "I love it. So, you know, my father gave me this chain and star before he died. How can I lose? I'll be wearing the gifts of two special men."

"I'm glad," said Brent.

They embraced briefly, each realizing a new sensation of familiarity and warmth.

"Come on, we have reservations and don't want to be late," said Brent,

"Where are we going?" asked Mandy.

"The Town Steakhouse."

"I love that place. They have a live band and great food."

"And they're waiting for us," said Brent.

"Just let me grab my coat," said Mandy.

"Allow me, madam," said Brent gallantly stepping behind her to assist with her short faux fur jacket.

"All set." He ushered her down the path to the parking lot to a new Cadillac sedan.

"Wow, new Cadillac," said Mandy.

"Well, when you're a partner you have to look the part."

It was a short ride to the Town Steakhouse. As always, the parking lot was jam-packed. Brent pulled up to the entrance to be met by an attendant wearing goblin ears.

"Oh, how could I have forgotten? It's their annual Halloween week. They're famous for it." The attendant assisted Mandy out of the car. Brent slipped a tip to the attendant and took Mandy by the hand.

"Our table awaits," said Brent with a smile.

The couple entered a restaurant festooned with hanging bats and skeletons, lit jack-lanterns, ghosts floating above. They waited at the front desk for the hostess and watched as employees dressed in costume as Fairies, witches, angels and a host of other characters bustled about servicing their guests. Finally, they heard, "Mr. Maxwell, so good to see you."

Startled, Brent turned to face a Marilyn Monroe look alike. "Gloria? That's a convincing outfit. You're as beautiful as the original. And, as always, it's a pleasure to see you too.

"Thank you for the compliment," Gloria blushed. "Your table is ready, and David will take you there."

David, sporting a simple clown's tie and red wig, grabbed two menus and Brent and Mandy followed closely behind to a band playing a smooth jazz tune.

"Well so much for a quiet evening together," issued Brent from the corner of his mouth.

David led them to a back corner booth, set with a candle cradled in a wreath of skulls and bones instead of flowers. Mandy and Brent slipped into their seats. David placed their menus on the table and took out his notepad.

"Would you care for anything from the bar?" he asked.

"A glass of pinot noir would be nice," said Mandy.

"Bring us the bottle," said Brent, "and two glasses."

"Well, well, the scotch drinker now drinks wine," Mandy laughed. "Weren't you the one who told me that old, grape juice stomped in a vat, laced with foot fungus, would kill me?"

"Well, even I can have a glass or two with a great steak. Now after dinner, I will kill all those wine toxins with a healthy glass of 18-year-old Scotch and a fine cigar."

"Keep drinking and I'll be driving that new Caddie home," smirked Mandy.

"So, how many lawyers does it take to screw in a light bulb?" asked Brent.

"Brent, please," she sneered.

"Four. One to screw in the light bulb, two shake the ladder and one to file the lawsuit against the ladder company." Brent laughed, not at his own joke, but because Mandy's expected reaction.

"OK, that's your one for tonight," Mandy deadpanned, "You are incorrigible."

David returned with the bottle of wine and showed the label to Brent. He uncorked it and poured a taste into Brent's wine glass. Brent swirled the wine in the glass and sniffed the aroma. He swallowed the wine in one gulp and nodded to the waiter to pour them each a glass.

"Give us a few minutes before we order," said Brent.

"As you wish," said David as he turned and left the table.

"Slange Var," said Brent raising his glass.

"Slange Var?" questioned Mandy.

"That's cheers in Scottish,"

"OK. Slange Var," said Mandy raising her glass and clinking it against his glass.

"I don't know about you, but filet mignon is definitely in my future."

"I second that motion," said Mandy, taking another sip of wine.

Brent waved David over. He came to the table with notepad in hand to take their orders.

"Filet for the lady, medium rare and a Caesar salad on the side. I'll have the same, except well done. Caesar too."

David restated their order, bowed, and left.

"Why would you cook a perfectly good piece of meat into shoe leather," quipped Mandy.

"I prefer my cow cooked, not mooing at me from my plate."

"To each his own."

They fell into free and easy conversation. What had been a business relationship had become personal. They were like two old friends chatting and catching up on recent events. Mandy told Brent how gracious Mike, her broker, was when she told him she was "retiring." Brent told Mandy about his swanky new corner office and how Pauli, his intern, was now his paid assistant. Pauli was so excited he proposed to Cherylann and they're now engaged.

It seemed like they just ordered when their steaks arrived. The aroma of the sizzling steak filled the air as David put down the plates.

"Thank you," said Mandy, "it looks wonderful."

"Will there be anything else?" asked David.

"No, I think we're good," said Brent.

Mandy sliced into the succulent meat and the juices flowed onto her plate. She held the piece of beef on her fork and examined it. It was done perfectly for her taste. "Now this is the way steak was supposed to be eaten."

"You must be part vampire," laughed Brent.

"Ah, you've guessed my secret," Mandy chuckled. "And I come out on Halloween."

The couple savored their meal and finished off the bottle of wine. While they enjoyed themselves, Evangelina, cloaked in her invisibility, sat on the corner of the bandstand, watching. She began to appreciate the attachment humans have for one another. As she surveyed the room, she saw couples eating, drinking, and laughing together. She thought this was the reason why people held onto life so dearly. It wasn't so much the physical beauty of the world as much as the beauty they created when they were together.

The band continued to play and several couples moved to the dance floor. They played a couple of fast songs, but then slowed it down. They began to play "Lady in Red" and more couples made their way to the floor for a slow dance.

"I believe this is your song," said Brent with a smile.

"What?" said Mandy, a bit confused.

"You're my lady in red. May I have this dance?"

"Did you order this to be played? It's a wonderful gesture Brent, but what you don't know about me is my dance skills are lacking."

"Don't worry. I'll lead," said Brent standing to take her hand, "Come, it will be fun."

Reluctantly, Mandy stood and walked with Brent to the dance floor. When they arrived, Brent took her in his arms and they began to sway with the music. "The lady in red is dancing with me, cheek to cheek, there's nobody here it's just you and me . . . " Brent softly sang the words into her ear. She'd forgotten how it was to be wrapped in a man's arms. With Brent it was more than comforting. He had a protective strength that brought her a sense of security and peace. With the end of the song, Brent leaned over and kissed her. And she kissed him back. Electricity shot through them both, a deep flow of energy melding them together. Mandy stepped on her tiptoes and they continued to kiss. When the next song was a fast song, they mutually ended their kiss and returned to their table. They sat silent for a moment or two.

"Wow," said Mandy.

"Indeed, wow," said Brent.

Brent reached across the table and took her by the hand. She looked into his smiling eyes and shook her head.

"Why would you be interested in me? We don't have a future . . . Well, at least I don't have a future," Mandy said somberly.

"Let's not worry about that now. Let's just enjoy this moment." His fading voice trembled lightly.

While his words resembled the same thoughts others had spoken with good intentions: live in the moment because you don't know how many moments you have left; enjoy what life you have left; throw care to the wind, and so on. Suddenly their significance shined brightly. Their impact held new power. She didn't ever want to say good-bye to Brent.

"You're right, Brent," she answered.

"Now, let's get me a cigar and a Scotch and you, a chocolate martini," smiled Brent.

"Sounds like a plan," laughed Mandy, "Where are we going?"

"My favorite hideaway," Brent said, "Capone's Library."

"Sounds interesting," said Mandy.

"It's my favorite cigar bar in town," said Brent.

"Let's do it," said Many, thrilled for another new adventure.

Brent raised his hand and called David to the table. He asked for the check, looked it over a second and then handed him cash. When Brent told him to keep the change, David smiled ear to ear.

Once in the car, Brent instructed her to buckle up. "Just sit back and relax, we'll be there in no time."

Brent put the car in gear and drove out and headed north on Rochester Road to the on ramp of I-75. Brent merged into traffic and cruised along in the center lane. Traffic was light, so Brent was making good time.

"Go fast," said Mandy.

"We're going 75 mph."

"No, go fast . . . really fast," she implored.

"Um, you know we've been drinking and if we get pulled over, I'm not sure what I'd blow. I'm a good lawyer, but I'm not good enough to refute that," said Brent.

"If we get pulled over tell the officer that I'm your client and you're rushing me the hospital. Believe me, if you drop me off at the emergency room they will admit me immediately," said Mandy. "Go fast."

Brent stomped the accelerator pedal and watched the digital speedometer rocket to 100 mph. The lines on the road became a blur, but he remembered to keep both hands tightly on the wheel. "It truly is exhilarating." Was it Brent who said that or Brent on wine speaking?

"Go faster," said Mandy.

"What?" questioned Brent glancing over, concerned for Mandy's sobriety.

"Go faster. It makes me feel alive," said Mandy.

Brent hesitated and then said, "Your wish is my command."

Brent crushed the accelerator pedal to the floor. The speedometer shot up to 120 mph . . . 130 mph . . . 140 mph. As they merged onto M-59, Brent spotted the flashing lights of a state trooper ahead on the road. The trooper had already pulled over another car and was standing alongside it. Brent immediately pulled his foot off the accelerator and applied the brakes. By the time he came upon the trooper, he dropped to the speed limit.

"Thank you, Brent."

"Whoa, that was close," he said, his heart rate slowly declining.

"It was a concoction of invigorating, mind-blowing, terrifying, and kind of kinky passion—Thank you for indulging me."

"It's the least I can do," said Brent, "and now I know this new baby has some guts."

Brent reached over and grabbed her hand and squeezed. She rested her head on his shoulder. They exited the highway and drove along the top streets to Capone's Library. By the time they entered a space in the parking lot and Brent popped out to open Mandy's door, he found her doubled over in her seat, coughing.

"What's wrong? What's wrong?" Brent questioned urgently.

Mandy continued to cough and hack. Brent kneeled beside her and rubbed his hand vigorously on her back attempting to ease the cough.

"Are you in pain?"

Mandy could only nod yes.

Finally, minutes later, the coughing subsided and Mandy accepted Brent's handkerchief, almost certain she'd find a repeat from her earlier spasm. And she did—a blood-soaked handkerchief. She began to cry.

"You need to go to the hospital," said a startled Brent.

"No, no, no," Mandy said hoarsely. "Just take me home so I can get my pills."

"Are you sure?" said Brent with concern as he took the handkerchief from her hand and dabbed the blood from the corner of her mouth.

"Yes," said Mandy.

Evangelina arrived on the scene a bit out of breath. She had sped, but couldn't compete with a 140 mph car. She lighted down on the "Capone's Library" sign and observed the couple. She marveled at Brent's loving compassion for Mandy.

Evangelina understood more and more why mortals hung on so dearly to life. The bond of love between them was worth the pain and suffering they endured.

Chapter 29

S HE AWOKE SLOWLY TO a thumping pain in her head, as if she had been in a bout with a punching bag. It was when she inched her head up, she saw bloodstains on her pillow and a dark blue bruise on her forearm that she peeked under her covers, confused to find herself still in her red dress. She closed her eyes and strained to put a memory to the night before. Her last cloudy picture was of her unending coughing fit at the Capone Library parking lot and getting sick. Flashes of Brent reoccurred. She remembered he drove her home and helped her into the house. She remembered Brent bringing her the pills from her coat pocket. After that, everything was blurred. She definitely had to call Brent and apologize. She checked her digital clock and remembered her meeting with Ev, but fogged at the time.

Mandy sat up slowly and groaned. A parched mouth drove her from her bed, only to be swept into a whirl of imbalance. She stood still until the wave of dizziness passed, and she could walk without a prop. As she turned, she caught her reflection in her dresser mirror. Her dress was wrinkled, hair in disarray and make up smeared her face. She rotated her head to get a full view and shook her head slowly.

"Wow," said Mandy aloud, struggling to undress before padding to the shower to wait for the water to warm to her touch. Craving liquid, she ran the faucet until the water turned ice cold and greedily gulped a glass down.

She stepped into the tub and let the warm water caress her face and slowly revitalize her body. She reviewed her schedule for the day, grateful for only two appointments. Visiting Grace at the hospital came first on her agenda. But this was the big night. She'd meet up with Ev again to retrieve her clothing from that whorehouse. She knew what she had to do, she only hoped she had enough fight in her to last the day.

———

The black limousine pulled into Mandy's condominium parking lot and sat idling at the rear. Inside, Satan sat silently with Belphegor. Blisdon put the limo into park and looked back at his passengers.

"Masters, we're here," said Blisdon.

"I can see that, you idiot," growled Satan.

"Belphegor," said Satan, "you are our last hope. If you can't get this mere mortal to voluntarily commit the deadly sin of sloth or apathy then we may have to revert to other more violent means."

"Don't worry," said Belphegor, "in her condition it will be easy to make her lazy and indifferent to all mankind. I'm amazed she isn't already depressed and uncaring. Disinterested in everything but herself. She'll be a quickie, believe me."

"Just do your job, imbecile," Satan growled.

Blisdon opened the limo door and Belphegor slid out, his eyes and concentration directed at Mandy's condo. As he walked, he slowly faded into his invisibility cloak until he vanished from sight. Evangelina, atop the condo roof, watched Belphegor move directly to Mandy's condo. She shook her head and scowled at the demons' next attempt to steal Mandy's soul. She needed to protect Mandy without alarming her.

"Hello, Ev," said Mandy, answering her phone. "I was just thinking of calling you."

"Hi. What's going on?" said Ev maintaining a casual, steady voice.

"I'm still trying to recover from last night's episode with the big 'C,'" she said

"Uh-oh."

"Yeah, it got messy, but I'll tell you about it when we meet this afternoon."

"This afternoon? I thought we were going to see your neighbor, Grace, this morning. I was hoping you were getting ready," said Ev.

"Ohhh, that's right," said Mandy. "Forgive my major brain fade. Last night I had to take one of those pills Dr. Fineman prescribed and I'm just coming out of the fog."

"I take it there were problems. You needed a pill? For pain? Are you clear-headed now?" It concerned Ev that Belphegor, at this moment, was moving toward Mandy. She may need to act quickly once she determined his plan.

"Eh . . . I'll be OK as the day wears on. Give me a little extra time to have breakfast. I'll be in survival mode before I leave the house. But when you get here, play like you're not shocked when you see me. I look like the wreck of the Hesperus."

"Gotcha. See ya' soon," said Ev.

Mandy slipped into grey slacks and black pullover sweater. She all but fled down the stairs to whip up a scrambled egg. *Who knows when I'll eat next?*

Evangelina entered the condo cloaked in invisibility and positioned herself on the loveseat just prior to Belphegor entering. He showed no surprise to find her sitting, waiting for him. He winked and grinned at her and she, in kind, gave him her finger as he made his way to the kitchen to interact with Mandy. Evangelina sat back and scowled; she'd wait patiently to identify Belphegor's ploy.

Belphegor sidled up to Mandy as she pulled eggs and orange juice from the refrigerator. He shadowed her every move in lock step. She brought a loaf of bread from the pantry and set to work on breakfast. Belphegor stood behind her, cloaked in invisibility, and introduced thought transference into her brain via her ears.

She's just an old lady, whispered Belphegor.

Mandy cracked the eggs and put them in a bowl and began whipping them with a fork.

She's probably all right.

Mandy turned and pulled the little carton of half and half from the refrigerator and added a tablespoon to the egg mixture and continued to whip.

Her sisters are probably taking care of her; you just might be interfering, he continued.

It delighted him to see her slowing her pace. Taking deeper breaths.

Mandy opened the loaf of bread and took out two slices for the toaster. She returned to the refrigerator to get the butter and stood motionless to breathe in the cool air before closing.

All the while Belphegor kept pace. *She may not even want visitors seeing her ill.*

Mandy hunched over and grabbed a small frying pan from the cupboard, set it on the stove, and fired up the heat. She took a spatula and scooped a dollop of butter and put it in the frying pan.

You hate hospitals.

With the butter melted, she grabbed the bowl of egg mixture and gave another whip before finally pouring it into the frying pan. But this time he noticed her wrist didn't have the same quick flick as earlier.

You'll have to park in that gloomy parking garage. Somebody will probably scratch your car. Belphegor heckled with joy, proud of his clever technique to reach Mandy's inner consciousness.

"She's cracking, just like one of her eggs," he said only to himself.

As the eggs began to sizzle, Mandy folded them over to cook them through. She turned off the stove when she heard the toaster pop.

The best way to get even sicker is to be exposed to all those germs in the hospital.

Mandy pulled the toast from the toaster and spread a thick coating of butter on each slice before plating it.

You're going to spend enough time in the hospital yourself. You don't need to go there today.

Mandy poured herself a glass of orange juice and took her plate of eggs and toast to the living room coffee table, seating herself on the two-seater sofa, directly next to Evangelina. Belphegor, not to be outdone, managed to squeeze between the two, sticking out his tongue at Evangelina.

Evangelina sat with her arms folded looking at the ceiling.

You know, you could always go tomorrow.

Mandy retrieved the television remote from the end table and pushed the ON button and aimlessly exchanged stations, watching a little here and a little there, flipping out every commercial. Still feeling the fatigue from the night before.

He could see she was "done," "cooked," ready for his masterpiece—the pièce de résistence. He wrung his hands together in complete joy and supreme confidence he could show those other imbecilic demons how a master such as himself could get things done.

He clamped his eyes shut and breathed out a head-wrenching thought transference: *Call Ev and tell her to forget about going to the hospital today. Tell her you're tired. Too lazy to go. Tell her you'd prefer to lie around the house for a while after such a rough night. Grace can wait.*

Mandy took a bite of toast. She put down her plate and grabbed her phone. Ev's last call was first on the list and she clicked redial. The phone rang a few times before Evangelina picked up.

Evangelina may have just been sitting on the end of the couch, but her side of the conversation to Mandy was muted within the room. Mandy could only hear what was coming through her phone.

"Hi, Mandy, what's up?" said Ev.

"Change of plans."

"Huh? What are the changes," asked Ev?

Belphegor sat up straight and offered Ev an evil grin of satisfaction. *She's bending. She's comin' with us. Wait til the boys see her with me.*

"I'm ahead of myself. Let's make it as soon as you can get here," said Mandy.

"Any particular reason?" said Ev.

"Yeah, I want to go to the hospital a little earlier so I can stop in the gift shop and get something nice for Grace," said Mandy.

"Gotcha," said Ev, "I'll see ya soon."

Belphegor stood and threw a menacing look of daggers at Evangelina. He shook a finger close to her face and his eyes turned savage with rage.

"It's an easy job when you have a woman of character and integrity to watch over," chuckled Evangelina, "You look silly," she said adding to his humiliation. "It's hilariously funny to see a grown demon trying to out-smart two young females."

"It's not over yet," spit Belphegor. Turning to mist he dematerialized through the closed front door.

Ev evaporated through the door, adding flounce to her movement.

CHAPTER 30

S HE HEARD THE DOORBELL ring from the kitchen.

"Come on in,'" she shouted out, certain it was Ev.

"How'd you know it was me?" Ev called out.

"Who else?' she said, entering the living room, drying her hands on a kitchen towel. "Hey, is that for me?" she asked, seeing Ev holding out a coffee from Starbucks.

With a nod Ev acknowledged the dirty dishes still out on the coffee table.

"I know. I had to cram in a lot of stuff since we upped the time. Food comes first. Who knows when I'll eat again?"

"No need to explain. Do you need more time?"

"Nope. Just let me get a jacket. I'll tend to the dishes later," said Mandy.

Once settled in their seats and driving, Ev opened the subject, "So, tell me what happened last night"

"Well, Brent came over and brought me flowers," said Mandy.

"Aw, so nice," said Ev.

"And he gave me this," said Mandy, indicating the gold Celtic knot heart pendant.

"Oh, that's beautiful," said Ev.

"He said it would bring me luck and, at this point, I need all the luck I can get," said Mandy.

"And then? . . . " quizzed Ev.

"And then we went to the Town Steakhouse."

"Ooh, fancy-smancy," said Ev.

"And we had fabulous steaks and after dinner we danced and . . . " she paused.

"Don't stop," said Ev having already seen this movie, but enthralled by Mandy's joy in telling it.

". . . and he kissed me on the dance floor," Mandy blurted. "Let's just say there was electricity. We both felt it."

"Ooh, tell me more," said Ev.

"And then I ruined the evening." How quickly her joyous face fell to one of stress and vulnerability.

"What happened?" asked Ev. She knew what was coming next, nevertheless experienced dread in the telling.

"He wanted to get a scotch and a cigar so we went to this place, Capone's Library, and I had one of my episodes of coughing and pain, compliments of the 'Big C,'" explained Mandy. "It was awful. Brent took me home and I blacked out after taking one of Dr. Fineman's pain pills."

"Oh, that's terrible," said Ev.

"Well, at least I know he's a gentleman. I woke up this morning fully clothed in my bed. Obviously, he put me there and left," said Mandy.

"Did you call him today?" asked Ev.

"No, I didn't want to bother him at work, but I'll call him later this afternoon and apologize," said Mandy.

"I don't think you have to apologize," said Ev.

"Yes, I do. I ruined a wonderful evening."

Mandy's cell phone rang and Brent's name popped up on her onboard car screen. Mandy pressed "Answer" on her touch screen and said hello.

"How are you doing today?" asked Brent.

"I'm doing much, much better," said Mandy, "Thank you for calling. I was going to call you later after you left the office. I didn't want to bother you while you were working."

"You're never a bother, Mandy. You had it pretty rough last night. I tucked you in. You know, I wanted to take you to the hospital, but you refused. You really need to see a doctor, kiddo," Brent said.

"I have to call Dr. Fineman on Monday," said Mandy, "for my weekly update."

"That's good. Listen, I drew up all the papers necessary to do all the financial stuff for your mother," Brent continued.

"That's great. Can we get together on Sunday to do the signing?" asked Mandy.

"Can we do it any sooner? I'd like to see you again," asked Brent.

"I'm kinda booked today and tomorrow. I have to go to Mom's on Halloween to help her hand out candy. She's looking forward to it," explained Mandy.

"I understand," said Brent. "So, Sunday brunch sounds good?"

"I'm looking forward to it," said Mandy.

"I'll call you about 11 a.m.," Brent said.

"Great. And, again, thank you for everything, Brent."

"My pleasure. See you Sunday."

"Ooh, he'd like to see you sooner," Ev teased.

"Stop," said Mandy. "It's too late in my life to blush and get the schoolgirl giggles. But I think I'm about to."

Mandy turned onto 13 Mile Road and headed toward Royal Oak Beaumont Hospital. A mile before she reached Woodward Avenue she ran into bumper-to-bumper traffic. Progress was excruciatingly slow. Frustrated, she pounded the steering wheel.

"When did they start construction here?" Mandy asked rhetorically.

"I don't know," said Ev.

"I was just down this way a week ago and there was zero construction," said Mandy frustrated.

Far up ahead they could see a construction worker, dressed in fluorescent orange, holding a "Slow/ Stop" sign. After what seemed an eternity, they drew near to the sign-bearing worker.

"I don't see any work being done here. Why is this guy holding up traffic?" Mandy asked.

Ev looked out her window at the construction worker holding the sign and didn't know whether to laugh or cry. It was Belphegor still trying to discourage Mandy from making her visit to Grace. Belphegor looked into the car at Ev and laughed, simultaneously sticking out his demon-forked tongue.

"Drive," said Ev.

"But the sign says 'Stop,'" said Mandy.

"This guy doesn't know what he's doing. Just go," said Ev.

Mandy hit the gas and blew off Belphegor and his "Stop" sign. They made the light at 13 Mile Road and Woodward Avenue and turned into the visitor's parking lot. They rushed from the car, Mandy looking behind for police car sirens to be on their tail. Once inside the main entrance, they gained composure and casually headed to the reception desk.

"We're here to see Grace DiDia," Mandy said to the receptionist.

The receptionist scanned her computer screen and found the entry for Grace DiDia. She reached down and handed out two visitor passes.

"That's room 3314. The elevators are to your right," said the receptionist.

"And the gift shop?" Mandy asked.

"It's right around that corner. You can't miss it," said the receptionist.

Mandy handed one of the passes to Ev and they walked to the gift shop and browsed the aisles. Ev picked out flowers while Mandy browsed the stuffed animals. Finally grabbing her two favorites, walked to where Ev was shopping.

"Whaddya think?" she asked, holding a stuffed bear with a heart that said "Get Well Soon!" and a stuffed piglet with an apron and chef's hat that read "Hope Ur Bacon the Kitchen, Bacon Soon!"

"Which one?"

"No, you choose. It's your gift."

"Oh, the piglet is so cute and is so, so like Grace." Mandy's cheerful laugh brought color back to her cheeks. "I'm sure she needs a laugh after what she's been through."

Ev chose a "Get Well Soon!" Mylar helium balloon to go with the flowers and Mandy's gift. They paid for their purchases and left the gift shop smiling, especially when they looked at the little piglet. They made small talk while waiting for the elevators.

"Why is it hospital elevators are so slow?" Ev asked.

"Funny, I never noticed." As Mandy was saying that, the door dinged open and the two stepped in, pressed the third-floor button.

The elevator began a slow rise, and they settled in for a short climb, until it came to an abrupt stop, jerking them against the back panel. It stopped mid-floor. Mandy looked at Ev, wide-eyed and panicked, while pounding the number three button with her finger. Nothing changed.

"Belphegor," shouted Ev.

"What?" quizzed Mandy.

"Oh, just a U.P. expression. It's our swear word," explained Ev, calmly pushing the alarm button. "They'll be here in jiff." Then an ear-piercing peal of the bell reverberated off the walls sending Mandy into sheer panic and to maniacally pushing all the elevator's buttons.

"Just stay calm," said Ev.

"I've never been stuck in an elevator," said Mandy all but calm.

"Don't worry. Help is on the way," said Ev.

It took a while, but eventually the elevator car began to move again, at last opening on the third floor and the ladies stepped out. They followed the directional arrows down the hallway and found room 3314. Ev looked for traces of Belphegor hiding in invisible sight. When they entered the room, nobody was there. It was obvious there was an occupant, but Grace was nowhere to be found.

"I wonder where she is?" asked Mandy.

"Let me find a nurse," said Ev.

Ev headed out the room to the nursing station.

The nurse looked up almost surprised to see someone standing before her. "Can I help you?"

"I'm Ev and you are?" asked Ev.

"I'm Lisa," said the nurse. "Let me apologize, I didn't see you standing there."

"That's fine. Can you tell me where Grace DiDia, room 3314, is now?" asked Ev.

"Let me check," said the nurse. "Ah, she's on her way back from X-ray. She had surgery on her hip earlier this morning and they should have her back here shortly. You may wait in her room. It shouldn't be long."

"Thank you," Ev said, turning to walk back to fill Mandy in on the situation, still on the lookout for the wearisome Belphegor.

They stood back from the bed, by the windows to leave space for Grace to be rolled in, and waited patiently, each lost in their own thoughts. It wasn't long before the orderlies wheeled Grace into the room and carefully situated her on her bed. Lisa, the nurse, entered to ask her if she needed anything. She placed a tall, waxed cup of cold water with a straw on the bed table and indicated to Grace that it was there and also pointed out the call button. Just buzz if you need anything else. When the commotion subsided, Grace turned her attention to Mandy and Ev.

"My goodness, so much ballyhoo for a little old lady," said a surprisingly perky Grace. "Oh, I'm so glad to see you," she said.

"I couldn't let my favorite neighbor go without a visit. We brought you some things to cheer you."

Ev put the flowers in a water pitcher she found in the room and then allowed the balloon to float to the head of the bed. But when Mandy handed Grace the stuffed piglet, she clutched it to her chest and burst into sharp chirping sounds.

"Sorry, girls, that's my version of a laugh. Stitches, ya' know. But really, so much? Unfortunately, it'll be awhile before I'm running around my kitchen again."

"What did you do to yourself?" asked Mandy.

"Oh, stupid me. I spilled a glass of water on the kitchen floor and didn't wipe it all up. My eyes aren't what they used to be. I slipped on the floor, fell and broke my hip."

"Are you in any pain?" asked Mandy.

"Not much. Whatever they're giving me works really well. They say they're going to have me up and walking today or tomorrow. I hope it's tomorrow," Grace groaned.

"I understand," said Mandy. "I was so worried about you. They wouldn't tell me anything when they took you."

"Well, the doctor says I should fully recover after doing my therapy."

"Where are your sisters?" asked Mandy.

"Oh, they were here for the surgery and they'll be here after dinner tonight," said Grace.

"Oh, that's good," said Mandy, "You have a wonderful support system."

"Will you look after my home while I'm gone?" asked Grace, "Did I give you a key?"

"Yes, you did and I still have it," said Mandy. "I'll keep a close watch for you."

"Oh, you're such a good girl," said Grace, fighting to keep her lids up.

"Oh, um, well, I think we should leave. With the surgery and your pain pills kicking in, you must be worn out," said Mandy now standing.

As Mandy reached over and squeezed Grace's hand and Ev patted her on her shoulder they turned to an odd voice squeaking, "By-bye you two. See you soon." They turned to see the cushy piglet waving good-by.

Mandy said, "If that's your version of a pig's voice, Grace, you need to practice."

Mandy laughed. But not Ev, for when she turned back to Grace, she could swear she was already fast asleep and that it was the voice of Belphegor issuing the "by-bye you two," and a threatening "See you soon."

"She is the sweetest old lady," said Mandy.

"She certainly is," said Ev. "She's had a great life."

"I just wish I had the time she had," said Mandy, followed by a quiet melancholy.

Chapter 31

"Hey, you definitely look the part," said Mandy, opening the door to Ev fully dressed in her Bubb's kitchen worker's disguise. "For heaven's sake, Ev, put those bags down," indicating a sack of potatoes on one shoulder and a bag of onions on the other. "Sorry for laughing, but they weigh more than you. Set them down on the stoop and come on in while I finish dressing."

Happy to relieve herself of her baggage Ev slowly made her way to the sofa with a groan and a plop.

"Hold on, I've got a few more finishing touches."

Ev watched Mandy dash up the stairs, only to return minutes later.

"Well, what do you think?" asked Mandy modeling her kitchen uniform as she proceeded down the steps, a glass of red wine in her hand. She did a small ballerina's pirouette, and nearly tripped on her low curtsy. "So? Do I fit the bill?"

"I think your outfit is great, but your dancing needs developing," said Ev.

"You think that's bad, you outta see my cha-cha-cha."

Mandy laughed. But Ev's face stood unmoved. She recognized the tension in her friend's body being fueled with alcohol.

"Ah, this is just what I need. Laughter is a welcome catharsis to whatever brings you down." She lifted the half bottle of wine for another glass.

Ev offered weak smile. "Mandy, you can't go on a secret mission while under the influence. It's in the rule book."

"Is there a rule book?"

"My rule book. Put the wine down and let's get out of here. We're on a mission. I'll grab a sack, the heavier potatoes. Do you think you can handle the onions?"

"No problem. In fact, I can carry them both," said Mandy. "Remember, I was a jock."

It was a short drive to Bubb's Rejuvenating Rubs. Mandy drove around to the back, to the loading docks, parking behind a dumpster to obscure dockworkers from seeing her car.

"Perfect. See there," Ev said pointing to the door next to the docks, "that's where we go in. When you get your stuff make it back through that same door. Keep going even if we get separated."

"Gotcha," said Mandy. "What time is it?"

"It's 9:45," said Ev.

"You think we should get started?" asked Mandy.

"Well . . . yeah, do you have a problem?" said Ev.

Mandy answered hesitantly. "No." With that, she opened the car door and stepped onto the concrete. Immediate pain exploded in her abdomen, like lightening hitting a transformer. She fell to her knees and began to cough and moan. Ev rushed around the back of the car and knelt by her side, placing a protective hand on her shoulder as she heaved. When the spasm subsided Ev helped Mandy back into the driver's seat.

"Breathe," said Ev.

"I'm fine," said Mandy, her voice raspy. "Give me my purse."

Ev ran around to the other side of the car to retrieve Mandy's purse. She sprinted back and offered to open it.

"Could you? I don't have the strength." Once open, Mandy reached for her prescription bottle and handed it to Ev. "Open it and give me one," Mandy said breathlessly.

Ev did as she was told and watched Mandy insert the pill into her mouth and grab the days old water bottle from the console, downing her painkiller with a long swig.

"Listen, do you think you'd be OK if *I* retrieved your stuff?" said Ev.

"No, no . . . give me a minute," rasped Mandy closing her eyes. "The pill is fast acting."

No sooner had she said that, the pain pill kicked in.

"I can do this," said Mandy.

"Are you sure?" said Ev. "This may be our only time to do this, so if you're not able, I'll go it alone. Trust me."

Mandy got out of the car and stood. "Let's do this."

Ev helped her remove her coat and threw it in the back seat.

"You're still unstable, kid," said Ev, steadying her at the shoulder.

With that, Mandy stood tall and straight, and popped the trunk.

Ev seized the bag of potatoes and Mandy made a reach for the bag of onions, but fumbled her grip and the onions fell to the ground. Ev picked up the bag and threw it back into the trunk.

"You don't need to carry a bag," said Ev. "Just focus on putting one foot in front of the other and follow me."

"Oh, O . . . kay," garbled Mandy.

Ev clutched Mandy's hand and the two walked slowly toward the door. Her staggering gate slowed their progress. "Do you have the key?" Ev asked urgently.

"Yep, ga it riiight here," slurred Mandy, awkwardly holding out her wrist displaying the key on its stretchy wrist coil.

Lord, give me strength, prayed Ev, letting go of Mandy's hand to open the door. She guided her through the doorway and closed the door behind her. Inside, they walked up the steps onto the floor of the loading dock and made their way to the double door entrance to the main building. They walked along the carpeted hallway to the kitchen door where Ev gladly dropped the sack of potatoes.

"Follow me to the locker room," said Ev.

"Shhhure."

Ev started down the hall toward the locker room. When she reached back for Mandy's hand, it wasn't there. She turned to see Mandy staring into the window of the kitchen door. She shook her head and grabbed Mandy's hand to yank her back. It didn't take much to recognize the interaction of pills with her intake of wine was impacting Mandy's ability to function.

"Focus, Mandy, focus," said Ev.

"Rrright," said Mandy. "But choo dun half to be a mean person."

Ev led Mandy down the hallway to the locker room access door. She cracked the door open and peeked inside. The locker room was deserted, so Ev entered with Mandy in tow. "Which locker?" asked Ev.

"Um, ah, I think . . . maybe, ah that one." Mandy made a random point with a wobbly finger.

"Give me the key, it'll have a locker number . . . Damn, it's too dark in here."

Ev tried the key and it didn't work. She tried the key on the two lockers on either side with no success. Ev put her hands on her hips and looked at Mandy. She shook her head and laughed.

"Look at you. You are pitiful. I need you to concentrate. Which locker is it?" said Ev sternly.

At that moment, the back locker room door opened and in walked an attendant with a cart of towels. He took one look at the pair and knew they didn't belong.

"What are you doing here?" asked the attendant. "Are you trying to break into the lockers?"

"No, no, no," said Ev, "She left her clothes . . . "

"Yeah, right," said the attendant, "I'm calling Ms. Lilith."

The attendant rushed to the red phone on the wall and began dialing. Ev grabbed Mandy by the hand and charged toward the front door of the locker room. The two burst out into the hall then out of the door leading to the foyer. They started towards the front doors, but were intercepted by a hoard of demons that appeared, instantly blocking the front door exit. Confronted by this host of demons that included Satan and others she'd dealt with recently. Ev bravely stepped in front of Mandy, shielding her from their view.

With her chin out, Ev commanded, "Begone you beasts of abomination!"

Satan laughed and motioned to Dolos. Dolos stepped forward and drew his fiery sword. With both hands holding it upright, he approached Evangelina.

"And what will you do? You must be puniest of pathetic angels," Satan laughed uproariously.

"I'll send you all back to the hell hole you slithered out from," Evangelina said defiantly as she morphed into her angelic form in full battle regalia.

Satan laughed a contemptuous laugh. He raised a swirling ball of fire in his hand and hurled it at Evangelina. Evangelina ducked and the ball of fire exploded on the opposite wall. The angel slowly stood up and looked into Satan's fiery eyes.

"So, it's a fight you want," Evangelina said with resolve.

"I believe you have a bone to pick with this urchin, Dolos," laughed Satan.

She pulled her sword of righteousness from its scabbard and pointed it at Dolos, who stepped back and feigned fear. He grinned and then attacked with a chopping blow of his fiery sword. Evangelina parried the blow and swiped it away.

Dolos charged Evangelina but she stepped aside, letting him attack air. Furious, Dolos turned and jabbed his sword at her face but Evangelina swirled and ducked, avoiding the blow. Evangelina stood with both hands on her blade, her base wide and stable and motioned with her sword to Dolos that she was ready for whatever he had.

Dolos roared and ran at the angel. But Evangelina, with the agility of whirling star, spun away, leaving herself positioned behind Dolos. She swung her blade precisely and chopped off Dolos' leg at the knee.

Dolos cried out in agony. He lay on the ground cradling his amputated appendage. He looked up at Evangelina and spit at her. Evangelina drove her blade through his heart. Dolos' body crumbled into dust.

Before she had any time to regroup, Satan unleashed another fireball at her. Once again, she sidestepped the fireball and it exploded on the marble reception desk.

"Put away your tiny dagger," Satan teased. You can't slay me. I'm immortal. What are you going to do with that piece of tin?"

As the words left Satan's lips, Leviathan shot bolts of lightning from his fingers at the angel, momentarily taking her off guard. Evangelina thought quickly and jumped safely out of the way. Unfortunately, her move left poor Mandy exposed, the bolt narrowly missing her. Evangelina raised her sword, but not before a ball of Satan's fire knocked the sword from her hand.

Standing defenseless against the hoard of demons, Evangelina's only thought was to protect Mandy from the demons' onslaught. Quickly she moved behind Mandy and enveloped her with her angel wings, protecting her from the perilous fury of the demons.

The other demons joined in and pummeled the huddled ladies with balls of fire, lightning, and fiery brimstone. Each strike singed Evangelina's wings a little deeper. The merciless onslaught burned through layer by layer, leaving them reduced to smoldering cinders, rendering little protection.

The onslaught suddenly stopped when Evangelina unfurled what was left of her wings and stepped around Mandy. She struck a combative pose in front of Mandy. With tattered wings, no sword of righteousness, and in virtuous defiance she resolved no demon would get to Mandy without destroying her first. Arms spread wide and eyes closed, she stuck out her chin with a smile on her face. She waited patiently for the demons' final blows. She waited for the end.

Time passed and curiosity got the best of her. Evangelina opened her eyes to find the demons standing wild-eyed in a defensive posture hissing and growling, but not attacking her.

Puzzled, she shook her head in disbelief. She heard the unmistakable sound of a steel blade being removed from a scabbard. Slowly she turned and saw the psychedelic mist, a characteristic of the Choir of the Power Angels. The first member of the Choir of Power, Petram the Rock, had already manifested and stood there, sword in hand. Next, Fulgar, the Angel of Lightning arrived followed by Ventus, the Angel of Wind. Altum, the Angel of Tides arrived with trident in hand. Ignis, the Angel of Fire and Glacies, the Angel of Ice arrived together. Monsigneus, the Angel of Volcanoes, arrived with his glowing red complexion. Genus, the Angel of Birth, came next. The lights in the foyer dimmed and an ominous whooshing filled the room. Mors, the Angel of death had arrived.

Mandy, in a crouching position, turned and watched as the Choir of the Power Angels assembled. What she was witnessing evoked both awe and terrifying fear.

"I hope they're here to help," Mandy said to Evangelina.

"Say hello to our cavalry," a soot-stained Evangelina said.

Satan gave the command and one by one, the snarling demons marched to Satan's side. They reached out and touched him to be instantly absorbed into his demon self. Their upper bodies still recognizable and protruding from Satan's torso; with each addition Satan grew taller and more formidable. When the last demon was absorbed, Satan stood twenty feet tall and all the demons snarled and growled at the Angels of Power.

"We have to get out of here," Evangelina said urgently.

She grabbed Mandy under her arm and helped her to her feet. As they stood, the Angels of Power moved forward and past them to surround the snarling beast. They stood at ready with weapons drawn. Evangelina and Mandy fell back and stood behind the smoldering marble reception desk.

"We could avoid all of this if you'd just hand over the girl," said Satan.

"We could avoid all this if you just went back to Hell," said Petram.

"That's not going to happen," said Satan.

"Oh, you're going back to Hell without the girl," said Petram.

Satan laughed and hurled the first fireball. It was deflected by Petram. Fulgar let loose a lightning bolt that seared Satan's horn. Leviathan hurled his own lightening and Monsingneus fired a stream of hot lava from his fingertips. Ignis breathed fire into the mix while Glacius fired frozen icicles at Satan's eyes. The demons hurled fire and brimstones in return. The Angels of Power continued their onslaught. A haze of smoke and noxious fumes filled the entryway.

"I've got to get you out of here," Evangelina shouted over the din.

Petram raised his sword and the Powers ceased their attack. Satan, befuddled by their action, called for his demons to pause. Petram made eye contact with each and every Power. One by one, each Power raised their weapon. In unison they drove their weapons into the marble floor.

The Earth began to shake violently. The roof began to crumble and fall. Evangelina grabbed Mandy by the arm and dragged her to the door to the spa.

"We're going out the back," Evangelina shouted.

The floor of the foyer began to crack and fissures blew hot steam into the air. The floor around Satan began to fracture. A great fiery gorge opened and Satan teetered on the edge. Altum, the Angel of Tides, flew up and drove his trident deep into Satan's chest. Satan staggered and fell into the fiery chasm. The building continued to shiver, shake and crumble. The debris was sucked into the fiery hole.

As the Powers of Angels rose in the air more and more of Bubb's Rubs was engulfed into the chasm. The paintings, the plants and the marble reception desk were all fell into gaping hole. The inner walls began to crack and fragment and the pieces were sucked into the fiery chasm. The entire structure began to groan under the pressure.

Evangelina dragged Mandy through the hallways toward the back door exit. The interior walls were groaning and cracking as they stumbled through the dark passages. The floors buckled and rolled as they burst through the doors into the rear tavern. The television monitors were shorting and sparking. A fire burned behind the bar. All the mortal patrons fled in terror when the battle began. They stumbled through the upended tables and chairs to the exit. The two blew through the doors into the brittle October air, staggering their way to Mandy's car. Evangelina pushed her partner into the passenger seat, ran to the other side and morphed back into Ev before she got in.

Ev watched spellbound as the Power of Angels rose above the din and stayed suspended around the building until the gaping chasm inhaled the debris from the building like a mammoth vacuum pump until nothing remained. The Power of Angels settled to the ground and extracted their weapons. The Earth rumbled and the chasm closed up leaving nothing but a vacant parking lot. Petram raised his sword and he and his cohorts in combat disappeared.

Ev smiled and looked down at Mandy slouched down in the passenger seat, passed out. A thin trickle of blood stained the corner of her mouth. Mandy's breathing was labored and she looked a bit grey. Ev shook her head and frowned. She knew she had to take her to the hospital.

CHAPTER 32

E v CAREENED DOWN the city streets of Royal Oak, narrowly missing two pedestrians crossing the street and a parked car, rushing to get Mandy to the Royal Oak Beaumont emergency entrance. She sped with surprising precision, stopping only when she reached her destination. She hopped out and ran around to Mandy propped up in the back seat. Holding her up with one arm, she waved for help with the other. Immediately two orderlies blasted out of the emergency room doors pushing a gurney. They arrived at the car and took charge.

"What happened?" the orderly asked.

"She's a cancer patient. She had sudden burst of extreme pain in her abdomen and took some prescription pain pills. She's coughing up blood and passed out. Please, please help her," cried Ev.

"What did she take?" asked the orderly.

Ev ran around the car and retrieved Mandy's purse. Hurriedly, she returned fumbling for the prescription bottle and handed it over to an orderly. The orderly read the label and looked at Ev.

"Wow, these would knock out a horse."

"She's not a horse. Help her," Ev commanded.

The orderlies placed her on their cart, strapped her down, and whisked her inside the hospital. Ev followed closely behind until a security guard blocked her from going further.

"Sorry, lady, you can't go in there," said the security guard.

"Why not?"

"You have to register her at the desk."

"What desk?"

"Right over there. They're waiting for you," said the guard.

"What's your name, young man," demanded Ev.

"My name is Ross."

"Well, Ross, my friend needs me and I intend to be there with her," scolded Ev.

"But not before you register her at the desk," said Ross. "It's the way things are done."

Ross gently turned Ev around and guided her to the registration desk. She sat down, placing Mandy's purse on her lap and waited to be addressed.

"How may I help you?" asked the receptionist.

"The young lady they just wheeled into emergency," said Ev.

"Name?" questioned the receptionist.

"Amanda Abbessi," replied Ev.

"Address?"

"Wait a minute," said Ev fumbling through Mandy's purse. "Here's her driver's license."

"Thank you . . . insurance provider?"

"I don't know," said Ev. "You're going to have to wait until she regains consciousness for that."

"Well, OK, you can wait over there," said Daria pointing to the visitor's lounge.

"Wait? Can't I go see her?"

"They'll call you when you can go back and see her; just be patient."

Easy for you to say thought Ev walking out of the emergency room. She looked to the outside to survey the surroundings for a suitable area to make her transformation. She faced nothing but short and tall buildings with windows and ten thousand eyes. The bathrooms? They, too, now have security cameras. Same with the parking garage. Inside the car? Perfect. She returned to her car and drove to a secluded area in the parking garage. Certain she couldn't be seen, she faded from sight under her cloak of invisibility and floated through the doors to emergency, then through the lobby and into the emergency room itself. It was a typical Friday night so all the cubicles were filled. Evangelina floated from one bed to the next looking for Mandy.

She found her lying in a bed, hooked up to an IV with a nurse taking her blood pressure. An emergency room doctor stopped by her bed and spoke with the nurse.

"What do we have here, Nurse Jackie?" asked the doctor.

"Hemoptysis, bradycardia, bradypnea and she is taking 100 micrograms prescription fentanyl," reported the nurse.

"Give her 2 mg of naloxone, get her stabilized and send her to x-ray. Give me an AXR, stat," directed the doctor before exiting the room.

The nurse noted the doctor's directions on Mandy's chart then walked briskly to the nurse's station to place the order. While the nurse was busy, Evangelina morphed back into Ev. She stood at the head of the bed stroking Mandy's hair.

"It's not your time, dear girl. Hang in there," soothed Ev.

The nurse returned to Mandy's bedside with a syringe and a vial. She saw Ev and smiled. Nurse Jackie drew the appropriate dosage into the syringe, and administered the shot.

"What did you give her?" questioned Ev.

"And you are . . . ?" questioned Nurse Jackie.

"I'm Ev. I brought her to emergency," Ev explained.

"Are you related?"

"Yes, you could say that," said Ev.

"She just received a shot of Narcan. Do you know if she has an opioid problem?"

"No, she's a cancer patient," said Ev.

"I see," said Nurse Jackie noting that on Mandy's chart. "They're coming soon to take her for X-rays. You can stay with her now, but you can't go to X-ray with her obviously. Why don't you go to the visitors' waiting room, get a cup of coffee and I'll contact you when she's back. That is unless she's admitted to the hospital if a room is available. Either way, I'll let you know."

"I understand," said Ev.

As the nurse finished, an orderly with a gurney arrived at Mandy's bedside to wheel her to X-ray. Mandy showed signs of coming round, although agitated and confused. She murmured something unintelligible and then popped open her eyes. She looked from the nurse to Ev.

"Where am I?" Mandy asked, still groggy.

"You're at the hospital, dear, you passed out and I couldn't wake you," said Ev.

"I had the weirdest dream."

"I'll bet you did."

"I dreamed we were at Bubb's and there were demons and the devil and they threw fireballs and angels showed up and . . . and it was crazy," said Mandy.

"Well, we were at Bubb's and, unfortunately, we couldn't retrieve your stuff. The rest of that, well I don't know," said Ev.

"Wow, it seemed so real. You had wings, Ev . . . like an angel."

"Wow, you were really trippin'."

"I guess so," said Mandy.

"This nice young man is going to take you to X-ray," said Nurse Jackie, interrupting their conversation. "You'll be able to talk to your friend soon."

The nurse and orderly helped Mandy out of her bed and into the wheelchair. She slumped down, obviously weak and still tired. They repositioned her up and strapped her down for her protection.

"I'll be here when you get back," Ev said, squeezing Mandy's hand.

"You're so good to me," said Mandy. "You are my rock."

The nurse exited the room alongside Ev.

"You two seem so close."

"Yeah, we are."

"Looking at her chart, it seems to me she's going to need someone like you."

The nurse reminded Ev she had to sit in the waiting room, so she made her way out of emergency to the waiting room and made herself comfortable, if possible, facing the flat screen television.

The television droned constant information about diabetes, its symptoms, treatment, and how a healthy diet and exercise was the best way to avoid the disease. She watched for a short while before moving to another part of the room, away from the television.

Sitting in a nearby corner was an elderly woman. A young woman seated next to her moved in close, and placed her head on the other's lap, each feeding on the other for support. The elderly woman fingered her rosary beads, while a young man knelt on one knee at her feet talking softly to her. A middle-aged woman stood behind the three talking softly into her cell phone.

A doctor emerged from an access door to the emergency ward and the middle-aged women approached him. He gave a simple "no" nod of his head and the middle-aged woman let her cellphone drop the floor. When she began to cry, the two young people stood wide-eyed, asking for answers they already knew. The middle-aged woman walked over to deliver the grim news to the aged woman. They made a small effort to comfort her, knowing she could not be consoled. She wailed in her grief. The doctor picked up the woman's cellphone and stood back, holding open the door, waiting for the group to assemble for a walk down the hall to say their good-byes to someone they held dearly. As they passed, the doctor handed the woman her cell phone and extended a gentle pat on the shoulder.

Ev's heart was heavy. She felt their grief and loss of the family member. There would be a permanent hole in their family structure, not one that another person could ever fill. She thought how death was harder on the living than the deceased.

CHAPTER 33

A NURSE WITH A CLIPBOARD emerged from the emergency ward access door and called out Amanda Abbessi's name. Ev raised her hand and approached the nurse and smiled.

"Yes?" asked Ev.

"Are you family?" questioned the nurse.

"You could say that," said Ev, hoping that answer would suffice. *It worked earlier. I'm not telling a lie, maybe a fib.*

"We admitted Amanda and she should be in her room shortly."

"Do you have the room number?"

"Let's see . . . " said the nurse checking her clipboard, "ah, she'll be in room 5195. Give her a few minutes to get settled and then you can go up and see her."

"Thank you," said Ev.

Ev bided her time walking around outside in the brisk and invigorating night air, looking up to the stars, certain Archangel Zadkiel was measuring her adequacy on Earth. She reminisced about her old job. After visiting Earth, she considered her old job to be unfulfilling and very lonely. She hoped that Zadkiel would allow her to continue as a guardian angel in training. She loved helping Mandy and helping mortals was a job she loved to do. She'd do anything to stay on Earth.

Ev said a prayer for the family in the waiting room. She decided enough time had passed and made her way back into the hospital, to the elevators and up to room 5195.

160

A low spirit consumed Mandy. To say she lacked hope would not be truthful. She was reminded her of her father's words that she promised to remember: When the going gets tough, the tough get going. But now, dressed in a hospital gown with an IV inserted into her arm, and plastic tubing running up the side of her bed and connecting to a harness that supplies oxygen to the nasal prongs she's wearing, she admitted second thoughts. Looking up, she uttered aloud: "I don't think I can do it this time, Dad. I don't have the strength."

Her face lit up and her depression lifted at seeing Ev enter the room. "Ev, I'm so happy you're here," said Mandy, suppressing a cough.

"Don't let yourself get over-excited; I'm happy to see you're doing better," said Ev.

"What happened?" rasped Mandy.

"You do remember taking that pill, right?" asked Ev, "Obviously, your pills and the wine you drank before I picked you up didn't mix very well."

"I didn't intend to take any pills," explained Mandy.

"I understand," said Ev, "but none-the-less after you took your pill it was downhill from there. I think you lost it when that attendant found us in the locker room."

"We made it to the locker room?" questioned Mandy.

"Uh huh, and he thought we were robbing lockers," said Ev, "and that's when we got out of there. When we got back to the car you passed out. I could see you were having trouble breathing. That's when I decided you needed to go to the hospital."

"Wow," said Mandy clearing her throat, "like I told you, the images in my dreams were more than images, they were real and wild and included demons coming for me. They wanted me. They tried to draw me into a battle with angels—I think they were angels."

"Well, you'll be happy to know that Bubb's Rejuvenating Rubs burned to the ground tonight," said Ev.

"Wow, what happened?" rasped Mandy.

"I don't have any details, but I heard about it. It's big news," said Ev.

"Well, so much about recovering my stuff."

"Exactly," said Ev. "So, how do you feel?"

"I'm groggy, but better."

"That's good," said Ev. "Can I get you anything?"

"I hate this hospital gown. Can you get me something from home with more, ah, coverage? And I need my cell phone and charger."

"Certainly, I'll grab something from your house. Your cell phone is in the car. What should I tell your mother?"

"Oh yeah. Mom. We're supposed to go over there tonight. Obviously, we can't. I don't know, Ev. What do you think?"

"Don't you think your mother would want to know her daughter is in the hospital?" asked Ev.

"But I don't want her to worry," coughed Mandy.

"She's a mother. That's what mothers do. And don't you think she'll be worried when you don't show for Halloween without a reason? And, what about Brent?"

"Oh, Brent. I was supposed to meet him this Sunday to sign papers. Yes, tell him I'll meet him another time," said Mandy.

"OK, you stay here and don't go anywhere and I'll be back," smiled Ev.

"Ha, ha, very funny," deadpanned Mandy.

She exited the hospital doors, instantly taken in by the brilliant colors of orange and pink and violet streaking across the sky. Its captivating natural beauty inspired her with awe, bringing her gentle tears. Sunrise was imminent and a new day was beginning. But with this new day so much pain would be visited upon them

Ev hopped into Mandy's car and drove out of the parking lot. It was early Saturday morning with very little traffic. Ev stomped the accelerator and flew down the road. The exhilaration was intoxicating. She learned to love driving and would miss it when her mission was complete. Until such time, she would just sit back and enjoy the ride.

It didn't take long before Ev arrived at Mandy's condo. Using Mandy's key, she entered the eerily empty condo and immediately took to the stairs leading to the bedroom, dead silence following. She started with the drawers and rummaged through them, grabbing anything comfortably appropriate for hospital wear, including underclothes. She found a small tote bag in the closet and filled it. It hit her that Mandy might want her own toothbrush and toiletries, so she went to the bathroom to collect them. She returned and stuffed them in the bag. She was about to leave when she felt a strange push against her leg and quickly looked down to brush it away.

"Oscar. Oh, Oscar." She bent over to lift the forlorn-looking cat and cradle him close. "Oh, Oscar. You poor dear. You know something is wrong, don't you?" She wondered of his future. She couldn't take him with her. Was there a protocol for pets?

And then inspiration hit. "Hey, buddy. Have you met Hope? You two could be great companions." With that, Ev started for the stairs with Oscar on her tail. She changed his water and opened a can of salmon cat food. Once he was preoccupied, she headed to the door, her package complete, and left.

Breaking the news to Mandy's mother that her daughter was in the hospital was going to be tough. While Mandy wanted to protect her mother, Ev knew she relied on her for support. She was determined to break the news as gently as possible.

The fallen leaves crunched under her footsteps as she approached the Abbessi home. Was it her imagination that the fall decorations from Ev's first visit, which seemed to honor the season and express fun and celebration, now appeared dismal and dying in preparation for what was to come? Ev stepped on the porch and rang the doorbell, to which Hope responded with eager barking. Ev waited patiently for Mrs. Abbessi to open the door.

"Well, hello. What brings you here so early? Mandy's not here. I think she spent the night at her condo."

"That's why I'm here, Mama Marie," said Ev.

"Why don't you come in, dear? It's chilly out there. I just made a fresh pot of coffee. Please, come and sit on the sofa while I pour you a cup. I baked some cookies last night. Pumpkin spice . . ." She spoke rapidly, almost babbling, as if she stopped something bad would enter her morning.

"No, no thank you," said Ev. "Listen, Mrs. Abbessi, I came to tell you that I took Mandy to the hospital last night and they admitted her."

"Oh no, no, no, figlia mia," said Mrs. Abbessi, her eyes widening.

"No, no, no, she's OK," said Ev quickly to avoid an onslaught of crying that couldn't be stopped. "She's awake and comfortable."

"What happened?"

"She passed out last night and was having trouble breathing, so I took her to emergency."

"Oh my, where is she?" Mrs. Abbessi instinctively knew this was not the time to show weakness.

"She's close. Royal Oak Beaumont."

"That's good. Ev, do you think you'd mind taking me there?"

"That's why I'm here."

"Give me just a minute to change," said Mrs. Abbessi.

"Take all the time you need."

Mrs. Abbessi quickly scampered out the room.

Ev sat and quietly patted Hope. *There is nothing in the world like a mother's love for her child.* She turned slightly weepy when her eyes fixed on Hope's adoring stare. Almost begging for an explanation. "It's gonna be OK girl."

"I'm almost ready," said Mrs. Abbessi, obviously flustered by this event. Ev's eyes followed as she moved about gathering her things, straining to maintain a steady demeanor.

"I need my black wool coat. Oh, and probably a headscarf. Where are my gloves?" She donned the scarf and slipped on the coat. She reached in her pocket and pulled out her gloves. "Oh, here they are. My purse, where'd I put my purse? I need my keys."

"Mama Marie, you calm down," said Ev. "Take a deep breath and remind yourself that one of the best ways to help Mandy is to let her see you are the strong woman who raised her."

"Hope, you go lie down. Momma will be back," said Mrs. Abbessi pulling the door shut on a whimper.

They drove the short distance to the hospital in silence. Ev snaked through the parking garage, waiting for Mrs. Abbessi to open up. But her face remained a stoic mask, disguising her thoughts.

"I can't lose Mandy," said Mrs. Abbessi softly, finally breaking through the heavy quiet. "I lost my parents when I was young. I lost my sister not long ago. I lost my husband. I can't lose Mandy, too. I'll be all alone. I'll have no one left. Why does God hate me?"

"God does not hate you, Mama Marie," said Ev patting her hand, "he just loved them and wanted to reward them for leading such good lives. You haven't lost them, Mrs. Abbessi. They're just waiting for you."

Mrs. Abbessi reached into her purse and grabbed a tissue to dry her eyes.

Chapter 34

Blisdon ran down the lava tube with an urgent message. The sides of the tube glowed red hot from the last load of lava that squirted through the passage. He raced along the way as it wound and curved through the underworld until he came to a screeching halt when he reached the chamber where Beelzebub was torturing a group of deceased mortals.

"Master, I have an urgent message," said Blisdon breathlessly.

"Can't you see I'm busy, imbecile?" raged Beelzebub.

"Forgive me, but the Prince of Light demands your presence."

"What now?" hissed Beelzebub.

"I don't know, but he is not happy," said Blisdon.

"So, what's new?" growled Beelzebub.

"He also summoned Satan, Belphegor, Mammon, Leviathan Asmodeus and Lilith," said Blisdon.

"Sounds like another one of his bitch sessions. When?"

"Now."

"All right. Dip these souls in pig excrement while I'm gone. Better yet, let them soak until I return," laughed Beelzebub.

"As you wish, Master," said Blisdon.

Beelzebub made his way to the royal chamber. Lucifer sat on his throne of skulls with Cerberus at his feet and his cohorts in crime in front of him on bended knee. Beelzebub walked to front of the throne.

"Emperor," greeted Beelzebub.

"So glad you could make it," said Lucifer. "Now kneel, you incompetent piece of male bovine fecal matter!

Beelzebub slowly kneeled before the throne and bowed his head in submission. Lucifer, clearly agitated, shifted back and forth on his throne. He shook his head and then bit his own thumb.

"You . . . all of you . . . together," spit Lucifer, "couldn't defeat . . . one, yes just one . . . puny insignificant angel? One puny untried, rookie angel beat you? And then, on top of it all, the Choir of Power kicked your collective asses? Is this a joke? No . . . *you* are the joke."

"Sire, the condition that she *voluntarily* commit one of the deadly . . ." began Beelzebub.

"Silence," screamed Lucifer.

Lucifer sunk back into his throne and stroked his beard. Deep in thought he mumbled unintelligible words to himself. Coming to a decision, he looked back at the assembled subordinates.

"I don't want the soul of the mortal anymore, although I will have it eventually." Lucifer laughed diabolically. "I want the scrawny angel to become one of my minions."

"I'm not sure that's possible," blurted Lilith.

"Silence, wench," screamed Lucifer.

Lucifer wiped the spittle from his beard with the back of his hand. He reached down and scratched one head of the three-headed dog, Cerberus and studied his audience. Finally standing, he stepped off his altar to address the assembled demons.

He threw his head back and in a booming voice that reverberated throughout the chamber he raged at his demons. "You are all incompetent fools," he began, "and this is much too important to entrust to any or all of you. This is going to be ultimate slap in the face to that tight ass archangel, Zadkiel. The only one smart enough, savvy enough, and clever enough to pull this off is . . . " He flourished his arms in a circular motion, ". . . is ME."

CHAPTER 35

Toting the duffel bag of clothing and Mandy's cell phone, Ev led Mrs. Abbessi from the elevator to room 5195. They hurried along the hallway, dodging food carts, med carts, wheel chairs, and bustling nurses and orderlies going about their business.

"Stop. Please stop for a moment. It's the smell of pine-scented disinfectant and the flowery scent of air fresher. I'm drawing up bad memories from all the days I've spent here with loved ones. Just give me a little time to adjust, I promise, I'll pull it together."

"Of course," said Ev. "We can find a place to sit for a while if you want."

"No. I'll be fine. I just need seconds to steady my land legs."

With that she nodded forward, indicating she was ready.

They entered the room on tiptoes.

"Figlia mia," cried Mrs. Abbessi upon seeing her daughter sitting up, attached to lines of medical equipment and watching television. She ran to her side and lunged for a big hug.

"Mom, Mom, be careful, Mom," said Mandy, pointing to her attached medical lines. "Mom! I'm so glad to see you."

"Your friend told me what happened," said Mom, settling to give her daughter a peck on the cheek. "What did the doctor say?"

"I haven't seen him yet. He won't be here until eleven," said Mandy.

"Maybe he'll release you today," said Ev. "If not, I have some clothes and your cell phone to bide you over."

"Oh, good," said Mandy, "Did you call Brent?"

"No, I thought you should make the call," said Ev.

"Ugh, Ev. I didn't want to talk to him in my condition," whined Mandy.

"I guess you'll have to put on your big girl pants and make the call," smiled Ev.

"Who is Brent?"

"Hold on, Mom. I'll tell you later. Hand me the cell phone, I need to get this call out of the way. It's important."

"I just got here and you're calling some guy? Did you eat?"

"I had coffee, orange juice and broth earlier, Mom. Lunch is coming at noon."

Mandy dialed the phone and listened to it ring numerous times before going to voice mail. "Hi, Brent, it's me. Listen, I can't make it Sunday. Call me when you can. I'll explain. Thanks." His call back was immediate.

"Hello, Brent, that was fast," said Mandy. "I just called to tell you that I can't meet with you Sunday."

Mandy listened to Brent and responded with an occasional "yes" or "no." She thanked him for the work he was doing for her and tried to hang up.

"If you must know, I'm in the hospital, Royal Oak Beaumont. I'm waiting to hear from the doctor so I don't know. I'm in room 5195. Yes, my mother and Ev are here. OK, uh-huh, thank you."

"Everything's all right?" asked Ev.

"He is persistent," said Mandy.

"Well, he is a lawyer," smiled Ev.

Just then, a nurse came in to take Mandy's vitals. She studied Mandy's chart before laying it aside.

"Well, hello, I'm nurse Olivia and I'll be watching over Mandy for the next eight hours." Her warm smile exuded hope, but they knew better than to try and read too much into it. "How are you feeling today, Mandy?"

"Well, a lot better than this morning."

"Let's check your blood/oxygen rate and BP," said nurse Olivia attaching a monitor to her finger and a blood pressure cuff on her arm.

"How am I doing?" asked Mandy, watching the nurse record the readings to her chart.

"Your blood pressure's normal, but your blood/oxygen is low," said the nurse. "We'll wait until the doctor sees you to adjust any medication."

"OK."

"Is there anything I can get you?" asked the nurse.

"No, I'm fine."

"If you need anything, just push the red button and I'll be here shortly," said nurse Olivia exiting the room.

"She seems nice," said Mom.

"They're all very attentive and understanding here," said Mandy.

"Well, they better take good care of my baby."

"Oh, Mom," groaned Mandy.

Ev hoisted up the duffel bag of clothing and plopped it on the bed.

"Oh, good," said Mandy.

"I rummaged your closet and drawers and here's what I came up with," said Ev emptying the bag in a heap. "Sweatshirts, t-shirts and sweatpants. Take your pick." She held out a small bag of undergarments and another of toiletries, "You can check these out later."

"Great," said Mandy, "I'll wear the MICHIGAN sweatshirt and the navy sweatpants."

"OK," said Ev, "I'll hang the rest in your little closet."

Mandy reached over and pushed the red button, calling for the nurse.

"What are you doing?" asked Ev.

"I need the nurse to get me to the bathroom with all these hanging things connected to me."

Nurse Olivia responded just as promised. She appeared in just minutes. "Well, how can I help?"

"I want to change into more comfortable clothing. Can you get me to the bathroom?"

"Certainly, and I'll help you maneuver into your clothes."

Ev gathered the sweatshirt, and sweatpants, along with the toiletries, and carried them to the bathroom for Mandy, and returned to the task of hanging the remaining clothes in the closet.

Mom waited patiently, her worn, sad face forming new deep wrinkles. She looked so alone. Ev continued to monitor Mrs. Abbessi for signs she might need help. Kneeling before her she searched for words to offer comfort. "There are many of us who love Mandy. They'll be praying for her and looking out for you."

Mrs. Abbessi closed her moistened eyes. In spite of Ev's words, she felt no optimism.

"I feel so much better," Mandy announced from the bathroom doorway.

"You look better, too," said her mother.

Nurse Olivia guided her back to her bed, fluffed her pillow, cranked the bed to sitting position and prepared to leave, reminding her she'd be back later. As she exited, she crossed paths with the doctor entering.

"Hello, Miss Abbessi. Am I pronouncing that correctly?" asked the doctor. "I'm Dr. Bernard, your attending physician."

"Pleased to meet you, and call me Mandy."

"You know you're quite ill, Mandy," said Dr. Bernard scrutinizing her chart. "I talked with Dr. Fineman earlier."

"Yes, I know," said Mandy.

"And who are these lovely ladies here with you today," asked Dr. Bernard.

"This is my mother and my best friend, Ev," said Mandy.

"May I speak frankly about your condition in front of them?"

"Yes, Doctor," said Mandy.

"Well," began Dr. Bernard as he listened to Mandy's heart through his stethoscope, "it appears that your underlying condition has spread to your lungs and you have pneumonia. There is a mass in your lungs that may be cancerous, but we will not know for sure without a biopsy. We are treating your pneumonia with intravenous antibiotics. I would like to start you on chemo, but I need your permission."

"No, I don't think so," offered Mandy. She said it blithely, almost like turning away a door-to-door salesman.

"Why not?" Mom interrupted.

"Mom," said Mandy, "not now."

"I understand," said Dr. Bernard, meaning it, "but if you change your mind, please let me know immediately. Whatever your decision, there are a few forms you will need to fill out which includes a "Do Not Resuscitate" directive. We need your signature on all of them. A representative will be in later to bring them to you."

"I understand, Doctor. Thank you."

After recording notes on Mandy's chart, the doctor paused. He considered addressing chemo again, but Mandy understood his hesitation and firmly fixed her eyes directly on his, warning him not to go further. His smile indicated he got the message. With that he squeezed her hand and left the room.

"What is wrong with your head, Mandy?" demanded Mom, suddenly coming to life.

"Oh, Mom," groaned Mandy.

"You're turning down chemo is stupid."

"Mom. We've been through all of this and I don't see the need to go over it again in front of others. Besides, don't you remember promising me you'd agree with any decision I choose? There is no help. There is no magic bullet. There aren't going to be any miracles."

"Tu . . . tu . . . sei pazzo," exclaimed Mom.

"I just want to get out of this hospital and live what time I have left. Please allow me to determine the rest of my life."

"Amanda Abbessi?"

All eyes turned to the door.

"Mandy Abbessi?" he asked.

"Yes."

"This is for you." A delivery boy held out a gift box wrapped in pale gray paper with a luxurious, iridescent sunset-orange bow on top.

Ev passed the box to Mandy then offered a gratuity to the boy.

"No tip necessary. It's been taken care of," said the young man, turning to leave.

"Whoever sent this thought of everything," said Mom, obviously impressed. "That wrapping is gorgeous. Hurry, let's see what's inside."

"Slow down, let me read the card."

Mandy opened the envelope attached to the ribbon first.

Then pulled open the card and read it out loud.

"Nothing could ever detract from your beauty—both inside and out. Love, Brent."

Under layers of gray tissue paper, lay one pink rose atop a gray flannel nightgown, sporting dancing cats, all resembling Oscar.

Slow on the uptake, Mom exclaimed, "Oh, I get it. You'd look good in anything. How cute."

Chapter 36

MANDY PICKED THE SINGLE pink rose and inhaled the fragrance. She attempted a broad smile for her mother and Ev to camouflage her true commingling feelings of love, confusion, and regret. She now understood what others meant when they said "My heart is breaking."

"Who is Brent?" asked Mom.

"He's just a friend," said Mandy.

"I don't think 'just a friend' sends nightwear," said Mom.

"Mom," Mandy whined, "OK, I have been seeing him, but just recently."

"And you don't tell your mother?"

"Mom, it's too new to even think about," said Mandy.

"And when will I meet this young man?" asked Mom.

"I don't know."

"Is he Italian?"

"Ah, I don't think so," said Mandy.

What does he do for a living? "

"Mom," exclaimed Mandy. "Stop!"

"Does he have a job?"

"All right, he's an attorney," said Mandy.

"Oh, I see. Is he influencing your decision to refuse chemo?"

Thankfully an attendant entered the room carrying a tray with Mandy's lunch. He put the domed plate on Mandy's tray, along with a container of apple juice, a carton of milk and plastic eating utensils wrapped in plastic. He checked his list and quickly left the room.

"What did you order?" asked Mom.

"Well, I was going to order the mac and cheese, but there's no way they can match *your* mac and cheese, so I asked for a grilled cheese sandwich and tomato soup . . . remember? One of our Friday night comfort foods?"

When she removed the lid, she uttered, "I guess this isn't the Four Seasons." She sat looking at a bowl of chicken broth.

"Now, back to 'Brent,'" said Mom. "How old is he?"

"Let me drink in peace." The ladies chatted while Mandy drank her lunch.

Mom talked about the memories she had of her daughter growing up. Of course, she had to include tales of her embarrassing moments, which Mandy wasn't happy about, but it beat the "Brent" topic.

At some point, Mandy pushed her tray away. "What I wouldn't do to have a juicy hamburger right now. These people must have thrown away the salt and pepper shakers."

"They're just looking after your health, dear. When I come tomorrow, I'll sneak in a little something for you."

"I'm looking forward to it," said Mandy, secretly hoping for Mom's mac and cheese.

It was Mandy's quick intake of air and the startled look on her face that jolted Mom and Ev up to face the door. Brent stood in the doorway, grinning broadly, his eyes directed only at Mandy. Despite her best efforts she couldn't speak or control the tears flooding her face.

"Hello, ladies," said Brent to six eyes fixated on him. He waited, but when no one spoke up, he said "Aren't you going to invite me in? . . . I guess I'll invite myself."

Brent walked directly to Mandy's side. His cool hands brushed away a lock of hair from her face before he bent over to kiss her warm, wet cheek.

"Oh, my, yes, hello." Mom flustered out the words, "Pardon my manners. I'm Mandy's mom, Mama Marie. And you are?" asked Mom, knowing who this was judging by Mandy's reaction to him.

"Brent . . . " he answered.

Mom jumped in, "Oh, yes, Amanda's attorney. So nice to meet you. And this is Ev, Mandy's closest friend."

Mandy made an effort to speak, but she choked on her words. Tears never came easily for her.

"Pleased to meet you, ladies," said Brent. Turning to Mandy, his voice low, almost a whisper, he said, "Since we couldn't get together to sign papers on Sunday, I thought I'd come here to make it easier for you,"

"Ooh, he's handsome," whispered Mom to Ev.

Brent dragged a chair to Mandy's bedside. "So, what brings you to this place?" Brent's sober face showed deep concern for her.

"Pneumonia," interjected Mom.

"I can answer for myself, Mom," coughed Mandy, slowly regaining self-control. "Yes, pneumonia."

"Are you getting the best care here?" and retrieved a file from his briefcase placing it within Mandy's reach on the bed.

"Yes, they've taken good care of me, so far, although the food has much to be desired."

"What? Don't they serve filet here?" joked Brent.

"Let's just say chicken broth is an adventure."

Brent leaned in closer to Mandy, his lips touching her ears, and said something in a hushed tone, causing her to giggle.

"Mama Marie, let's take a walk, give them privacy," said Ev quietly. "Maybe get a coffee or a light lunch."

Mrs. Abbessi had confusion written across her face. "Huh? Why?"

"To be frank, they need to be alone. And I need a coffee."

"Oh, OK . . . I guess."

With that, they excused themselves, with no objection from Mandy, and headed into the hallway.

"While they're gone, I have papers for you to sign."

Brent handed Mandy a pen pulled from his vest pocket and held it out to her. He pulled the first document out and explained it to Mandy, clause by clause. She nodded her head, acknowledging she understood its meaning. He continued to pull documents from his file and reviewed each one meticulously with her. Mandy signed each one as asked. The final document was a quitclaim deed, which put her mother's name on the title to her condo. Mandy signed the deed. Brent took the collection of documents and replaced them in the file. He took the file and placed it back into his briefcase.

"I will file all of these docs for you and send you copies as soon as I can," smiled Brent.

"Thank you, Brent," said Mandy. "How much will this all cost?"

"Cost? No, no, no," said Brent. "This is on me, dear and I won't have it any other way."

"Brent, at least let me pay the filing fees," said Mandy.

"I would have spent more if I took you out to dinner, Mandy. I won't hear of it," said Brent.

"Are you sure?" asked Mandy.

"Absolutely. And let's not talk about this again. Said, signed and done."

They both looked up to the voices returning to the room, in better moods than they had left with. "Did you miss us?"

"Oh, sure, can't you tell . . . " began Mandy and suddenly everything froze.

Ev stood up and looked around. She knew for certain that she did not freeze time. Some other being was responsible. Ev morphed into Evangelina. She walked the room waiting for the presence to manifest itself. She was unhappy thinking there was another battle to be fought. She readied herself for the next confrontation.

CHAPTER 37

HE APPEARED AT THE DOOR to room 5195 and leaned in brandishing a sense of accomplishment across his face, twirling his trademark walking cane with the golden handle. Always dapper, he wore a cream-colored suit, accented with a red pocket square, cream-colored fedora and red snakeskin shoes. His beautifully handsome and intriguing face with a chiseled chin and golden eyes either drew people to him or repelled them. He slithered into the room and sat, crossing his legs.

His chilling smile prompted Evangelina to address him. "Well, well, if it isn't the "Morning Star" himself, Lucifer. What inspired you to slither out of your hole?"

"I had to meet the puny little angel that bested my demons," said Lucifer. "It was, let's say, a matter of pride."

"They say pride comes before the fall and you can't have fallen much farther than the dregs of Hell," poked Evangelina.

"Let's pause this exchange of slights. I have brought you a peace offering," said Lucifer opening his coat to reveal Evangelina's lost sword.

"My sword," exclaimed Evangelina.

Lucifer grabbed the sword by its blade and handed it to Evangelina, handle first. She grabbed the handle and swung into a defensive posture with the blade high over her head. Her body armor morphed over her body and she stood erect, ready for combat.

"And what do you think is going to happen next?" laughed Lucifer.

"I'm ready for anything you got."

"I did not come here to fight you, young lady," said Lucifer, "I came to make you an offer."

"An offer?" said Evangelina. "You don't have anything I want."

"Well, let's explore that thought," said Lucifer calmly. "I've noticed there are some earthly pleasures you have or would have loved to enjoy."

"Like what?" questioned Evangelina relaxing her pose.

"Well for instance, I've noticed you have not had even the slightest bite of mortal food or a drink, other than, maybe, water," explained Lucifer, "There are things on this Earth so good they would make a tear come to your eye. There are steaks and fish and other seafood. There are fruits and vegetables, like corn and peas and apples and peaches and pineapple, that are so sweet they would make your mouth smile. And, speaking of sweet, there are cakes and pastries and pies that are so sublime you could not stop eating them. Mortals around the world have mastered this bounty and have created all their own cuisines. Then there are the drinks from cow's milk to wines to aperitifs to bourbon that would delight your palate."

Evangelina stood silent, showing no emotion. Lucifer continued.

"I've also noticed your love for driving automobiles. It seems you like to go fast. Well, that little car that Mandy owns is nice, but if you want speed there are many others that would make that car look like a snail by comparison," said Lucifer.

"What's your point?"

"Let me finish," said Lucifer. "Look at what you're wearing. It's nothing more than a uniform. A being as beautiful as you should be robed in mulberry silk, vicuna wool, baby cashmere and Egyptian linen. You should have closets full of beautiful attire so that you never wear the same thing twice. Look at those trashy sandals. You should have a room full of shoes that match each and every outfit you wear."

Evangelina's scowl started to soften. She stood expressionless, listening to Lucifer pontificating the wonders of the world.

"And what of love?" Lucifer continued. "Don't you deserve to be held in the arms of a loving man who puts you on a pedestal and gives you children?"

Evangelina started to shuffle her feet nervously. Lucifer sensed her uncomfortable state. He decided to make his pitch.

"I can give you all of that and more," said Lucifer. "I can give you immortality and a new set of wings and you can remain here on this beautiful Earth. There are wonders on this planet that will take your breath away. You will have the time and means to see it all."

"And what do you want in return?" questioned Evangelina.

"I only ask one thing and one thing only. You must renounce heaven and pledge loyalty and fidelity to me and only me," said Lucifer.

Evangelina stood thinking. Lucifer's smile looked like warped evil, carved into his face with a putty knife. He folded his bejeweled hands together and waited.

"So," began Evangelina, "I want to make sure I understand you and your offer. You want me to give up the honey and ambrosia of heaven to eat burgers on Earth? You want me to give up flying across the universe, to be able to drive a car? You want me to give up the robes of heaven to be able to wear blue jeans? You want me to give up the love of our Lord for the embrace of a mortal man? Children? I tend God's children already. The beauty of the Earth? I already have the beauty of the universe. Lucifer, your offer is inferior to what I already have. So, my answer is no, now and forever."

"You impertinent wench," growled Lucifer. "I will make you sorry for even thinking you could best me and my minions."

Slouched in his chair, Lucifer raised his hand above his head and snapped his fingers. *Mandy, alone, reanimated.* Her eyes flicked open and she looked for a familiar place to land. The room seemed foreign until she saw Ev. Evangelina seeing the anxiety in her eyes, quickly morphed back into Ev.

"Ev, who is this gentleman?" asked Mandy, "And why is everyone frozen in space?"

"This is no gentleman," said Ev.

"Now, now, young lady," said Lucifer, "let's not judge so hastily."

"This being is the scourge of humanity. He is the messenger of hate and destruction," said Ev.

"Ignore this woman, Mandy," said Lucifer. "I bring you hope and a future."

"What, Ev? What's he talking about?"

"Don't listen . . . " Ev began.

"Silence, you bellicose brat," growled Lucifer. "I have an offer for you, Mandy."

"Offer? What kind of offer?"

"This condition you are suffering . . . what if I could make it all go away and you could have a long and normal life. You could marry your young gentleman. You could help your mother through her golden years," proposed Lucifer.

"You can do that?" she asked with piqued interest.

"I most certainly can," said Lucifer.

"Well, then, do it. Do it now," smiled Mandy ear to ear.

"Tell her what it will cost her, Lucifer," said Ev.

"Lucifer? Ev, who is this guy?" asked Mandy.

"It's the Devil himself," said Ev.

"Well," began Lucifer, "I will visit you from time to time and require you to do my bidding. Also, if you agree, I will make certain you have a first-born male son that, well, will be mine."

"Is this guy for real Ev?" asked Mandy.

"Yep, he's the real deal, Mandy."

"You've got to be kidding me."

"No, I'm not joking," said Lucifer, "I'll give you back your life if you agree to my terms."

Befuddled, Mandy looked to Ev who stood with her palms straight up and shaking her head, indicating she was unable to interfere with Mandy's decision. She could only hope her charge would make the right choice.

"So, you say you could cure me of this cancer and I would live a long life?" Mandy restated his offer.

"That's exactly right," answered Lucifer.

"And all you want is for me to do your bidding and offer you my first-born male son?"

"A paltry price for all the joy you would experience," smiled Lucifer.

Mandy thrust herself forward and shouted, "Fuck off, asshole. I'd rather be dead."

Ev smiled at her courageous little friend.

"I see," sighed Lucifer stroking his chin, "as you wish."

Lucifer deliberately raised his hand above his head and snapped his fingers. Mandy grabbed her chest and, with wide eyes, fell back into her bed, gasping for air.

"What did you do?" screamed Ev.

"Well, you know ovarian cancer tends to throw off a lot of blood clots," laughed Lucifer, "I'm guessing, but I think that just happened."

Lucifer snapped his fingers again and the world returned to normal. He faded away and was gone. The alarm went off on Mandy's heart monitor. Ev ran to the Mandy's side of the bed and pounded the nurse call button.

"What's going on?" said Brent panicked.

"Mia bambina, mia bambina," wailed Mom over and over.

Chapter 38

N<small>URSE</small> O<small>LIVIA WAS SEATED</small> at her desk, entering data into the computer when the alarm went off at the nurses' station flagging room 5195. She picked up the internal intercom phone and spoke.

"Code Blue! 5-1-9-5," she spoke rapidly into the intercom internal phone. Bolting from her chair she sprinted down the hall. Her heart quickened and her thoughts rushed to her last image of Mandy sitting up and smiling.

Entering the room, she found Mandy surrounded by her loved ones.

"ALL OF YOU, OUT," shouted the nurse.

Ev motioned for Brent to lead Mama into the hallway. He grabbed her resisting hand and stood with her braced against the wall to clear a pathway for the hospital's crash-cart racing down the hallway to Mandy's room. Before the nurse pulled the drape to encircle Mandy's bed and close the door, Mom and Brent watched the scene in horror. They did not see that Ev was not with them.

A resident sliced open Mandy's sweatshirt while another jellied the paddles of the defibrillator. The resident then put his ear to Mandy's chest and listened carefully for a heartbeat. The whine of the machine charging covered the room. Evangelina stood at the foot of the bed waiting patiently.

Mandy's essence rose from her body and hovered over the bed watching the resident apply paddles to her and fire an electrical current through her chest, causing her body to involuntarily jerk then fall back to the bed.

The crash-cart crew all looked at the heart monitor, hoping to see evidence of a responding heart. But the line was flat.

"Charge!"

Once again, the machine whined up its charge again. The resident applied the paddles to Mandy's chest again. "Clear," he commanded and pulled the trigger and applied a massive charge to Mandy's chest. Mandy involuntarily arched her back, then fell back to the bed. All eyes rotated to the monitor. Nothing.

"Turn it up," commanded the resident. "Charge!"

The defibrillator whined to its top charge and the attendant nodded to the resident.

"Clear," commanded the resident and fired the defibrillator's charge into Mandy's chest for the last time.

Mandy's body jumped at the charge. Her essence looked to the foot of the bed where Evangelina stood, invisible to mortal eyes. Dressed in angel's garb and tattered wings, Evangelina smiled back at Mandy.

"Ev?" questioned Mandy, not sure who or what she was seeing.

"Yes, Evangelina," corrected Evangelina.

"Are you a . . . a . . . angel?"

"I am *your* angel."

"Was all that stuff real last night?"

"Indeed, it was."

"Wow," said Mandy, who paused to understand. "Am I . . . dead?"

"That's up to you," said Evangelina.

"What do you mean?" said Mandy, confusion and fear clouding her thinking.

"Well, it's not your time, but you have a choice," said Evangelina.

"A choice?"

"You could return to your body and continue to your eventual demise. You would suffer the pain and a slow death. Brent and your mother would be by your side each day until you pass. Or, you can come with me," answered Evangelina.

"I don't know," said Mandy, "what would you do, Ev?"

"It is not up to me and I am not here to influence you. I am here to help you with whatever path you choose," explained Evangelina.

"There are so many things I want to say to my mother. I want to thank her for all she did for me. I want to share memories with her. I want to kiss her one more time," whispered a teary Mandy.

"I understand," said Evangelina.

"And Brent," said Mandy, "I want to tell him that he was the best thing that has ever happened to me. I want to tell him that his love and kindness has helped me so much over this tough time," said Mandy. "I want to tell him . . . I want to tell him . . . I love him."

"Yes, I understand," said Evangelina. "He already knows."

"And what will become of my poor mother?"

"Of course, she will mourn your loss, but Brent will take good of her. He will treat her like she was his own mother."

"Did I leave her enough to get by?" asked Mandy.

"Oh, my, yes. In fact, Brent helps her to invest and she will live quite comfortably for the rest of her days," said Evangelina.

"And what of Brent?"

"He will do very, very well for himself," said Evangelina.

"Will he marry?" questioned Mandy.

"Unfortunately, no," said Evangelina.

"I see," said Mandy.

"Will I ever see them again?" asked Mandy.

"Of course, you will."

"Where are you taking me?" asked Mandy.

"I'm taking you to see your Father," said Evangelina.

"Daddy?" said Mandy excitedly.

"Yes, him too."

"How much time do I have?"

"Now would be good," said Evangelina.

"Are you sure about Mom and Brent?"

"I'm as sure as I am that you are Amanda Abbessi," said Evangelina.

"Are you sure I'll see them again?"

"Absolutely."

"Will you be with me?"

"Whichever scenario you choose, I will be with you. I am here to guide and protect you," explained Evangelina.

"Then, Ev . . ." began Mandy, thoughtfully, "I choose to . . . "

CHAPTER 39

A SMALL WHIRLWIND CARRIED COLORFUL autumn leaves across the hospital parking lot. Evangelina stood on the front lawn of the hospital taking in the beauty of the day. Bright sunshine warmed her face as a brisk October breeze blew through her hair. Fluffy cumulus clouds rolled across the crystal blue sky. Evangelina marveled at the beautiful colors of the leaves that desperately clung to the half bare trees.

"I'm going to miss this beautiful time of the year," said Mandy dressed in layers of sheer white linen.

"It will be replaced by the most beautiful place you have ever seen," said Evangelina.

"So, what's next?"

"What would you like to do? Is there any place you'd like to visit? Is there anyone you'd like to see," asked Evangelina.

"I don't know. Let me think," said Mandy, "I'd like to see how Grace is doing."

"Certainly," said Evangelina who whisked Mandy off to Grace's hospital room.

The three sisters, Rose, Eva and Katie, sat in Grace's room and they were laughing about a memory they all shared. Grace looked to be in wonderful spirits. She munched on homemade pizzelles from her sisters and sipped cappuccino from the in-hospital barista.

"I'm so glad to see she is doing well," said Mandy.

"She's one tough customer," said Evangelina.

"And what of Michael and my office?"

"Well, let's check it out," said Evangelina.

In a blink of an eye, Mandy and Evangelina were standing in the middle of Mandy's old real estate office. She looked around and saw the usual hustle and bustle of a regular day working in-office. She walked over to her old office and, much to her surprise it was vacant. There was a note taped to the door that read:

"RESERVED FOR MANDY'S RETURN"

Mandy smiled, "I guess Mike had high hopes for my return . . . I hate to disappoint him."

"I'm sure he will grieve your loss. He always thought so highly of you."

"He was a friend and mentor. He took me under his wing and taught me the business," said Mandy, "He's a good honest man. God, I'm going to miss him."

"Well, if he truly is a good and honest man, you will see him again, Mandy," said Evangelina.

"And what of Sam?"

"You were a good influence on him, Mandy. He idolized you, believe it or not. Sam will grow up, finish college and become an influential voice in America."

"Makes sense to me. His smile could take him to the White House."

"Yes, indeed," said Evangelina, "Is there anywhere else you'd like to go? Would you like to see your funeral?"

"My funeral? No, I couldn't stand to watch it."

"Are you sure?"

"Yes, I'm sure. Do you know what I'd really like to see?" queried Mandy. "I'd like to sit on the dock at 10 Mile Road. My dad used to take me there when I was young and we would fish from there. It's been over 25 years?"

"As you wish," said Evangelina.

Mandy looked down and found herself standing on grey, weathered wood planks, surrounded by tall weeds, cattails and the sounds of frogs tuning into the day. "This is it, Ev. Our dock, mine and my dad's, right here at the 10 Mile Road pier overlooking Lake St. Clair." The water was choppy, driven by the northwest wind and Mandy peered out at the horizon. A large cumulus cloud covered the sun and Mandy watched as the shadow traveled across the lake.

"Wow, a lot of wonderful times were had on this dock," said Mandy.

"Tell me about them."

"I remember catching my first fish with my dad here," Mandy said wistfully. "It was just a little thing and we put it back in the lake so it could grow big and strong. I can't count all the times we caught fish, took them home and had a fish fry. Dad's beer batter fish recipe was the best I've ever had."

"What kind of fish did you catch," asked Ev.

"My favorite was the yellow perch. I don't think there is a better eating fish than that . . . except maybe walleye. A walleye is just an overgrown perch anyways," said Mandy. "We also caught blue gill, sun fish and crappie. They were good eating, too, but kinda small."

"I can't imagine you as a fisherman," said Evangelina.

"Well, not since I started playing soccer competitively," said Mandy.

"Well, from now on, you will have all the time you want to fish or do whatever you can dream up."

"It would be a dream to fish with Dad one more time," said Mandy.

"Mandy, you have people waiting for you. Are you ready, yet," asked Evangelina?

Mandy looked out over the water and, with a sigh, closed her eyes and took a deep breath bringing in the earthy smell she remembered so well. She opened her eyes just as the cloud cleared the sun. Its radiant glow glinted off the waves and warmed her face. She turned and looked at Evangelina.

"I'm ready," said Mandy.

"As you wish."

Evangelina reached for Mandy's hand and took hold. With her other arm she pointed up and the pair lifted off from the dock. They slowly spiraled higher and higher in the air. Mandy looked down and marveled at the beautiful aerial view.

"Evangelina, look."

"What is it?" Evangelina followed the extended point of Mandy's finger.

"Dip down, please. Close to Mom's back yard. Can you see what I see?"

They took a drop and focused in on Oscar and Hope romping like two playful friends.

"Now I'm happy. Goodbye, world, I'm ready."

"Don't look behind you, Mandy. Look at the wonders that await you ahead," said Evangelina.

Mandy raised her eyes above them and saw a bright white light emitting a beam of incredible warmth and love. Higher and higher they travelled. The higher they rose the more intense the shaft of light encapsulated her. They travelled through the clouds following the light. Finally, they broke through the clouds and stood at the gates of heaven.

CHAPTER 40

MANDY AWOKE TO A FLURRY of delicate sunbeams circling her, nudging her to rise up and prepare for the day. Her eyes open wide, surprised to see Evangelina sitting cross-legged at her side and smiling.

"How wondrous," Amanda cried out, reaching for the miniature beams edging her to stand.

"Welcome home," said Evangelina.

"Home?"

"Yes, heaven," said Evangelina. "There are many waiting to see you."

"Me? Who?" Amanda asked eagerly.

"You will meet them soon enough."

"How exciting. I'm looking . . . " Before she could finish her sentence, she gave out an alarmed gasp. " . . . look," she said, pointing ahead.

A lone figure sporting a flowing grey beard magically emerged from the mist ahead, dressed in a pristine white toga that sparkled in the sun. With outstretched arms he welcomed them to come forward. Evangelina approached the man with Amanda on her tail.

"Greetings and peace unto you, Peter," said Evangelina.

"Peace unto you, Evangelina," bowed Peter. "Who do we have here?"

"This is my charge, Amanda Abbessi."

"I see," said Peter. "And who assigned you this underling?"

"The Archangel Zadkiel, head of the Dominions," replied Evangelina.

"I see," said Peter. With that said he raised his arms and shouted out "Amanda Abbessi."

An oversized book majestically appeared and hung suspended midair before Peter. "Amanda Abbessi," he called full volume into the book. As he pronounced her name, the book opened on its own. The pages rapidly flipped along, directly to the page bearing her name. "Here is her name." The air grew silent as he read the pages to himself. "Seems you had a rough time on Earth."

"It got a little rough, but we overcame the adversity and we are here now," smiled Evangelina.

"Welcome. You may enter," said Peter, "and may peace be unto your spirit."

"And also with you," said Evangelina.

Evangelina took Amanda by the hand and the pair walked through Florentine gates. They followed along the pathway that wound its way through the clouds. The pair came to a place surrounded by clouds, but bathed in sunshine and Evangelina stopped and turned to Amanda.

"Amanda, there some souls that want to welcome you," said Evangelina.

The first two souls who walked out of the cloud bank were Grandma and Grandpa Abbessi. They moved toward Amanda, their wide smiles exposing their happiness at seeing their granddaughter.

"Oh me, oh my," exclaimed Amanda. Evangelina gave her a soft nudge to assure her it was permissible to run to them. The hugs, and tears and kisses were abundant and unending.

"There are others who would like to greet you," said Evangelina.

Another couple emerged from the cloudbank—her mother's mom and dad. Though having passed long ago when Amanda was in grade school, she still had warm memories of them. They walked toward the group with smiles and open arms. As Amanda hugged both Grandma and Grandpa Polizzi the distance in years fell away and she evoked clear memories of them from her earliest years.

"And, there's someone else," said Evangelina.

A female figure slowly walked from the mist. Amanda recognized her Immediately and joyously broke from the group and ran to her side.

"Auntie, Auntie, Auntie," Amanda cried, "I've missed you so much."

"And I have missed you, too," said Auntie Virginia.

"I am so happy," Amanda said burying head into her bosom.

The group converged together and they chattered and laughed about the fond memories they shared together. They reminisced about the old days and described life in the area each had chosen to spend their heavenly days. While the group continued to chatter, Mandy broke away and returned to Evangelina.

"Where's Daddy?" asked Mandy.

"Ah, yes, your father," began Evangelina, "Well, um, he couldn't make it here."

"What do you mean?" said Mandy.

"Just what I said . . . he, uh, well. Come with me."

"What about my Grandmas and Grandpas and Aunt Virgie," asked Mandy.

"Oh, they'll be here when you return," said Evangelina with a smirk.

"Where are we going?"

"We're going to take a special trip," said Evangelina. "Trust me."

"I've trusted you so far; I guess I can continue trusting you."

Evangelina grabbed Mandy's hand and laboriously flapped her singed wings. Slowly they rose in the air and, as they gained altitude, Amanda's group of relatives turned, smiled and waved. Amanda waved back as the pair started across the sky.

Evangelina flew across the horizon for an extended period of time. In the distance Amanda saw an oval shaped building. The closer they got, the larger it loomed. Closer and closer they travelled until they set down next to the imposing edifice. They stood before a long tunnel that led inside and Amanda could see bright lights and green grass at the end of the tunnel. The pair heard cheers and chanting from inside.

"What is this?" Amanda asked in disbelief.

"Isn't this something you have always wanted?" asked Evangelina.

"I don't understand," said Amanda.

Evangelina stepped back and smiled. Amanda looked down at herself to witness her white linen garb be replaced by a white uniform trimmed in gold. A large "number one" adorned the front of her jersey.

"Huh," Amanda exclaimed.

"Welcome to Heaven's Annual Soccer Championship Game. You're starting at center, "laughed Evangelina, "and by the way, it's a lot bigger than the Olympics."

"You've got to be kidding me," said Amanda.

"Nope. No joke," said Evangelina, "Your coach is waiting for you. You better get along." Amanda reached out to overpower Evangelina with a new strength found in her angel body, then turned and started jogging toward the tunnel. Straining to see in the distance Amanda could make out a figure at the end of the tunnel, waving to her with a sense of urgency. She picked up her pace and began to run. Her bad leg gave her no pain and she accelerated to top speed. Closer and closer she came to the field. The waving figure seemed quite familiar. When she got within a hundred yards, Amanda recognized the figure. It was Daddy. Amanda screamed full heartedly and lunged toward him. She made a flying leap. Fortunately, he caught her before they both stumbled back. She wrapped her legs around him and he twirled with her in his arms. She kissed his face a hundred times. Finally, he brought her gently down on the ground.

"Well, it's about time sport. We've been waiting for our star player," said Dad.

"Oh Daddy, I've missed you so much," said Mandy.

"And I have missed you," said Dad, "Now we have a match to play. Make no mistake, these are top-notch players. You are playing with the best of the best."

Mandy hugged her Dad once again and said, "I'll do my best. I love you, Daddy."

"I love you, too, Sport," said Dad, "Now go have fun."

Epilogue

As Evangelina sat at the edge of the cloud, she leaned back and rested on her hands. She slowly kicked her feet as she took in the wonders of the universe.

Evangelina wondered how Mandy was doing and hoped she had adapted to her new life. Her happiness made the whole harrowing endeavor worthwhile. The experience would stay with her forever.

Evangelina had not heard anything from the Dominions or the Archangel Zadkiel. It had been so long Evangelina's wings had grown back. She wondered if they knew about the ordeal and that she completed her assignment. She wondered if she may have done something wrong or substandard and their silence reflected their anger. In any event, Mandy was home and happy. That was the most important thing for Evangelina.

Evangelina got up from her spot and walked back to her place among the clouds. She would continue her job cleaning up the universe's debris. As she began gathering her tools to leave on her rounds a messenger angel, Vangelis, arrived.

"Peace unto you, Evangelina," said Vangelis.

"Oh, Vangelis, you startled me. Peace unto you, also," said Evangelina.

"The Archangel Zadkiel requires your presence," he announced.

"Thank you, Vangelis," said Evangelina.

Evangelina was excited and nervous. She wondered if she would be criticized or commended. In any event, she had done her best. No matter what happened at her audience with Zadkiel she would always keep her fond memories of Mandy and her time on Earth.

Evangelina navigated her way across the clouds to the gates of the Dominion Angels. She walked along the misty path toward the purple glow ahead. She heard trumpets blare announcing her arrival and broke through the last clouds to stand in the presence of the Archangel Zadkiel, himself.

"Peace unto you, Zadkiel," said Evangelina kneeling.

"And peace unto you," he replied. "I have called you today to review your performance on Earth for your charge, Amanda Abbessi."

"Yes, sir," said Evangelina, "I hope it was satisfactory."

"The Dominions and I have reviewed your actions on Earth and evaluated your performance," said Zadkiel, "and we have a few questions."

"I'm ready to answer any and all questions." She stood erect and unafraid.

"What did you learn about the Earth?" asked Zadkiel

"The Earth is a beautiful place. It's trees and plants and animals are incredible creations," said Evangelina.

"What have you learned about human life?" asked Zadkiel.

"Life is precious because of the bonds humans form between their families and friends."

"What have you learned about death?" asked Zadkiel.

"Death is harder on the living than the people who die."

"And what have you learned about demons?" asked Zadkiel

"Demons are despicable and scary, but they're not very bright."

"I see," said Zadkiel, "I want you to understand something. I don't ever want to be forced into calling up the Choir of the Power Angels to protect you again. You will never put yourself in such a situation again. You'll get you and your charge out of the situation."

"I understand, sir," said Evangelina.

"With that said, after we saw your creativity, resourcefulness and resistance to the ultimate evil of Lucifer, the Dominion of Angels have empowered me to elevate you to the rank of Guardian Angel," said Zadkiel.

"Thank you, sir," said Evangelina.

"Now stand and go forth. There are souls that need to be protected," commanded Zadkiel.

Evangelina bowed her head and turned to leave. She began to retrace her steps back down the path. When she felt she was far removed, she peeked back over her shoulder. Once assured no one was watching, Evangelina jumped up and kicked her heels.